Fergus Hu

The Lost Parchment

Fergus Hume

The Lost Parchment

1st Edition | ISBN: 978-3-75235-260-3

Place of Publication: Frankfurt am Main, Germany

Year of Publication: 2020

Outlook Verlag GmbH, Germany.

Reproduction of the original.

The Lost Parchment

BY

FERGUS HUME

CHAPTER I

SCHOOLFELLOWS

"So this is your kingdom, Hendle?" said the visitor, looking round the garden which glowed with rainbow tints in the hot July sunshine; "and a very jolly kingdom it is. When did you enter into it?"

"When I was fifteen, twelve years ago," replied the Squire, smiling. "Don't you remember how I wrote and told you of the death of my father? You had just left school for the 'Varsity. Those were capital days at Rugby, weren't they, Carrington?"

"They were. I have had few capital days since."

"But surely at Oxford—"

Carrington shrugged his shoulders and made a frank admission. "Oh, yes! Oxford was all right until my father died and left me without a sixpence. It was hard work, I can tell you, qualifying for the Bar on next to nothing. And I can't say that I have made my fortune as a barrister. You, lucky dog, don't need to bother about pounds, shillings, and pence."

"I have certainly nothing to complain of on that score," said Hendle in a satisfied tone and extending his cigarette case. "It was a pity we drifted apart, Carrington, as we were such chums at Rugby. I might have helped you."

"You were always a good chap, Hendle, and that is why I took to you, when we were in our teens. But we saw nothing of each other all these years because you had money and I hadn't. Besides, you went to Cambridge, while I patronized Oxford. It is my fault that our friendship has not continued unbroken, as I never answered your many letters. But you see I was always too much involved in law studies to bother. You, I presume, were looking after your snug little kingdom."

Hendle nodded. "I am a very stay-at-home person, and the place requires a good deal of supervision."

"Lucky dog!" repeated the barrister. "You have a fine income, too."

"So-so. Four thousand a year."

"The deuce! And, like Bottom, I support life on sixpence a day, which, unlike Bottom, I have to earn. There is no Theseus to give me a pension."

"You didn't seem to be so very hard up when I met you six months ago in the *Criterion Restaurant*," said the young squire dryly.

"Oh, one has to keep up some sort of appearance and dress in purple and fine linen, even if one cannot afford to do so," answered Carrington easily. "It is only your rich man who can dispense with Solomon-in-all-his-glory raiment, old fellow. Anyhow, poor or rich, I was delighted to meet you again."

"Were you?" Hendle appeared to be a trifle sceptical. "You didn't hurry yourself to come down to Barship anyhow."

"I didn't; that's a fact. I thought you might fancy that I would borrow, if I came too speedily. Hence the six months' hesitation."

"Oh, rot! You know that I'm not the sort of fellow to grudge a loan to an old school chum if he asks for it."

"You were always a good chap, Hendle," said Carrington again. "But I am not going to ask. I have bread and butter, if not jam, and one must be grateful for the necessities of life in these hard times."

Hendle nodded with a lazy laugh and the young men lighted fresh cigarettes as they crossed the lawn to gain the avenue which sloped gradually for a quarter of a mile in the direction of the village. Behind them they left a delightfully ugly mansion of Georgian architecture mellowed by time into positive beauty. The Big House—its local name—draped itself majestically in dark trailing ivy, showing here and there the bland softened hue of its ruddy brick walls.

"My mind to me a kingdom is," quoted Carrington with a backward glance at the peace and beauty they were leaving. "A poetic, but truly unsatisfactory saying, Hendle. Your acres are a more tangible possession than the stuff of which dreams are made. Let us go hence."

The Squire in his simple honesty laughed at the fantastic remarks of his visitor, not guessing that a considerable amount of acid envy underlay the amiable compliments. Hendle was one of those honorable, good-natured creatures, who believed that his fellow-men were as open-minded and straightforward as he was himself. His florid complexion, fair crisp hair, big limbs and general air of latent strength revealed plainly his Saxon ancestry, and he resembled a good-natured bull content with plentiful grass and water and the freedom of wide meadows. He was markedly good-looking, with sleepy blue eyes and a heavy moustache of a russet hue, which he usually tugged at to help on his slow-moving thoughts. His name, Rupert, suggested swift dash and impetuous daring. But there was nothing of these things about this somewhat drowsy giant, although he had ample courage when necessary. It took much to rouse him, but once the dam of his self-restraint broke, everything and everyone were swept away like straws in a torrent of Berserk fury. When Rupert did fight, nothing could stand against his enormous physical power; and the use of this, being tempered by strong common-sense, invariably gained him the victory. But he usually preferred peace to war, and it took much to stimulate his passions to an outbreak.

Dean Carrington himself was to his friend like a Georgian rapier to a Crusader's sword. He was small and lean, quick-witted and nimble, with dark hair and dark eyes and a swarthy complexion. His clean-shaven face with its regular features and keen expression suggested the born intriguer, who gained his ends rather by cunning than force. Always perfectly dressed, always amiable, an accomplished squire-of-dames, well-read and yet a man-of-the-world, Carrington was the exact opposite of Hendle, and perhaps had made him his friend because of the vast difference in their natures. Having a more alert though not a stronger mind, he dominated Rupert in a most dexterous manner, never showing the iron hand without its velvet glove. Nevertheless, this ascendency had been achieved at Rugby, and owed its strength to the admiration of the dull boy for the clever boy; to the hero-worship of the younger for the older. But if Carrington was now thirty, Rupert was now twenty-seven, and might not be so easily mastered, presuming, as might be the case, the latter had developed qualities with which the former could not cope. This remained to be seen, and it was to see, that Carrington had come down for a Saturday to Monday rest. Now that he judged Rupert to be much the same and saw how luxurious were his surroundings, the astute barrister determined to reëstablish his sway over a wealthy friend too long neglected. Therefore he made himself delightfully agreeable. He had spent Saturday and Sunday with the Squire, and now was strolling through the village on Monday afternoon, before catching the evening train. So far, owing to Rupert's frank intimacy, he foresaw no obstacle to his making use of the young man. But there was one possibility to be reckoned with, which had to be looked into, and this Carrington approached in a roundabout manner, after his usual custom.

"A delightful place," said the barrister with a sigh of pleasure, as they sauntered along the cobblestone street, with its quaint houses on either side. "You are a king here. When you conduct the queen to the throne at the Big House, the serfs will lie down and allow you both to walk over them."

"I haven't any wish to walk over them," said Hendle, shrugging his mighty shoulders, "and I don't think the villagers would like to hear you call them serfs, Carrington."

"Pooh! They wouldn't know the meaning of the word. And, after all, it is only my picturesque way of speaking. But you evade my question."

"I didn't know you asked any. You simply made a remark."

"The Lord mend your wit, then. I must be plain, I see. What about a wife?"

"Oh, that's all arranged for," replied the Squire stolidly, and with never a blush, so matter-of-fact was he.

"And you never told me," murmured Carrington reproachfully.

"You never asked me."

"No," said the other, wondering at this phlegmatic nature. "I didn't." Then he lapsed into musing, and Rupert, never a talker at the best of times, strode beside him silent and comfortably happy.

So the possibility had become a probability, and a feminine influence had to be reckoned with after all. This was what Carrington had dreaded, and he blamed himself for not having asked the question before. Had he done so, he might have been introduced to the lady and then would have been able to judge what sort of a marplot she would prove to be. However, he hoped to meet her when he next came down, which would be very soon, and meanwhile, true to his plan of campaign, he laughed amiably at Rupert's reticence.

"You always did take things stolidly at school, Hendle," he said, arching his finely penciled eyebrows, "and you have not changed in this respect. Who is she?"

"My cousin—a third or fourth cousin. We have known each other all our lives, and that is why we know we will be happy."

"Familiarity doesn't breed contempt in this case, then," said the barrister lightly. "As you have known her all her life, I presume she lives hereabouts?"

"Oh, yes. At the other end of the village."

"I should like to see her," suggested Carrington persuasively.

"Next time you come down you shall. I shall ask her father and Dorinda to dinner at the Big House."

"Who is her father?"

"A second or third cousin of mine."

"What is his name?" "Mallien—Julius Mallien."

"I am little the wiser," said the barrister ironically, "and I don't want to exercise my profession of cross-examining people in the country. Can't you give me details?"

"I am," said the other, slightly surprised. "I am giving you details."

"Yes, when I ask you incessant questions. But make some sort of a speech. I want to know what kind of a person Mallien is; I want a description of the lady; I desire to learn what the father does, and if he will give his daughter a dowry. In fact, I wish to know all about it, as naturally I take the greatest interest in the welfare of my old school chum."

"Good old man," said Rupert, giving Carrington's arm so affectionate a squeeze that the barrister winced with the pain. "Well, Mallien's a beast, like Timon of Athens—you remember the play we read at school. I don't like Mallien, as he's always grousing at everyone and everything."

"You give me the key to his character by mentioning Timon. Your future father-in-law is a misanthrope."

Rupert nodded. "Very much so. And Dorinda is—"

"An angel. I know what you are about to say."

"I don't think you do. Dorinda is a good sort."

"Is that all the praise you can bestow on your future wife?"

"It's all she wants. Dorinda doesn't like compliments."

"What an unnatural girl!" laughed Carrington, "and her looks?"

Hendle filled his pipe while he replied and halted in the village square while he did so. "She's got black hair and blue eyes and a ripping figure and is heaps cleverer than I am."

"What a bald description! Has she two eyes and a nose with a mouth under it?"

"How you chaff, Carrington. However, when you come down again, you will see Dorinda for herself. Hallo, here's Kit."

"Who is Kit?" questioned the other, as a smart motor car slipped easily out of the crooked street to halt in the square, as the village green was grandiloquently entitled.

"The son of my housekeeper, Mrs. Beatson."

"That sour-looking woman with the hard eye?"

"The same. She has been hammered hard by misfortune, but is a lady born and bred for all that. Morning, Kit."

"Good morning, Squire. Hot, isn't it? I can only get some sort of wind by running the machine at top speed."

"You'll be roped in by the police if you don't mind your eye, Kit. My friend, Mr. Dean Carrington. This is Mr. Christopher Beatson, Carrington. He's a reckless hero, who plays with the whiskers of death on all and every occasion."

"That is the habit of the present generation," said Carrington, with a nod to the handsome young fellow in the car. "Motors, aeroplanes, scenic railways and looping-the-loop. Youth enjoys nothing nowadays unless it has in it an element of danger. To go out and never know if you will be home to supper, Mr. Beatson: that is your delight."

"There is much truth in what you say, Mr. Carrington," returned Kit, laughing. "After all, it's life."

"This is the frantic age," said Hendle sententiously. "How's business, Kit?"

"Ripping! I sold three cars last week on behalf of the firm. One to a lady."

"Who was taken with your good looks, I suppose. Take care Miss Tollart doesn't grow jealous, Kit."

"You will have your joke, Mr. Hendle," answered Beatson, his bronzed skin growing crimson and his brown eyes sparkling. "But Sophy knows that I have to play up to the customers to get the stuff sold." He turned from the wheel to look round generally. "Have you seen her? She's to meet me here and go with me for a spin."

Just then Miss Tollart appeared hurrying to the rendezvous as fast as her hobble-skirt would permit. She revealed herself as a fine-looking and decidedly flamboyant young woman with an independent air which suggested the suffragist. It could easily be seen, and by a less observant person than Carrington, that Kit would be known as "Mrs. Beatson's husband" when the ring was on the lady's finger. His chin betrayed a rather weak nature, and his eyes had much too kind a look in them to hint at mastery, while the tall black-browed young woman, who swung toward the group with the air of conquering Semiramis, appeared quite capable of dominating an empire, much less a husband. Carrington did not envy Kit's approaching connubial bliss.

"Mr. Carrington, Miss Tollart," said the Squire, introducing his friend to the new arrival. "Carrington, Miss Tollart is the daughter of our doctor."

Sophy winced at the mention of her father and Carrington wondered why she should. However, the emotion passed in a flash and Miss Tollart inspected the barrister much as a naturalist inspects a microbe under the microscope. The sniff with which she concluded her scrutiny hinted at dissatisfaction, if not at contempt. But then Sophy as an ardent suffragist never did think much of the male, and straightway flew her colors in the face of this particular one. "I am going to Elbowsham to speak at a meeting, Squire. Have I your good wishes?"

"That you will come home safe and sound?" queried Hendle with twinkling eyes. "You have. Don't insult the crowd more than you can help, Miss Tollart."

"I shall not conceal my opinions," retorted the lady, tightening her lips.

"Ah!" Carrington looked her up and down, "in that case I am glad Mr. Beatson and his car will be at hand to rescue you."

"I can fight my own battles," said Miss Tollart coolly. "But I see that you don't believe in Votes for Women."

"My dear lady," replied Carrington smoothly, "when I am in your presence I believe in anything you like to advance."

Sophy sniffed. "Hedging!" she observed aggressively. "Men never can give a straight answer. I only wish," she continued as she turned to Hendle, "that I could infect Dorinda with my ardor. But she won't uphold the banner, and sulks in her tent."

"I am afraid that I have exhausted all my persuasive power in inducing her to join me as my future wife," said the Squire politely.

Sophy nodded her approval. "Dorinda's a nice girl and a good girl, and a very pretty girl," she said, in her deep-toned voice, "but she is as weak as any man in this village. As weak as you are, Squire, as the vicar, as my father, and you know what he is." She winced again, then turned aggressively on Kit. "But I can't stay here all day, as the meeting at Elbowsham is waiting. Five miles,

Kit; you must do it in five minutes."

"What about the police?" asked Carrington.

"I despise the police," cried Miss Tollart, as she was borne away hurriedly by her lover to prevent further trouble. "They know me."

Carrington looked leisurely after the machine until it vanished and Sophy's trumpet tones of defiance died away. "What an uncomfortable young woman," he observed, turning toward his friend.

"Oh, Sophy's a good sort," said Hendle soberly. "She's had heaps of trouble."

"It doesn't seem to have knocked much sense into her, anyway. Trouble. Bother, I see. Her father, I expect?"

The Squire looked astonished. "Yes. But how you guessed—"

"I saw her wince when you and she mentioned Dr. Tollart," explained the barrister.

They crossed the green, passing an ancient cross of worn stone, which stood in the center of a vast expanse of grass burnt brown with the long-enduring heat. Round the square were various cottages with white-washed walls and thatched roofs, each standing in its own tiny garden brilliant with flowers. *The Hendle Inn*, with the arms of the family swinging from a signpost, was the largest building in sight, and presented an attractive sight to an artist, since it dated from Tudor times, and its upper story overhung the lower. With its red-tiled roof and dark oaken beams deeply embedded in its flint and stone walls it caught the eye of Carrington straightway. He had seen it before, but its quaint beauty lured him again to contemplation.

"That's a delightful old inn," he said, looking backward as they passed out of the square. "Quite the place for an adventure."

"There are no adventures in Barship," replied the Squire heavily. "We are very dull people hereabouts. Leigh is our bright and shining light, as he goes in for old manuscripts and ancient buildings and queer customs and—"

"In a word, Leigh is an archæologist," interrupted Carrington, who found Rupert somewhat prolix. "And who is Leigh?"

"If we had gone to church yesterday, you would have seen him in the pulpit, Carrington. He is the vicar, and, if you don't mind being blamed for nonattendance, we are going to look him up now."

"Oh, I don't mind in the least," said the barrister briskly. "If he talks religion, I can talk science. Argument is always amusing with a fanatic."

"I don't think Leigh is a fanatic. He is fonder of his hobby than of his profession. But he's all right as a parson, although he doesn't visit his parishioners as often as I could wish. Yonder's the church where all my people are buried. Picturesque?"

The barrister gave the building his grave approval "But everything is picturesque about here in the best style of art. You ought to be happy."

"I am. Very happy. But I shall be happier when I marry Dorinda!"

"Amen to that. And let me be your best man," said Carrington gaily.

"If Dorinda doesn't mind, yes," replied Hendle, exasperatingly matter of fact.

CHAPTER II

THE VICAR

By this time the Squire and his friend were approaching a rickety five-barred gate which stood wide open, as the hinges being useless, it could not easily be shut. Passing through this, they advanced up a wide untidy drive overgrown with grass, and this dismal path conducted them to a weedy stony expanse, girdled by an uncultivated jungle. Flowers, shrubs, herbs, trees, docks and darnels were all mixed up together in a way, suggesting only too clearly the sluggard's garden and almost aggressively presented an aspect of decay. The vicarage thoroughly matched this desolation, although in skilful hands it could have been made into a most charming residence. Carrington viewed this deadly solitude with disgust.

"Are you taking me to see the ruins of Babylon?" he asked, noting that even the blazing sunshine could not impart an aspect of cheerfulness to the place. "Is your vicar an owl or a jackal that he can live here?"

Hendle laughed deeply and pulled at his pipe. "Leigh is too much wrapped up in his hobby to care about the necessaries of life."

"He might care for the decencies, anyway," retorted the barrister. "As the lord of the manor, why don't you insist upon his keeping the place in repair?"

"The living is not in my gift, Carrington, and I have no right to interfere in any way. Leigh is the last descendant of an old family who camped ages ago in this parish. The living is all that remains of what they once possessed, and the vicar exists on a miserable stipend of two hundred a year."

"And you have four thousand per annum.—What about your tithes?"

"Tithes come from land, and save the park I have no land. My grandfather sold what we owned and invested the proceeds in various companies. My income is derived from stocks and shares. My tithe represents a small amount."

"Still, you might house your spiritual adviser better, Hendle."

"I don't think so. I look after the poor in the parish, and as one of the churchwardens I see that the church is all right. If Leigh choses to live in this way I can't prevent him. He's quite happy so long as he has a bed and a fire and a roof, with bread and cheese and his beloved books. What is the use of my giving him money to buy more volumes?"

Carrington nodded comprehendingly. "I understand. There are some people you cannot help, however much you may wish to."

"Precisely," murmured the big man indolently. "Leigh knows that I am willing to do anything in reason, but that I don't hold with his wasting money on books. His time also. The parson is here to look after his cure of souls; not to encourage a selfish hobby. Leigh loves books and dreams books and lives books and would spend a fortune in buying books. There is nothing he would not do to purchase more."

"A kind of clerical Eugene Aram?"

"Oh, no," replied Rupert hastily. "Leigh would never do wrong even to gratify his craze for books. He is a gentle soul."

"A character at all events, if nothing else," observed the barrister dryly.

In response to Hendle's loud rapping on the rusty panels of the door with the knob of his walking stick a slovenly, fat, old female waddled into sight, wiping her hands on a coarse apron. Her stout looks were in direct contradiction to the lean appearance of the place; but, judging from her inflamed countenance, these might have been due to a constant consumption of beer. She was arrayed in a dingy cotton gown, so dirty that it was difficult to guess at its original color, and her gray hair was as dishevelled as her shoes and stockings were untidy. This frowzy lady, who answered to the odd name of Selina Jabber, received the visitors with a good-natured smile which twinkled all over her plump face.

"To think, sir, that you should find me like this before I'm smartened for the afternoon," she cried, volubly addressing Rupert; "but washing has to be done, say what you like, though I do say that the master don't give me more to do than my weakness can deal with."

Talking all the time, the housekeeper had conducted the amused men through an entrance hall, narrowed by books heaped on the oilcloth, through a passage lined with crowded shelves and into a large bare room which appeared to be built up of many volumes. The walls could not be seen for these, and they were also piled in little heaps on the uncarpeted floor. The only articles of furniture were a large round table covered with green baize, standing directly in front of the undraped window, and a chair before it in which Mr. Leigh sat with a heavy tome on his knee. In spite of the sunshine pouring in, the apartment looked bleak and dreary, as there was no fireplace and no adornments or comforts of any sort. The vicar, a tall, lean, dreamy man with an ascetic, clean-shaven face and calm blue eyes, raised his head in response to the continuous ding-dong of Mrs. Jabber's voice:

"Mr. Hendle and a gent from London, sir; Mr. Hendle and a gent from London, sir; Mr. Hendle and—"

"That will do, Mrs. Jabber," interrupted the vicar in a dignified manner, and revealing the pundit in tone and accent. "You can go."

"You mustn't mind Mrs. Jabber, Rupert," said the vicar mildly. "She is quite a character. And this—"

"Is my friend, Mr. Carrington. I wished him to meet you before he went away."

"I am pleased to see you, Mr. Carrington," said Leigh, offering a dry, cold hand and giving the barrister a more searching glance than one would have expected from so mild a man. "I fancy I remember Rupert mentioning you as an old schoolfellow of Rugby days."

"Oh, yes. We were great friends at school, and I am glad to renew our acquaintance, as you may guess, Mr. Leigh."

"Quite so, quite so. And what's doing in London?" inquired the vicar in a weary manner as if he felt it incumbent upon him to manufacture conversation in which he took not the slightest interest.

Rupert sat down on one pile of books—as there were no chairs—and Carrington on another pile, while the barrister gave the latest metropolitan gossip and the squire smoked stolidly. Mr. Leigh drew up his threadbare black trousers, showing socks of different color and pattern, and sat down to take his book again on his knee. His face was handsome in a refined and gentle way: he had scanty white hair and excellent teeth, which looked genuine: hands and feet slender and elegant, suggested race, and he had the stooping shoulders of a student. Carrington, observing him narrowly while he talked in a desultory manner, saw that here was the last withered branch of an ancient family tree. The sap of the race was exhausted in Simon Leigh, and he looked as though his frail organization could not last much longer. There was no fire in him: only the slowly fading heat of dying ashes. Remembering what Hendle had said about the vicar's craze for books he attempted to interest him in that direction, as Mr. Leigh appeared to be wholly indifferent to news of the busy world.

"You are fond of archæology, I believe, sir," mentioned the barrister, glancing round the truly scholarly room.

"I am devoted to it, Mr. Carrington," replied the student, his calm eyes flashing into vivid life. "Antiquities, ancient customs, the usages of the Middle Ages and Classic times, together with the traditions of religious belief and ceremony appeal more to my understanding than anything else."

"Humph!" grunted the Squire pointedly, "surely as a parson—"

"We have frequently argued on the subject, you hint at, Rupert," said Mr. Leigh hastily. "But as your views differ from mine, we have, as yet, not arrived at any agreement. As a parson I trust that I do my duty, though it may be that I am not the ideal of a parish priest."

Hendle colored at this dignified rebuke. "I apologize, sir, but you rather mistake my true meaning. What I implied was that you are more of a scholar than a parson."

"I admit that, Rupert. Had I lived in monastic days, I should have been a hermit or a monk. My wants are few, and I do not seek the loaves and fishes of ecclesiastical preferment. The services of the church; occasional visits to my parishioners and giving of what alms my small means allow are my duties as a Clerk in Holy Orders. But what time otherwise is at my disposal I give to books, to the examination of old buildings, to the study of ancient customs, and such-like matters. You see I am frank, Mr. Carrington."

"And very original," said the barrister heartily, "it is a great pleasure to meet one whose views are other than commonplace. And what a tremendous number of books you have."

"You are like that clergyman in Scott's novel, *St. Ronan's Well*," said Hendle, removing his pipe for a moment. "What's his name—Cargill."

"I never waste my hours reading novels," said Leigh loftily.

"I should think they would be more entertaining than these parchments," suggested Carrington, looking at the writing table, which was littered profusely with dusty documents covered with crabbed characters.

"No! No! No!" cried Leigh vivaciously, and laid a thin hand on his beloved dry-as-dust pamphlets. "Nothing can be more entertaining than deciphering these deeds. Leases and proclamations, accounts and registrations: all of various reigns and all written in the dog Latin of knightly days. And it ill becomes you, Rupert," added the vicar in a mildly jesting way, "to reproach me with my besetting sin, when you pander to it by permitting me access to your Muniment Room."

"Muniment Room," echoed the barrister.

"It would not interest you, Mr. Carrington, believe me," said the vicar jealously, "as young men do not care to inspect such treasures. I can tell you all about the most interesting documents and can show you what is worthy of note, if indeed you care for such lofty learning. But don't meddle with the chest and its contents, I beg. They are too valuable to be lightly handled."

Rupert laughed and nodded. "I believe that Mr. Leigh grudges even me meddling with the deeds and documents. He thinks that I am an unworthy guardian of such literary treasures."

"I think they are quite safe," said Carrington, looking with disdain on the time-worn and soiled parchments rustling under the vicar's thin fingers. "No one will seek to deprive Mr. Leigh of his weary delights."

"Weary! Ah, my dear sir, you don't know what joy it is to pore over these glorious relics of monkish days. They give in wonderful detail the history of Barship, when it was quite a noted port."

"Port? Why, it's an inland parish."

"Now it is," cried the vicar eagerly and now settled in the saddle of his hobby-horse, "but in the reign of Henry III, Barship was built round a commodious harbor. The sea has retired these many miles, and the village which was once a bustling town is now scarcely known."

"Well, I must say that information is very interesting," said Carrington.

"Isn't it? And there are many other things just as interesting. I am writing a history of our parish from these documents here and others which are in the Muniment Room of the Big House. It will take me years to complete, but when ready it will form a book of surpassing interest."

At this moment, Carrington heard the door open softly. He turned his head, as did Rupert at the sound, to see a stout, black-bearded man standing on the threshold. He came in with a padding step like a cat, and scowled when he saw that the vicar had visitors.

"How are you, Mr. Mallien?" said Hendle with a good-natured nod. "This is my friend Carrington, who was at school with me."

"How do," said Mallien gruffly, and with an air of resenting Carrington's return greeting. "Beastly day—far too hot. Pouf! how this room smells of sheepskin. Why don't you drag Leigh out for a walk, Rupert?"

"The age of miracles is past," said the young Squire dryly. "You see that even your entrance cannot rouse the vicar from his studies."

"Vicar! Vicar!" said Mallien gruffly and tapped the parson's shoulder.

"Go away! go away! I'm busy," said Leigh peevishly; then, keeping his finger on a line of crabbed writing he had reached, he looked up. "Oh, Mr. Mallien, I beg pardon. What do you want?"

"Dorinda has brought you some flowers for the altar," said Mallien, "so I came with her. She *would* drag me out, although I didn't want to tire myself on this hot day."

"Is the day hot?" inquired the vicar absently. "Flowers. Thank you. Mrs. Jabber has the key of the church."

"Is Dorinda here!" questioned Hendle, making for the door with alacrity; "I must go and see her. Look after Carrington," he called back as he disappeared, and the vicar shook his head irritably at the sound of his raised voice.

Mallien did not obey his cousin's request by making himself agreeable to the visitor who was thus given into his charge. He stared at Carrington and Carrington stared at him, while Mr. Leigh droned in an undertone like a bee over his newly discovered fact of military occupation. The barrister saw before him a little man, less in height than himself and considerably stouter, dressed comfortably in a suit of loosely fitting gray homespun. Mallien's most noticeable point was the extraordinary quantity of jewelry he wore, which suggested Jewish blood. And indeed his face with its hooked nose and deeply black eyes hinted at the Hebrew. His dark hair and dark beard were flecked with gray, but his fresh, unwrinkled complexion made him appear much younger than he really was. He did not look at all an amiable person. And Carrington quite believed that Rupert had spoken truly when he had hinted at his cousin's misanthropic nature. Here assuredly was Timon of Athens in modern dress, glaring at the barrister as if he wondered why he presumed to exist. The man's manner was disagreeable and when he spoke his speech was pointedly aggressive.

"I know why you are staring," said Mr. Mallien in abrupt and unfriendly tone. "Everyone stares in the same way, confound their insolence. It's my jewelry, isn't it?"

"Why, yes!" said Carrington, matching this insolence. "You are as bedizened as a Hindoo idol on its feast day."

"You speak plainly," growled Mallien with a crushing look.

"So do you," retorted Carrington, who was not to be crushed. "We are well matched, it seems."

"I am older than you and require to be treated politely," snapped the other.

"Because everyone has hitherto gone down before your bullying ways, confound you," replied the barrister, getting in his thrust. "Don't you find plain speech a refreshing novelty?"

"Ah! what," Mr. Leigh looked up. "Presently, Mrs. Jabber—presently. I am not yet hungry. Go away. Oh, Mallien, I beg your pardon! When did you arrive? Will you stop to luncheon?"

"And eat the potted tongue your housekeeper has been talking about to Dorinda?" queried Mallien with grim rudeness. "No thanks. I have more regard for my stomach."

The vicar scarcely heard the retort, as he had already returned to the study of his soiled parchment.

"Do you know of any spot in the parish where a circumvallation is discernible, Mr. Mallien?" he said, half to himself.

"No, sir, I don't. And as I have no aeroplane I can't soar to the clouds where your wits are at present. I shall take my leave straightway. Good day;" and he departed forthwith. Carrington, amused by Mallien's brusque leave-taking, picked up his cap to follow so judicious an example since the vicar, really being in the clouds, was unable to attend to chance visitors. "Good day, Mr. Leigh," he said, moving toward the door; but, no notice being taken, he repeated his farewell in louder tones. "Good day, Mr. Leigh."

"Oh, good day, good day, good day," snapped the student irritably.

Leaving Mr. Leigh murmuring comments, and fumbling amongst the flotsam and jetsam of the Middle Ages, the barrister walked leisurely along the book-lined passage, through the book-littered entrance hall and emerged into the desolation of the surrounding jungle. Rupert and Miss Mallien were conspicuous by their absence, and the gruff individual left in charge of Carrington was waiting restlessly. He waved his hand when the visitor appeared.

"Did you ever see such a pig sty?" he growled with the voice of an ourangoutang, which beast he greatly resembled, "and Leigh is exactly suited to it. As the man is so are his surroundings: his mind is as muddled as his garden. And this addle-pated parson is supposed to be the spiritual father of the parish. Pah! Come and look at the lordly pleasure grounds. Rupert asked me to look after you, so I must, I suppose. Did you ever see such a rotten place?" he asked contemptuously.

"Oh, yes! You are showing me nothing new," replied Carrington, who took a delight in exasperating the man's temper.

"I shan't show you anything more," growled Mallien sullenly, "and after all I'm dashed silly to bother myself in this way."

"Oh, I don't quite see—Oh!" His face twisted with pain as he spoke.

"What's the matter with you?" demanded Mallien crossly.

"Toothache! I have had a twinge or two lately and I expect that this damp place"—Carrington looked up at the dark overhanging boughs—"has brought back the pain. I shall have to see a doctor when I go to town."

"You can see a doctor here, if you like," said Mallien roughly, and pushed his way back to the avenue. "Dr. Tollart lives at the end of the village. Anyone will tell you where he is to be found."

"Thanks," said the barrister as they paused by the rickety gate. "You are kinder than you mean to be."

"I'm not. I want to get rid of you," fumed Mallien, turning on his heel. "You can go to the doctor or to the devil for all I care."

Carrington saw the little man vanishing with great speed round the corner and laughed at the oddity of his character. Then he walked through the village and soon found Tollart's house. The doctor proved to be within and speedily gave his patient something to take away the aching. It was only a makeshift of course, but Carrington was glad enough to get rid of the uncomfortable feeling. After paying half a crown he went away leisurely, and by the time he reached the gates of the park felt much better.

Strolling up the avenue, Carrington suddenly began to shiver in the warm sunshine, and was greatly surprised that he should do so. It seemed unreasonable and certainly was unexpected.

"Strange," he muttered with a shrug; "now a superstitious person would say that I was walking over my grave. Pooh!" he laughed, but nevertheless shivered again.

CHAPTER III

LOVERS

In justice to Handle, it must be said that he by no means intended to desert his friend, even though the enthralling society of Dorinda might have proved an excuse for his forgetfulness. But far from wishing for the barrister's absence, Rupert had left a message with his future father-in-law, requesting Carrington to see the church, after taking leave of the vicar. Out of what the Yankees term "sheer cussedness," Mallien had not delivered the message, and every moment Hendle expected the appearance of his friend, quite ignorant that Carrington was already on his way to The Big House. And thinking that the barrister was being entertained—as one of his cynical character would be—by Mallien's rudeness and Leigh's quaint ways, the young Squire forgot all about his old school chum for the time being. This was very natural, seeing that Dorinda was beside him, and he therefore had no eyes or ears save for her.

"Get a can of water," directed Dorinda, as they passed from the vicarage jungle into the trim slopes of the churchyard, "and bring it to me as soon as possible. You will find me in the porch arranging the flowers."

Readily consenting to this division of labor, the Squire went to find Mrs. Jabber and the necessary can, while Dorinda, already possessed of the key, unlocked the great oaken door under the porch. With her arms filled with roses, she entered into the chill twilight of the little fane: chill because the thick walls prevented the summer heat from penetrating into the interior of the building and twilight since the sunshine was more or less baffled by the stained glass of the windows. As the girl passed up the central aisle, round her were the squat Norman pillars, above her loomed the criss-cross rafters of time-darkened oak, and beneath her feet was the storied pavement inlaid with many a quaintly lettered brass plate praising the virtues of the dead in monkish Latin. Before her, under the glorious hues of the east window, rose the altar, draped in white and gold with single and triple silver candlesticks glittering on either side of the tall brass cross. The vases—also silver—were filled with mixed ill-chosen flowers gathered anyhow and arranged anyhow by Mrs. Jabber, whose eye was anything but artistic. After breathing a short prayer, Dorinda, who had left her roses on a convenient seat, took the vases off the altar and out of the church. Having shaken out the flowers, she brought her crimson blooms into the porch and sat down on the side seat to fulfil what was to her a very pleasant duty. Rupert arrived with the can of water, and the information—obtained from Mrs. Jabber—that both Mallien and Carrington had gone home.

"I expect your father forgot to deliver my message," said the Squire, setting down the green can and taking a seat opposite to the girl.

"It is more likely that my father never intended to give it," replied Dorinda with a shrug.

"Why shouldn't he?"

"Because it was a reasonable thing to do, and my father is never reasonable, as you know."

"Carrington will think me rude."

"Not if he can see through a brick wall. And from what you have told me about him, Rupert, I think his eyes are quite keen enough to do so. There is one thing to be said," observed Miss Mallien, rather piqued by the barrister's neglect, "that your friend isn't anxious to see me."

"On the contrary, he is very eager," Rupert assured her hastily.

"Does his going back to the Big House look like it?"

"Ah, I expect he had some delicacy in interrupting our *tête-à-tête*, Dorinda."

"There's something in that," replied Miss Mallien, dexterously binding her bunches of roses loosely together, "and his action speaks well for him. Perhaps I shall like him better than I expect to, Rupert."

The Squire looked up in astonishment from his task of brimming the altar vases with spring water. "Why shouldn't you like him in any case?"

"Well," Dorinda placed a bunch of flowers in a vase and put her head on one side to note the effect, "you say that Mr. Carrington is cynical, and I don't like cynical people. I have had so much cynicism from my father that it is impossible to stand more of it from another person."

"Oh, it's only a pose with Carrington. He's really a good fellow."

"If he is, why can't he show that he is? My dear Rupert, I never did believe in those people, who have hearts of gold and bad manners: who lend you money with a blow, and with the best intentions bully you into cheerfulness."

"What odd things you say, Dorinda," murmured Rupert, not knowing if she was speaking in earnest or in fun. "Carrington hasn't bad manners unless his going away without seeing you—"

"No! No! That may be delicacy," she interrupted swiftly. "I dare say he's really a nice man, and I shall like him very much. But remember, dear, that knowing you has raised my standard. I shall expect him to be very, very nice."

"Oh, Dorinda, don't put me on a pedestal," said Hendle, at once dismayed and pleased. "I am a very prosaic person."

"Then I like prosaic persons."

"And Carrington is very brilliant," went on Rupert stolidly, as he tugged at his moustache to induce thoughts for his friend's defense.

"You are quite brilliant enough for me, my dear boy." She rose suddenly, and taking his face between her hands kissed him twice. "There and there. Why are you so exasperatingly modest?"

"Am I?" asked Rupert, wondering why he had received the caress.

Dorinda laughed. Indeed, she could do nothing else, since Hendle was so very literal in his acceptation of her remarks. "You're a sweet-tempered donkey, my dear," she said lightly. "Now you take those two vases and I'll take these two. Come along."

Shortly the altar glowed with the crimson splendor of the roses, and their delicate fragrance was wafted through the chancel. Then the lovers left the church and sauntered back to the Vicarage, with the key for Mrs. Jabber, with offended dignity.

Miss Mallien was well worth looking at, as she was a gracious and stately maiden, well fitted to be the mate of the Saxon giant. Dorinda was as tall for a woman as Rupert was for a man, and carried herself with the same imposing dignity. Her dark hair and deeply blue eyes hinted at an Irish strain, and her vivacity was also Hibernian. But to this fascination, which had to do with the race of the sister isle, Dorinda added much English common sense, so that her romantic dreams never overrode her matter-of-fact instincts. She loved her cousin for his staunch honesty and attractive simplicity of character, since in these qualities he represented the exact opposite of her father. For this last-mentioned individual, whom she had the misfortune to call her parent, Dorinda did not entertain much respect, and hoped by marrying Rupert to escape from a companionship which was very disagreeable to her. It was only Hendle's wealth which induced Mallien to consent to the marriage; but, even had he objected, Dorinda would have held to her engagement. Rupert was her man of men, and, while he held her hands and looked at her with grave admiration, she thought how fortunate she was in securing such a mate. She esteemed his devotion more than much fine gold.

"My father will be waiting for me at the cottage," said Dorinda; as she strolled away again.

"A little disappointment won't harm him," said Hendle coolly, for he had not much sympathy with Mallien's selfish nature; "and I want you to meet Carrington. He leaves for London after dinner, and you won't meet him again for some time. Say yes."

"Yes," responded Dorinda, who really felt considerable curiosity concerning the object of Hendle's Rugby hero worship; "but father will be cross."

"I never knew father when he wasn't cross," retorted her lover, as they resumed their walk and entered the village square. "He's an infliction. I tell you what, Dorinda, the best thing we can do is to marry before the roses fade."

"Oh, Rupert, you are getting quite poetical."

"Am I?" asked Rupert, surprised. "That's strange, when I don't like poetry."

"I must teach you to like it, dear."

"Hum!" said Rupert, rather at sea, "you mean, I suppose, that we have much to learn from one another."

"Something of that sort."

"You shall do exactly as you like, dear," said her lover, as they came in sight of the house. "Why, here is Mrs. Beatson."

A tall, lean woman, with a sour and discontented face and an elegant figure issued from a side walk with a basket of flowers. Anyone could see that Hendle's housekeeper was a lady by birth, just as anyone could see that she was not an amiable woman. She was like Mallien, and had a tendency to look upon human beings as her mortal enemies, since, liking luxury, she had never been able to indulge her fancies. Left a widow with one son, she had taken the post of housekeeper some five years before Carrington's visit, and on the whole performed her duties admirably. But, being disappointed in not leading an idle life with sufficient money to gratify her whims, she always went about with an aggrieved air. It was only Rupert's kind-heartedness which permitted her to stay at The Big House, and visitors—Carrington among them—wondered how he could put up with such a wet blanket. Few people care to have a kind of Christian martyr at their elbow from morning to night.

"How are you, Miss Mallien?" said Mrs. Beatson, greeting Dorinda stiffly. "I am just gathering flowers for the dinner table. You will have an early dinner to-night, Mr. Hendle, will you not, as Mr. Carrington is leaving early?"

"Yes. I think I told you, Mrs. Beatson. We dine at six-thirty. By the way, I met Kit in the village; he looks well."

"He never comes near me to see if he's well or ill," rejoined the housekeeper bitterly. "He's a bad boy."

"Oh, no, Mrs. Beatson," chimed in Dorinda. "Kit is a very good boy. We are all very fond of him."

"Ah, you don't know him as well as I do," said Mrs. Beatson, shaking her head sadly. "He is—but I need not tell you, as you will find out soon enough for yourselves. Excuse me, Mr. Hendle, and you, Miss Mallien, but I must go in with my flowers. And there is Mr. Carrington at the drawing-room window."

With a stiff bow Mrs. Beatson disappeared, while Dorinda shrugged her shoulders. She never approved of Mrs. Beatson's martyr-like airs, which were wholly unnecessary, seeing what a comfortable situation she had. However, there was no time to think about the widow, for Carrington, slipping out of the front door, came down the terrace steps. He looked young and handsome and debonair, evidently presenting his very best side for the inspection of his friend's betrothed. Indeed, having caught sight of the couple from the drawing-room window, he had hastened to come out, with the intention of breaking the ice with the young lady in a light and airy manner. Mr. Carrington had a great belief in first impressions.

"I have eaten all the cakes and have drunk all the tea, Hendle," he said, gaily; "but, had I known that Miss Mallien was to honor the tea table, I should have restrained my appetite. How do you do, Miss Mallien? Since Hendle will not introduce me, I must do myself. Behold a briefless barrister, Dean Carrington by name, who is delighted to meet you."

"Thank you," replied Dorinda, shaking hands, and wondering why the man was so emphatically agreeable. Perhaps a touch of her father's misanthropy made her suspicious, or perhaps Carrington rather overdid his welcome. "I am glad to meet you. Rupert has often spoken about you."

"I hope he has said nice things," rattled on the barrister, as the trio returned to the house. "You see, he only remembers what a nice person I was at Rugby, and it is years since we met. I may have changed for the worse."

"I don't see any change in you," replied Hendle, with mild surprise. "Don't undervalue yourself, Carrington. Why didn't you come on to the church?"

"Perhaps you didn't know that we were there," suggested Dorinda. "My father may have forgotten to deliver Rupert's message."

"Oh no. The message was delivered right enough, Miss Mallien. But I have been young myself, and never, never, never spoil sport."

"You talk as if you were a hundred," remarked Hendle, as they began the meal.

"So I am, in experience of the seamy side of life. You, my dear fellow, are about five years of age. I expect you have found that out, Miss Mallien. He is the most unsophisticated youth, who has been wrapped up in cotton wool all his life, knowing disagreeables only from the newspapers and novels."

"I think that Rupert is less unsophisticated than you think," replied Dorinda, a trifle dryly, for she did not admire Carrington's easy tone of patronage toward her lover. "And why do you say that you expect I have found that out? I may be unsophisticated also."

"You are everything that is charming," said Carrington alertly, "but, having met your father, I think that you are not to be taken in by people."

Dorinda colored, knowing well what the keen-witted barrister meant. However, she endeavored to turn his point by altering slightly a well-worn quotation. "To know him is a liberal education, I suppose you mean," she said, lightly. "Don't take my father too seriously, Mr. Carrington. His bark is worse than his bite."

"Oh, I am sure of that," replied Carrington, who was sure of nothing of the sort. "We both barked at one another until the Vicarage jungle rang. We hope to meet again, Miss Mallien, and renew our contest of wits. By the way, to go to another subject—the Vicar. What a man, and what surroundings!"

"He is quite a character," laughed Dorinda, "but the dearest old man in the world."

The conversation continued, mostly in a bantering way, for some time, and then, tea finished, Rupert proposed to see Dorinda to the gates of the park. "If you don't mind being left alone, Carrington."

"Not at all; not at all. Gather ye rosebuds," said the barrister, lightly; "good day and good-bye until our next happy meeting, Miss Mallien."

With a smile which masked her true feelings—for she resented Carrington's manner; it seemed to her while having tea that he had attempted to make Rupert look small—Dorinda passed out of the drawing-room and into the hall. Hendle put on his cap and accompanied her down the avenue, while the barrister stood at the door and waved a farewell. But when they were far enough away to prevent seeing or hearing, his brow grew dark. "Confound that Hendle," he muttered; "he has all the good things of this world. A fine house; a large income; a delightful betrothed, and magnificent health. If I were an envious man—ha!" He drew a long breath, and then turned sharply, as some one passed through the hall.

It was Mrs. Beatson, who always had a habit of coming and going in a ghostly fashion. Carrington was not sure if she had overheard, as he always was suspicious of people's sharp ears. And he had spoken somewhat loud. However, if she had been eavesdropping, there was nothing for it but to risk the chance of her repeating his not very wise speech to Hendle. However, again, the barrister thought that if the housekeeper did babble, he would be quite able to deal with such a fool as the squire. Therefore he gave Mrs. Beatson a bland smile, which she returned with a sour one, and climbed up the stairs to his room.

Meanwhile, at the gate, Hendle was asking Dorinda a question. "I think you'll find me a dull sort of fellow after Carrington," he said ruefully.

"My dear," replied the girl, throwing her arms round his neck. "I would not exchange you for one hundred and ten Carringtons."

"You don't like him?" questioned Hendle, greatly surprised.

"No," answered Miss Mallien, "I don't. He's double-faced. We'll hand him over to father. He can deal with him," and in spite of Hendle's objections, she went away repeating her doubts of the brilliant barrister.

CHAPTER IV

THE COTTAGE

For a widower with one grown-up daughter, Mr. Julius Mallien was very well off on an income of five hundred a year, for which he did not do a stroke of work. Like the lilies of the field he toiled not, neither did he spin, and, if not quite a Solomon-in-all-his-glory, he was quite comfortable, enjoying some of the luxuries of life as well as all the necessities. Born lazy and idle, he had never earned a single penny for himself during the fifty-odd years of his existence. First he had lived on his father and mother; afterward on his wife. Now that all three were dead, he managed to exist in a pleasantly easy way on the accumulated moneys they had left him. His picturesque six-roomed cottage, standing in a quarter acre of garden on the outskirts of Barship, was rented from the Squire at twenty pounds a year, yet he grumbled like an Irish tenant at the exactions of his landlord. Dorinda, with the aid of one small servant, looked after the house, and Mallien was quite untroubled with domestic details. His daughter catered for him in strict accordance with his tastes, wholly setting her own aside, and from one year to another there was no change in the economy of the establishment. It therefore came about in quite a natural manner that Mr. Mallien spent the greater part of his income on himself.

"I shall allow you so much for housekeeping and so much to dress on," he said to Dorinda, when she returned from school to become his companion, or rather his domestic drudge. "One hundred pounds yearly must cover all expenses, food, servants, clothes and rent; and if you exceed that, you'll hear about it."

As it took Dorinda some time to get used to this scrimping, she frequently made mistakes, and did hear about it. In fact, she was scolded so often that she became quite callous to her father's tempers, and finally, when he went too far, the girl who was not lacking in spirit, told him what she thought of his selfish conduct. There was a royal row, in which Dorinda came off best, and when things were again settled Mallien was careful not to provoke her anger again more than his disagreeable temper could help. On the whole, father and daughter got on very well together, but there was little affection displayed by either of them: on Mallien's part because he hated what he called sentiment, and on Dorinda's because her egotistical parent always kept her at arm's length. The boy-and-girl love of Miss Mallien for her cousin, which had strengthened into the staunch love of man and woman, was the sole thing which enabled the girl to endure the drab existence at The Cottage. It was always something to look forward to that one day she would become Rupert's wife, and then would be quit forever of her father's uncomfortable whims.

Not that Mallien gave his daughter much of his society. His hobby was jewel collecting, and Dorinda took no interest in such things. For a woman, she was inexplicably indifferent to gems, and lace, and clothes and amusement, so that her father voted her a bore and went his own way. In his particular room—which was the most comfortable in the cottage—he remained, constantly arranging and polishing and admiring the precious stones in their many mahogany cases. Not being rich, his collection was necessarily a small one, although every jewel represented a bargain and had a history attached to it. But Mallien was always lamenting that he could not purchase historic gems, and envied the long purse of his cousin, the young Squire. However, he hoped to draw upon this when Dorinda became Mrs. Hendle, as Rupert had promised to double his income to make up for the loss of the girl. She objected.

"I feel as if father was selling me," she told Rupert when matters were settled on this basis. "He won't feel my being away a bit, except that he will miss his favorite dishes and the way in which I manage to make both ends meet. You shouldn't have agreed, Rupert."

"My dear," said her lover, with much common sense. "I think it is cheap at the price, to get rid of such a disagreeable man. What I give your father will enable him to indulge more freely in his expensive hobby; consequently, he will leave us alone."

"No, he won't," contradicted Dorinda, who knew her father's persistence. "When he hears of some particularly rare jewel, he will come and bother you for money to buy it."

"He won't get it," retorted Rupert, dryly. "I can be quite as obstinate as your father. With what he has, he will have one thousand a year, so he must do the best he can with that. I am doing my best to settle things fairly and peacefully, but if your father wants trouble, I am not the man to deny him any in reason."

Dorinda laughed and gave way, although she still resented her father making money out of her marriage. But Mallien, being one of those men who is a curse to himself and to everyone around him, could not be treated in any other way, and could make himself very disagreeable when on his mettle. Besides, Dorinda knowing what Rupert's temper was when aroused, dreaded lest there should be an open quarrel. Mallien would certainly have come off worst in any encounter; but, as he was her father, she did not wish for such a *contretemps*. She and Rupert had been engaged for two years when Carrington came down to Barship, and hitherto all had gone smoothly. But a few days after the barrister's departure, Mallien began to make himself unpleasant. "I don't see why Rupert can't marry you next month," he said, fretfully, one morning at breakfast. "You've been engaged long enough."

"So we both think," replied Dorinda, who was pouring out the coffee, looking particularly fresh and charming in a white linen frock. "But you have always objected, you know."

"I don't wish to lose my daughter," growled the misanthrope, clutching at his black beard and scowling.

"That is very sweet of you, father, but you mustn't sacrifice five hundred a year for my society."

"What do you mean by that, you minx?"

"Is it so hard to understand?" asked Dorinda coolly.

"It's not what a daughter should say to a father."

"Well, you see, so much depends upon the sort of father one says it to."

"Honor your father and your mother," quoted Mallien, crossly.

"Parents, be mindful of your children," retorted the girl. "Oh, I can match you, quotation for quotation, if you like, father; I have been exercising my memory in this respect when talking to Mr. Carrington."

"Carrington! Carrington. I forbid you to mention his name. I have already given you my opinion of that impertinent pig—"

"Frequently," interpolated Dorinda crisply.

"—And I won't allow him to be spoken of. You have just mentioned the reason why I think you should get married straightway."

Dorinda set down the marmalade with surprise. "What can Mr. Carrington have to do with our marriage?" she inquired, staring.

Mallien wriggled. "Rupert's a fool to bring the fellow down here," he burst out furiously. "He's a sponge, and a son of the horse-leech, who will get all the money he can from Rupert."

"I don't see why you should say that," protested the girl. "Mr. Carrington did not give me that impression."

"Well, he gave it to me," grumbled her father, eating sullenly; "and if you allow him to get hold of Rupert—who is a fool, as I said before—your marriage will be indefinitely postponed. I won't have it; I won't have it, I tell you," cried the stout little man, jumping up in a fine rage. "If Rupert's money should be given to anyone, it should be given to me."

"Well, as soon as I am Rupert's wife, you will have five hundred a year," said Dorinda soothingly.

"What's five hundred a year?" said Mallien, contemptuously. "I want the whole four thousand. There's a blue sapphire in Paris I wish to get hold of."

Dorinda shrugged her shoulders calmly, being quite used to her father's explosive nature. "You can't expect Rupert to give you all his income," she observed in measured tones. "He is paying a good price for me, seeing that I go to him without a dowry."

"You shall have my jewels and my income when I die," growled her father, as he sat down again. "Any money he gives me, comes back to you. But if Rupert was to die—"

"Father!" Dorinda uttered a startled cry of pain.

"There! There!" snarled Mallien testily. "I don't mean that he is going to die, you silly girl. But he's mortal and *may* die."

"God forbid! But if he did—" she hesitated, then uttered the word faintly, "—die?"

"Then I would have The Big House and the four thousand a year," said Mallien brutally. "You seem to forget that we are both descended from John Hendle, who died in the Waterloo year."

"I have never given a thought to it," said Dorinda uneasily, as she did not approve of her father starting this hare.

"Well, you ought to think of it. We descend from the elder son of John Hendle, and are the older branch."

"But Rupert descends through the male line, while we come through the female, father," protested the girl, puzzled by this genealogical conversation.

"Pooh! Pooh! There's no entail. Don't look so astonished, Dorinda; I don't mean to say that I have any claim, though, if everyone had their rights, we should be at The Big House and Rupert in his beastly cottage. There would be no need for you to marry him then."

Dorinda rose with great dignity. "I marry Rupert because I love him, and if he was a pauper, I should still love him."

"Oh, you could love him as much as you like," said her father, carelessly, "but if he were really a pauper, you shouldn't marry him. I'd see to that."

Dorinda walked round the table and bent over her father with a look on her face which made him push back his chair. "You would see to nothing," she said, very distinctly, and bringing her face close to that of Mallien. "It is my will and pleasure to marry Rupert, and nothing you can say or do will prevent my becoming his wife. You understand?"

"Who said anything otherwise," growled Mallien savagely, yet retreating dexterously. "As things stand, I am willing you should marry him. And, as you talk to me in that way, the sooner you become his wife and leave me alone the better it will be. Marry to-morrow if you like."

"I see," said Dorinda, whose face was perfectly colorless. "You want the extra five hundred a year to buy this blue sapphire you speak of."

"Partly. But I also want you to marry Rupert before Carrington—the beast—squeezes him like a lemon."

"There is no chance of any squeezing," said Dorinda coldly. "Rupert is quite capable of looking after himself, even if Mr. Carrington were after his money, which I see no reason to think that he is."

"I do! Carrington's a man on the market, if you know what that means."

"I don't. What does it mean?"

"One who lives from hand to mouth; one who is always on the make; one who doesn't mind what he does so long as he can extract a fiver. Rupert's a fool, and Carrington isn't. There, you have my opinion in a nutshell."

"I think you are making a great fuss over nothing, father," said Dorinda, with disdain. "But I am glad that Mr. Carrington's visit is likely to hasten our marriage. We can get married next month, and then you can buy the sapphire when we are on our honeymoon."

"Sensible girl!" Mallien stood up and wiped his bearded mouth. "Well, now that we understand one another—?"

"Do we understand one another?" asked Dorinda, irritated by the whole unnecessary conversation.

"Yes!" replied her father, tartly. "I have given my consent to your marriage taking place at an early date—"

"Because you want the five hundred a year to buy the blue sapphire."

"Don't be silly. And I have warned you against letting that flipperty-flap Carrington gain too much influence over Rupert."

"A quite unnecessary warning," said the girl, coldly. "You don't like Mr. Carrington, because he held his own against you."

"Insolent beast!" growled Mallien, bristling. "And I think you said that you did not like him yourself."

"I said that I did not trust him; but he is amusing enough to like as a companion for all that."

"You'll find him very amusing when he rifles Rupert's pockets," sneered the gentle parent, fuming at her opposition.

"I don't think that there is the least chance of his doing that, as Rupert—I said this before—is well able to look after himself. Besides, you have no grounds for saying that Mr. Carrington is a scamp."

"A look is enough for me."

"It's not enough to take away a man's character. And this talk of our being descended from John Hendle? What do you mean by that?"

"I don't mean anything particular," responded Mallien, honestly enough. "It was Leigh who put it into my head."

"The vicar. And what does he know of our family history?"

"Much more than we do. He has been scrambling through the papers in the Muniment Room at The Big House."

"Well, Rupert gave him permission to look out any documents likely to prove necessary for writing the history of the parish. You know he is writing a book."

Mallien nodded. "He found letters, written by John Hendle, which showed how much our ancestor regretted that the estates should go to Frederick Hendle."

"That is the younger son from whom Rupert is descended?"

"Exactly. He was a bad lot apparently, Leigh says. Walter, who was the eldest son and our progenitor, was killed in the Battle of Waterloo, and he seems to have been the old man's favorite. If Walter had lived, we should have inherited The Big House and the estates."

"Well, father," answered Dorinda with a shrug; "Walter didn't live, and we did not inherit the estates, so I don't see what is the use of talking."

"I didn't say that there was any use," retorted Mallien crossly, "only I thought that the piece of family history discovered by Mr. Leigh might interest you."

"It does in a way. But, after all, these family troubles happened nearly one hundred years ago." Dorinda was looking out of the window as she made this remark, and broke off suddenly. "Strange!" she said, staring into the garden.

"What is strange?"

"That we should have been talking of Mr. Leigh, for here he is with Titus Ark as his shadow, as usual. I wonder why he always has Titus at his heels?"

"It's a very necessary precaution," said Mallien, grimly; "otherwise, Leigh is so absent-minded that he would get lost. Leigh has only come to look again at that Yucatan diary, which my father left me."

"Does he want to see it?" asked Dorinda, forgetting that Leigh had seen the diary before.

"Yes. Your grandfather, as you know, was something of an explorer, and searched for hidden treasure among the buried cities of Central America. I was telling Leigh about the diary, and he wants to have another look at it," Mallien chuckled. "I shouldn't wonder if the old man wanted to go to Yucatan himself, since he is cracked on old buildings."

By this time, the vicar was knocking at the door, and Titus Ark was staring sourly round the garden. He was the sexton and the vicar's shadow, a dour ancient, who said little and thought much. Dorinda, not wishing to see the vicar, who rather bored her with his archeological discourses, went into the kitchen to attend to her domestic duties, while her father opened the front door to receive his visitors in his usual ungracious manner.

"What on earth brings you here, vicar?" he demanded brusquely, although he had just explained to his daughter why the visit had been made; "and why do you always have that old ass at your heels, Mr. Simon Leigh, parson of Barship Parish, God help the people?" grumbled Mallien, as he pushed his visitor into a chair and banged the door.

"Titus," said Leigh in his precise tones. "Oh, we were boys together—that is, he was a young man when I was a boy. Poor fellow, his generation lies under the ground, so I take him about to comfort him with talk about old times. He quite brightens up when we have our talks and walks."

"I'd brighten him if I had the power," growled the gracious host. "He ought to be under the turf with his confounded generation, or in the workhouse. I don't see any use for such a stiff-jointed old skeleton being aboveground."

"He is eighty," said Mr. Leigh, placidly. "Great age. A comfortable room this, Mr. Mallien; there is something of the sybarite about you."

"Don't call names, vicar. The room is less like a pig sty than yours, and that is the best to be said about it."

"I often wonder, Mr. Mallien, that with your bringing up, you have not learned better manners," said Leigh, putting on his pince-nez and blinking. "You are certainly a most ill-conducted person. You should marry, and see if the softening influence of the feminine nature—"

Mallien turned from a cupboard of black oak, in which he was rummaging, and answered viciously. "I have been married."

"Dear me," mused the vicar, as if aware of this for the first time, "so you have been. And how is Miss Dorinda?"

"I believe his wits are going," grumbled Mallien to himself: then raised his voice. "She's busy, and can't waste her time in seeing you. Here"—he flung a heavy sheaf of papers on the table—"this is the diary kept by my silly father when he was treasure hunting in Yucatan. Old fool, he got nothing but rheumatism. If he'd found gold and jewels, there would have been some sense in his explorations. Don't you think so? don't you think so? don't you? Oh, hang you, vicar; one might as well call the dead."

Leigh nodded absently, for the sound rather than the sense of this polite speech had reached him. Already he had opened the manuscript diary at random and, with his nose close to the pages, was pouring over the faded writing. Mr. Mallien growled as usual, and walked across to the mantelpiece to pick up his pipe for a morning smoke. When blue clouds made a haze round the eagerly reading parson, Mr. Mallien brought out a handful of precious stones of little value from his trousers pocket, and began to fiddle with them, after his ordinary fashion. He strewed ruby and emerald and moonstone about the table, where a shaft of sunlight struck across the room, and watched the many colored sparkles, emitted by the tiny gems. Leigh, taking no notice, turned over page after page with great interest. After a long while he grunted and spoke, maliciously anxious to spoil the scholar's pleasure if he could.

"Dull stuff my father wrote, didn't he?"

"Dear me, Mr. Mallien, are you there? Dull stuff. Oh, dear me, no. Most interesting. These Maya buildings are quite fascinating, and the manuscripts he discovered, and the stone carvings, and the hieroglyphics, similar to those of Egypt. Yes," went on the vicar dreamily, "I must go there."

"Go there; go to Yucatan," cried Mallien, staring; "an old buffer like you?"

"Yes, sir," said the vicar with dignity. "For quite a year since you mentioned the diary of your father, it has been in my mind to fit out an expedition to so interesting a place."

"How can you fit out an expedition on your income?"

"Money. Ah yes, I shall require money, of course."

"And a jolly lot, too. Expeditions are not fitted out for nothing."

"I believe not," murmured Mr. Leigh, again dipping into the manuscript.

"Well, well, the money will be forthcoming."

"Who will give it to you?" asked Mallien contemptuously.

"I thought that Rupert—?"

"Pooh! You might as well try and get blood out of a stone, Mr. Leigh. And why the dickens should he give you money to go on a wild-goose chase? Rupert is a wise man, and keeps his cash in his pocket, as I'd do if I had his income."

"Would you not give me the money if you had four thousand a year?" asked the vicar, with an extraordinarily keen look.

Mallien stared, quite unable to speak, so indignant was he at the audacity of the parson. "Give it to you?" he burst out. "I'd give it to nobody."

"Ah, then I hope you'll never get money," said Mr. Leigh, placidly, "you would make bad use of it."

"I would," retorted the gracious host, "if I gave it to you to make ducks and drakes of in expeditions. You can be buried less expensively in England than in Yucatan, believe me."

"I have no idea of being buried anywhere," said the vicar with dignity, and yet with a scared look which puzzled Mallien. "I am old, it is true, but my health is good and I live a reasonable life."

"You wouldn't if you went exploring Yucatan," retorted the other.

"I would take the risk of that, Mr. Mallien. The place is so interesting"—his nose was glued to the manuscript again—"that I really must raise the money and go. I have plans—oh yes, I have plans to get it."

"You won't from Rupert."

"Nor from you, apparently," said Leigh, who appeared to be much more alert than usual, "but I prefer Rupert's youth to your avaricious age. However, I shall come again and resume my reading of this manuscript—unless you will let me take it away."

"I'll do nothing of the kind, nor help your expedition," said Mallien grimly, "nor even give you the rubbish my father wrote."

"Rubbish," cried the parson indignantly; "that diary is worth all the property which John Hendle left to the son he didn't love. Well! Well, it's a case of pearls before swine," and, paying back Mallien in his own coin, by making this remark, the vicar departed with his shadow at his heels.

"Old fool," commented Mallien; "but I wish John Hendle had made that will."

CHAPTER V

A REVELATION

It was with joy and relief that Dorinda communicated her father's decision to Rupert, and he was as pleased as she was at the prospect of their speedy marriage. Hitherto Mallien, not wishing to make himself uncomfortable by losing his housekeeper—which Dorinda really was—had always objected to the performance of the ceremony. Certainly he gained five hundred a year when the two became one; but, during the twenty-four months of the official engagement, this fond parent had not been in particular want of money, and in any case had always borrowed what small sums he required from his liberal-minded cousin, at intervals. But now his heart was set upon purchasing the blue sapphire which he had mentioned to Dorinda, and it was not likely that Rupert would give him the price of that. Therefore, to get his new income assured, he allowed the young couple to have their own way. Also—and this had a good deal to do with the granted permission—he really dreaded lest Carrington should obtain any influence over the young Squire, and thought that the gaining of such could best be prevented by giving Rupert his desire. With Dorinda beside him, it was unlikely that Hendle would allow Carrington to draw on his purse.

Seeing that Miss Mallien had a small opinion of her father, and spoke to him pretty freely on subjects of dispute between them, it seemed strange that she should have laid such stress on obtaining his consent to the marriage. But Dorinda, considering that her father was her father, in spite of his unamiable nature, wished him to exercise this last act of paternal authority. She would not have been happy had she provoked a quarrel by going contrary to his views, and so had waited until he thought fit to issue his commands. Had Mallien, indeed, wholly forbidden the marriage taking place, Dorinda would have rebelled, but she gave way on the minor point of an unusually long engagement. She saw Rupert almost daily; they understood one another thoroughly, and, as both were young, there was no particular hurry. Nevertheless, the girl was pleased at the lordly permission of her irritating parent, and set about her preparations straightway. It was now July, and after a conversation with Rupert, it was decided that the Rev. Simon Leigh should make them man and wife toward the end of August. And Dorinda confessed to her future husband, that she would be glad to escape from the constant society of her father, who of late had been unusually trying. On his side, Rupert was extremely glad to get the dearest girl in the world all to himself. So the important matter was settled, and Hendle returned to The Big House very contented with the world in general and with himself in particular.

In his delight he called in Mrs. Beatson to the library to inform her of his intended change of life, although he rather dreaded the woeful looks and sad words with which she would receive his communication. Mrs. Beatson made her appearance, looking more like a Christian martyr than ever, but assumed her most gracious and lady-like manner to hear what her young master had to say. She greatly resembled that painfully well-bred gentlewoman, Mrs. Sparsit, in Dickens' story, and, like her, was a housekeeper very much against her will.

"Wish me joy, Mrs. Beatson," said Rupert gaily, when the martyr made her sour appearance. "I am going to be married."

"So I have understood for two years, Mr. Hendle."

"Quite so. I have been engaged to Miss Mallien for quite that time. But we are to be married toward the end of next month."

"Indeed!" Mrs. Beatson looked dismayed. "Isn't that rather sudden?"

"Sudden!" Rupert swung round his chair and looked puzzled. "How can it be sudden after my being engaged for twenty-four months?"

"I only mean, Mr. Hendle, that I should have thought it necessary for you to consider the matter carefully for six months before fixing the day. Marriage, Mr. Hendle, is a serious matter."

"It is a very delightful matter, Mrs. Beatson, considering who the lady is."

"Ah!" Mrs. Beatson crossed her hands and cast up her eyes with a melancholy expression, "so we all say until we are married. I suppose, Mr. Hendle, you intend to give me notice?"

"Indeed, I intend to give you nothing of the sort," said Rupert bluffly. "All the difference will be that my wife will give you orders instead of me."

Mrs. Beatson looked as though this would make a very great difference indeed, as she much preferred to have a master than a mistress. All the same, she looked relieved when she learned that her situation was not in danger. "I am glad to stay on, Mr. Hendle," she said, with the air of making a concession. "I look on The Big House as in some sense my home."

"That's all right. Continue to look upon it as your home, until Kit marries Miss Tollart and you go to live with them."

"Pardon me, Mr. Hendle," said Mrs. Beatson with icy scorn; "but you little know my nature when you suggest such a thing. I don't approve of Sophy Tollart, whose views regarding our sex are anything but pacific. Besides, young people rarely take the advice of those who are older and wiser than they are; consequently, it is best for them to live by themselves. Would you like Mr. Mallien to dwell at The Big House when you wed with his daughter?"

"Good Lord, no," replied Hendle hastily. "It is the last thing either I or Miss Mallien would desire. We can manage our own affairs."

"So you think, Mr. Hendle; but the mistakes you will make will be endless."

"Nonsense, I am not a fool, and Miss Mallien has plenty of good sense."

"Sense isn't experience," lamented Mrs. Beatson, shaking her head and smiling in a most dreary manner. "However, I am no prophetess of evil, and wish you and Miss Mallien well. But mistakes you will make, say what you will, and sorrow will come to you as it comes to all."

"There! There! Don't croak any more, Mrs. Beatson."

"Me croak," repeated the lady in surprise. "Why, I am trying to look on the bright side of things, for whatever you may say there is always a black side."

"Well, well," observed Rupert testily, for her words and manner irritated his usually steady nerves. "We'll wait and see what happens. Never trouble trouble till trouble troubles you, is a very good proverb."

"I annoy you by speaking the truth," remarked the good lady with a superior smile. "Ah, that is always the way with the young, sir. However, you have only to say the word and I go."

"I don't want you to go."

"You may not, Mr. Hendle, but Miss Mallien will."

"Not at all. She is quite willing that you should stay."

"So she says, but I have my doubts;" and Mrs. Beatson groaned, being quite sure in her own mind that Dorinda wished to turn her out to die by the wayside. "However, this is a world of sorrow, and when I am starved to death, perhaps you may be sorry for your harsh treatment."

"Wait until the harsh treatment takes place," retorted Rupert, who would have liked to shake her into common sense. "Meanwhile, I have told you of my intention to get married next month."

"There's many a slip between the cup and the lip," said Mrs. Beatson, mysteriously; "but the less talked about is the soonest forgotten." After which cryptic speech she drifted toward the door, as if her legs were taking her in a direction contrary to that expressed by her will. "The Rev. Mr. Leigh is in the Muniment Room, Mr. Hendle," she said, pausing on the threshold, "and expressed a wish to see you."

"You might ask him to stay to dinner," said Rupert, glancing at his watch.

Mrs. Beatson departed firmly convinced that her master really intended to dismiss her and had only broken the ice with his information about the marriage, so that she might be prepared to be turned out to die. With this in her mind, she hovered uneasily about the dining-room and drawing-room both before and after dinner, in the hope of catching some stray word, which might reveal Rupert's expected treachery.

Meanwhile Rupert, after a hearty laugh at Mrs. Beatson's cheerful manner of looking at the future, went upstairs to dress for dinner.

"Hang Mrs. Beatson," he thought, when he descended to the drawing-room. "I do wish she would keep her dismals to herself. She's about as cheerful as tombs, and not at all the person to have in the house of a young married couple," and from this mental speech it may be guessed that the dreary old lady was within an ace of being dismissed, as she dreaded, although such an idea had never entered her master's mind until she began her wailing.

Mr. Leigh, who had brushed and washed at Mrs. Beatson's request, for he was dusty and grimy after his work in the Muniment Room, was wandering about the big drawing-room, peering at pictures and statues and old silver through his pince-nez. He turned to greet Rupert in his usual mild absent-minded way, when the young Squire, smartly groomed and eminently handsome, entered.

"Quite Greek," murmured the vicar, balancing himself on his toes and with his hands behind his back. "I must say that your looks are in your favor, Rupert. For the well-being of the race you should marry and beget children."

"Well, I am going to," said Hendle, used to the vicar's eccentric speeches. "I make Dorinda my wife next month."

"Oh, indeed," said Mr. Leigh alertly. "Dorinda is a very desirable damsel. I hope you will be happy."

"You seem to have your doubts, from the tone you use," remarked Rupert dryly.

Mr. Leigh shook his head. "Life has its troubles," he observed sententiously.

"For heaven's sake, vicar, don't croak. I have had enough of that from Mrs. Beatson," a remark which the housekeeper, hovering outside the door, overheard and registered in her mind as a bad omen for her future continuance at The Big House. "I beg your pardon," went on the Squire, rather ashamed of his momentary irritability, "but I do wish people would look on marriage as marriage and not as a funeral."

"Of course, of course," ruminated Mr. Leigh. "One is always sure of a funeral, though not of a marriage."

"Vicar!" burst out the young man, much vexed at this persistent lamentation, "you are—well." He linked his arm in that of Mr. Leigh, knowing it was useless to argue, "you are hungry and there's the gong."

"Am I hungry?" Mr. Leigh asked, when he was being conducted into the dining-room. "Really I believe I am. For three or four hours I have been busy in the Muniment Room."

"I wonder you don't grow tired of fumbling amongst those dusty parchments."

"No! No! No! They are most interesting. Yet," went on the vicar, as he spread his napkin across his spare knees. "I may have to postpone my history of Barship Parish after all—until I return from Yucatan, that is."

"Yucatan!" Rupert nodded to the butler that he should fill Mr. Leigh's glass with sherry, for the vicar was too absent-minded to give the order. "Where is Yucatan?"

Mr. Leigh devoted his attention to the soup, and then looked up dreamily. "Yucatan," he repeated. "Dear me, Rupert, your geographical knowledge is limited."

"I never was a particularly good scholar," said the squire apologetically, "and Yucatan is some out-of-the-way place, I take it."

"It is in Central America, and is concerned with the Maya civilization."

"Oh, now I know what you are talking about. You refer to that diary of old Frank Mallien, which his son has. Dorinda told me that you went occasionally to see it at my cousin's cottage."

"Yes," said Mr. Leigh, more wide awake than usual; "and, although I have been many times for the last year, Mallien always tells me over again that it is his father's manuscript when he explored Central America. He thinks that I am wanting in common sense, I fancy. But I let him talk on rudely, as he does talk, Rupert. After all, the diary is so interesting, that Mallien's brusque manners are well worth putting up with for the sake of my acquiring the information it contains."

"What does it contain?" asked Rupert, more for the sake of promoting conversation than because he cared.

"An account of a dead and gone civilization," said the vicar in a dreamy tone, and scarcely knowing that fish had been placed before him. "Tombs, cities, stone carvings and manuscripts, deposited with mummies. Yes, there certainly must have been some communication between Yucatan and Egypt. Le Plongue says—dear me, I forget what he does say. However, I can see into the matter for myself when I go there."

"Go to Yucatan—to Central America," said Hendle staring. "Why, at your age, it is dangerous to attempt such an expedition."

Mr. Leigh only caught the last word. "Expedition! Yes! It will be costly, as Mallien, in his rude way, observed. But I have arranged how to get the money, Rupert. A thousand pounds—perhaps more. Really I am not sure what it will cost. But we can arrange the sum later."

"We?" Rupert stared harder than ever.

"You and I," said Leigh placidly. "After all, I am glad you have the money and not Mallien, as you are more likely to do what I want than he is. A dour man, grasping and avaricious."

Rupert glanced at the butler and the footman. "I don't quite understand," he said, in a puzzled way. "Perhaps you will explain."

In his turn Leigh, following Hendle's eyes, glanced at the servants. "When we are alone I can tell you all about it over our coffee."

More bewildered than ever and, in a vague way, sensing danger, Rupert would have asked for an explanation. But the servants being present, he decided to wait until he was alone with his erratic friend. Therefore the conversation passed on to other subjects connected with Mr. Leigh's discoveries in the Muniment Room, of various documents connected with the behavior of dead and buried Hendles toward the parish. Rupert said very little. What with Mrs. Beatson's gloom and the vicar's cryptic utterances, he felt as though some storm were approaching, and was anxious for the meal to end, so that he could go to the root of the matter. All the same, he laughed at himself for entertaining such a wild fancy. There was no quarter of the heavens from which any storm, big or little, could blow, as all was serene and bright. And, as Hendle happened to be one of those very material persons who only believe in what can be seen, heard or touched, he scouted the idea of any premonition heralding any possible evil. Yet the premonition was in his consciousness sure enough, and the young man, prosaic as ever, put it down to indigestion. A weaker explanation considering his splendid health can scarcely be imagined.

When the dinner was over, Mr. Leigh, who had contented himself with a single glass of port wine to round off the entertainment, rose more briskly than usual, and announced his wish to go.

"You must not mind my speedy departure, Rupert," he said, slipping his pince-nez into his waistcoat pocket; "but I have much work to do in connection with my proposed expedition. I hope Titus Ark is waiting to accompany me home. I told him to call for me about half-past six."

"Ark is waiting in the kitchen," said Rupert, after a quiet word with the pompous butler. "He came at six and has stayed on. There is no hurry for you to go, Mr. Leigh. Remember you have something to tell me," and Hendle, taking the old man's arm, led him gently but firmly into the drawing room.

"Something to tell you," repeated the vicar puzzled; then suddenly his face cleared. "Oh, dear me, yes; how fortunate you reminded me, Rupert. It has to do with John Hendle."

"John Hendle. Do you mean my great-great-grandfather—"

"Who died in the Waterloo year. Yes, I do. When we are alone,"—Mr. Leigh broke off and glanced meaningly at the footman who was bringing in the coffee. "It is lucky you reminded me," he ended aimlessly, "very lucky. My expedition, ah yes, this hangs on that and that on this."

"What on earth are you talking about?" questioned Hendle, much vexed at all this unnecessary mystery. "Sit down and drink your coffee and tell me all about it. You don't smoke, I know, but I shall."

"Certainly, certainly," murmured Leigh vaguely, "of course, your marriage with your cousin will bring together the two branches of the family. That, in the long run, will put things right."

"Put what things right?"

"Money matters."

Hendle echoed the word and stared. "I wish you would talk plainly," he said, with some irritation.

"Oh, certainly. I am rather apt to wander in worldly matters." Leigh cleared his throat and sat up briskly with all his wits about him for once in his dreamy life. "Mallien is descended from Walter Hendle, and you from Frederick Hendle, their father John being your common ancestor."

"Yes, that is so. But Mallien descends through the female line, although he is the elder branch of the family."

"There is no entail?"

"No. If there was, it would be in my favor, as I descend through the male heirs. But what does all this mean?"

"I shall tell you if you will allow me to collect my thoughts. While searching in the Muniment Room, Rupert, I came across letters of John Hendle, which show that he loved his elder son Walter and greatly disliked his younger son Frederick. Walter was a brave man, who fought for his country and who died at Waterloo. Frederick, as the letters say, was a scamp—what in those days was known as a blood. Reckless, extravagant and evil, he alienated his father's affections, and John Hendle desired to disinherit him."

"It is the first time I have heard of Frederick's iniquity," said Rupert with a shrug, "and I see little use in raking up the evil done by a man who lived about one hundred years ago."

Leigh took no notice of this observation. "John desired that his granddaughter Eunice, the child of his favorite son Walter, should inherit. As the property was entirely at his own disposal, he made a will in her favor."

Rupert jumped up so suddenly that he upset his coffee. "What?"

"Pray don't act in so excitable a manner, Rupert," protested the vicar, raising his thin hand. "You irritate my nerves."

"But—but—what you say—oh, it's absurd," stammered the Squire. "There was never any question about Frederick's inheriting the property. I don't know much about the matter, as the thing didn't interest me. But, if Frederick inherited wrongly, surely the question would have been raised before."

"How could it be when the will in favor of Eunice was missing?"

"Missing?"

"Yes. John made the will and apparently died suddenly before he could make it public. I found it," said Mr. Leigh slowly, "in the chest."

"In the Muniment Room?"

"Yes. It is a will drawn up quite legally on parchment as was the case in those days, although I don't think wills are drawn up now on—"

"Oh, never mind these minor points," broke in Rupert hastily. "You say that you found a will, made by John Hendle, leaving the property to Eunice, from whom my cousin Mallien is descended?"

"I did. Some weeks ago I came across the document. But I did not say anything until I ascertained for myself as to which of you two was the right person to have the money. I am inclined to think that you had better keep it, Rupert, since Mallien is so avaricious, and will not help anyone—not even me, when I desire money for my expedition to forward the cause of science."

"If this will is in order," said Rupert, rising to pace the long room, and feeling painfully agitated. "Mallien should have the property."

"I fear so; I fear so," murmured the vicar uncomfortably. "The same leaves the property unreservedly to his grandmother Eunice. I have not told Mallien, who would undoubtedly contest your right to the estates, as I do not consider him a fit and proper person to have much money."

"Right is right," said Hendle, whose face was pale and whose lips were dry. "If Mallien is the rightful heir, he must be placed in possession. But all this may be a mistake on your part. Where is the will?"

Mr. Leigh looked nervous and distressed. "Dear me, Rupert, I am afraid I have mislaid it. I took it home to study it at my convenience, so as to make sure that it really gave the property to Eunice. I did examine it, and became quite positive that Mallien is the rightful heir. Then, somehow—you know how absent-minded I am—I laid it aside and since have not been able to find it. I have searched without result."

"You should have given it to me at once," said Hendle, severely.

"But, my dear boy, I had your interest at heart," protested the vicar, wiping his forehead. "I know how quixotic you are, and guessed that you would give the property to Mallien without demur, if the will was correct, which I fear it is. For your own sake I took time to consider the discovery I had made."

"You must find the will at once," commanded Rupert manfully, "and it must be submitted to the lawyers. If Mallien is the heir, Mallien gets the money."

Mr. Leigh rose, much agitated. "I don't think he should get it, Rupert. He is a greedy man, who would only hoard up gold and make a bad use of newly acquired wealth. I tell you he declined to help me to fit out my expedition. I know you will, so you ought to keep the money."

"How can you advise me to be so dishonest," cried the Squire, indignantly, "you who are a clergyman of the Church of England?"

"I have the greater sense of right from being so," rejoined the vicar, quite tartly for so amiable a man. "And when I remember that you and yours have enjoyed the property for one hundred years, it seems ridiculous to hand it over to another man."

"Who belongs to the elder branch, remember," said Rupert swiftly. "And who is, according to your reading of this newly discovered will, the rightful heir." He took a turn up and down the room, then stopped to face the vicar who was fidgeting on the hearth rug. "You must turn your house upside down to find the will, Mr. Leigh, and it must be handed over to our family lawyers, so that Mallien may be placed in possession of the property forthwith."

"Rupert, I implore you not to act hastily or foolishly. Say nothing about this belated testament, which will do Mallien more harm than good considering his greedy and misanthropic nature. I will look for it and will give it to you. Throw it into the chest again."

"No! no! no! I would never have a moment's peace if I did that. I know that Mallien is not the man to have too much money, but I can't help that. If he is the rightful heir, he must enter into his kingdom. Besides, if I marry Dorinda, the property will come back to me, representing the younger branch."

"If Mallien gets the property," said Mr. Leigh deliberately, "he will not allow you to marry Dorinda."

"I can trust her," said Rupert curtly.

"Quite so. But you will have no money to marry her, and Mallien will cut her off with a shilling. He is quite capable of doing so."

Hendle knew this well enough and reflected for a few moments. "Say nothing to Mallien or to anyone," he remarked finally, "until you find the will and we can look over it together."

"Oh, I shall certainly hold my tongue," said the vicar quickly. "Believe me, it is only my esteem for you which makes me urge you not to notice the will. Sleep on the question, Rupert, for the morning is wiser than the night. This matter will remain strictly between ourselves. Now good night; good night."

Hendle shook hands, not objecting to the vicar's abrupt departure, and when alone groaned over the unexpected fulfilment of his premonition.

CHAPTER VI

COUNSEL'S OPINION

When Hendle, having a weight on his mind, woke shortly after dawn, he remembered the vicar's proverb, and thought that it might be true. Morning certainly was wiser than the night with him, as he began to ask himself why he should be so much disturbed over an unproven matter. Leigh certainly asserted positively that he had found a hundred-year-old will, made in favor of the elder branch of the Hendle family, and, undoubtedly, he spoke in a way which appeared to be genuine. But then, the vicar was a queer, eccentric person, who sometimes believed his visions to be facts, and who had on occasions some difficulty in distinguishing between the real and the unreal. In a perfectly honest way he might be making a mistake, and Rupert, turning over the matter before rising, hoped fervently that such might prove to be the case.

On the other hand, unless Mr. Leigh's statement had some foundation, in fact, it seemed improbable that he would even think of such a thing. There had never been any question as to the legitimacy of Hendle holding the property, and after a whole century had elapsed, it seemed strange that such an odd question should be raised. Assuredly the vicar must have found something which had to do with the inheritance of the estates by the elder branch, else the fantastic idea would not have entered his rather wavering mind. But the will might not be good in law; it might have been signed and not witnessed, or there might be some flaw in its drawing up which would nullify its provisions. If this was the case, Rupert was far too sensible to think of surrendering his lands and income to a man, who, on the face of it, would make a bad use of the same. On the other hand, if the will was quite in order, the Squire was honest enough to step down from his throne and allow the rightful king to take his seat thereon, evil as might prove to be his rule. The whole question of right or wrong turned on the production of the will.

Having reached this point in his meditations, Rupert arose, and cleared his brain by a cold bath. It would be foolish to say that he was not worried, for he felt very much upset, as was natural, seeing there was a chance of his being reduced to the condition of a pauper. Mallien was not rich, but he had enough to live on, so the acquisition of more money would only result in his greater extravagance in the purchase of jewels. But if the will proved to be legal, Hendle foresaw that he—the Squire of Barship—would be turned out of his pleasant home without a single penny and without any means of earning one. He had no profession; he had no trade; he was not over-clever, and Mallien— he was sure of this—would not allow him anything out of the estate. This was uncomfortable enough in itself for a young man who liked the good things of this life, but there was worse to follow. He would lose Dorinda, since her father would undoubtedly prevent the marriage with a pauper. The girl herself, as Rupert had said to the vicar, would remain true; but how could he ask her to become his wife, when he could not support himself, much less a helpmate? It was all very painful and very disagreeable, and Rupert descended to breakfast with a bad appetite.

"You don't look at all well, Mr. Hendle," remarked Mrs. Beatson, when she came for orders after breakfast. "Perhaps you are sickening for a fever."

"Not at all," replied her master, more crossly than he was accustomed to speak to this dismal woman. "I have had a wakeful night, that's all."

"Ah well, sir, it's natural, considering you are going to take such a serious step as marriage without thinking about it."

Rupert allowed Mrs. Beatson a certain amount of latitude, but here she overstepped the mark. He passed over her observation in silence, and gave his orders for the day. "I shall have dinner at eight," he remarked, having arranged matters, "as I am going to town and will not be back until late."

"Going to see the lawyers, I suppose, sir," mentioned the housekeeper with an odd look on her dreary face.

Rupert looked up suddenly, wondering why she had made such a pertinent observation, for it was in his mind to do what she had suggested. "Why do you suppose that, Mrs. Beatson?"

"Well, sir, it's only natural, as no doubt there are marriage settlements to be prepared, and all must be in order for the ceremony."

Mrs. Beatson said this glibly enough, and her reason appeared to be very plausible. Nevertheless, her glance was so significant that Hendle wondered if she had guessed his trouble. It seemed to be incredible, since Leigh had promised to hold his tongue until the matter was properly threshed out. Yet there was a certain malicious triumph lurking in the housekeeper's look, which hinted that she was rejoicing at his approaching downfall. After swift reflection Rupert thought that he was mistaken, and was in the position of a man who sees a bird in every bush. He therefore ignored Mrs. Beatson's remark and merely repeated that he would return late to dine. The woman hesitated for a moment, as if she wished to speak more plainly, then tossed her head and glided out in her ghostly way. Rupert frowned, for her behavior made him uncomfortable. Yet it was impossible that she should know anything of the thunderbolt which had struck him.

And after all, as the Squire reflected when he started to walk to the railway station, the thunderbolt had not yet reached its mark and might not reach it at all. Only an examination of the will would prove if he was a rich man or a pauper, and in his anxiety to learn this, Hendle called in at the Vicarage as he passed the rickety gate. Strange to say, Mr. Leigh proved to be absent, as he had gone to see a dying parishioner.

It was only a short walk to the little wayside station, at which the London trains stopped occasionally during the day. Rupert caught the ten o'clock train easily, and, although it was very full, managed to secure a compartment to himself. Here, when the engine started, he gave himself up to meditation, not, as it may be guessed, of the most pleasant kind.

Hendle, as Mrs. Beatson ignorantly or knowingly had suggested, really intended to consult lawyers. But, before going to his family solicitors, he thought that he would ask the opinion of counsel in the person of Carrington, as it struck him that there might be a Statute of Limitations in connection with long-lost wills. Even if there were, Rupert knew, in his own heart, that if Mallien proved to be the rightful owner of the property, he—the present owner—would never be able to take advantage of any law quibble. It all depended on the will, for, if not produced, he would not be required—even by his own uneasy conscience—to surrender his house and income. He wondered if Leigh had lost the will forever, in which case things could remain as they were; he wondered if there was a will at all, or, if there was, whether the vicar might not have made a mistake; he wondered if the will were found, if it would be all shipshape, so as to deprive him of his kingdom. Indeed, Hendle wondered in a more or less worried way throughout the journey to town, and stepped out onto the platform of the Liverpool Street station in anything but a happy frame of mind. Carrington had envied him his wealth and quiet existence; it was anything but quiet now, and the wealth—if the vicar proved to be correct—was about to take wings to itself and fly away into Mallien's gaping pockets. In a dismal frame of mind, Rupert took a taxi to Friars Inn.

It was in this set of tall buildings that Carrington had his chambers for business purposes.

"Hendle!" said the barrister, when his visitor was ushered into a bare room sparsely furnished and looking very businesslike, "this is a surprise. How are you, old chap; not up to much, from the look of you."

"I'm bothered out of my life," replied Hendle, taking the cane chair—a most uncomfortable one—which was pointed out to him.

"Oh, I think there is sufficient life left in you to stand a trifle more strain," was Carrington's flippant observation, as he resumed his seat at a very businesslike desk. "I can't guess in any way what can bother you."

"No one, but the wearer, knows where the shoe pinches," quoted Hendle grimly.

"Quite so, and no one ever will know unless the wearer explains the bad fit, my friend. Bothered? You! With beeves and lands and money, and the promise of a beautiful and desirable damsel to be your wife."

"That's just it," said the visitor, seizing the opening. "I may lose all these things, Carrington."

The barrister wheeled his chair round to stare, and his keen dark face was alive with curiosity. "Have you been outrunning the constable?" he asked; "has the lady changed her mind? Has—"

"You are wide of the mark. To put the matter in a nutshell, it's a will."

"A will! What about it?"

"This much. It exists and may disinherit me."

"The deuce. In whose favor?"

"In favor of Julius Mallien, my cousin."

"Then he will have his rights, if he has a leg to stand on," said Carrington grimly. "Mallien struck me as a man who would go through fire and water for himself. Why did your father make a will in his favor?"

"He did not. The will was made one hundred years ago, by John Hendle, from whom Mallien and I are descended."

"One hundred years ago," echoed the barrister puzzled. "Then how comes it you have to do with it now?"

"Leigh found it in the Muniment Room."

"Confound his zeal. But still I don't quite understand. Perhaps you will tell me the whole story from the beginning. I suppose you have come to ask my advice as a friend?"

"Yes, and as a barrister."

"My best forensic lore is at your disposal. Well?"

Hendle at once began his explanation, and, as he proceeded, became much too restless to remain seated. Midway in the recital he started to his feet and began to pace the narrow limits of the office. Shading his eyes with his hand and drawing figures on the blotting paper, Carrington listened to the rather amazing story of Leigh's discovery, and when in possession of the facts looked rather skeptical. "I understand that you have not seen the will?"

"No. Leigh, as is natural with so untidy a man, has mislaid it."

"Then how do you know the will exists?"

"Leigh says so."

"Humph!" Carrington threw down his pencil and leaned back with a doubtful look. "I think the vicar's wits must be wool-gathering. He has no enmity against you, I suppose?"

"Enmity?" Hendle stopped in his walk and stared.

"I mean he is your friend."

"Oh, yes. Leigh and I are great friends."

"And his attitude toward Mallien?"

"He doesn't like him overmuch. Mallien is so rude to him."

"And to everyone," finished Carrington with a shrug. "A most disagreeable person. Well, as Leigh likes you and doesn't like your cousin, I take it he could not have invented this story to do you out of the property in Mallien's favor."

"No. Leigh is the best of good fellows, though rather eccentric. He must have found the will; it is impossible that he could have suggested its existence otherwise."

"I suppose not," murmured Carrington vaguely; then glanced shrewdly at his client. "Does he know your family history?"

"Everyone in Barship knows that," replied Hendle, dropping again into his chair with a sigh. "There is nothing to know really, as we have always been a dull, homely lot of people."

"Tell me how your descent runs from John Hendle?"

"In the direct male line. Frederick, the son; Henry, the grandson; Charles, the great-grandson, and myself, the great-great-grandson."

"And Mallien's descent?"

"He comes in the female line from Walter, the eldest son of John Hendle. Eunice, the daughter of Walter and the granddaughter of John, married George Filbert. Mrs. Filbert had a daughter Anne, who married Frank Mallien, and her son is Julius, my cousin, who has, as you know, a daughter."

"Dorinda, to whom you are engaged," commented Carrington; "that marriage will bring the elder and the younger branches of the family together. A very good arrangement. Will Julius marry again?"

"I don't think so. He hates women."

"I should think every single member of the sex returned the compliment. But what I mean is, that when you marry Miss Mallien, the money will come to you and her when her father dies."

"It should, as we two represent the elder and younger branches of the family, joined, as you observed. But Mallien is quite capable of leaving the money elsewhere out of devilment. He tolerates me because I lend him money, and he has very little affection for Dorinda. We are to marry next month, because I have promised Mallien five hundred a year when I make Dorinda my wife, and he is now in a hurry for the money. But," added Rupert anxiously, "if he knew that he was the rightful heir, he would forbid the marriage."

"It is probable he would, since he has such a sweet nature," said Carrington dryly; "but would Miss Mallien obey him?"

"No. She loves me too well for that. But, of course, if I lose the property, I am reduced to pauperism pure and simple, and could scarcely ask the girl to share my nothing."

The barrister nodded sympathetically. "It's a beastly position," he said, after a pause, "especially as you haven't been brought up to earn your own living in any way. But, of course, we are building on sand. Nobody but this weird parson has seen the will, so it may not exist."

"I don't see why Leigh should think of such a thing if the will does not exist," said Rupert impatiently.

"True enough. Well, let us grant that the will does exist and leaves the property to Eunice Filbert, from whom Mallien traces his descent. Still, possession is nine points of the law, and your lot has held the property for close upon one hundred years. There is a Statute of Limitations."

"Oh!" Rupert looked up eagerly. "I had an idea that there might be. Then, if I take your meaning correctly, since this will has only been found after so long a period, the Statute operates against its being legal?"

"Well, it might operate or it might not; it all depends upon the circumstances of the case. Mostly the Statute of Limitations would operate. The will was never filed in the Probate Court, I take it?"

"No. Until Leigh found it I expect no one but its maker and his witnesses knew of its existence, and they are all dead, ages ago. But I thought wills were filed at Somerset House?"

"Now they are. But in 1815 they were filed at the Probate Court at Canterbury."

"Well," said Hendle restlessly. "The question is, what am I to do?"

"Well, obviously the first thing is to get possession of the will and in that way learn exactly how things stand with regard to Mallien. John Hendle may not have cut off his second son Frederick entirely."

"He may not," assented Rupert dubiously; "on the other hand he may. Leigh certainly gave me to understand that everything had been left to Eunice, who afterward married Filbert. If such is the case, you may be sure that Mallien will take everything, and will decline to give me a penny."

"Just like him. But the Statute of Limitations—"

"I shall not take advantage of that," interrupted Hendle firmly. "If the will does make Mallien the heir by descent, he shall have the property."

"But, my dear man," cried the barrister, starting to his feet, "that is quixotic. Why leave yourself without a penny, especially when Mallien is such an unamiable person?"

"It's hard, I grant," replied Rupert ruefully; "yet, as an honest man, what else can I do?"

"It seems to me that there is a limit to honesty," said Carrington tartly. "I scarcely think that I could act so quixotically if I had to do with the matter. However, we can discuss this point when the will is in your possession, and we can make sure that what Leigh says is true. When do you hope to get it?"

"Well, I don't know. Leigh said that he had mislaid it and would search for it, so I have called this morning on the chance that he might have found it. He was absent attending to a dying woman, and of course I couldn't interrupt him at his business. I left a message that I would call again when I returned this evening."

"When do you return?"

"By the seven o'clock train. I shall arrive in time for dinner. I told Mrs. Beatson that I would dine at eight."

"If Leigh finds the will, I presume he will bring it to you this evening at The Big House?"

"He might and he might not. And in any case I shall call."

Carrington considered the remark for a few moments and stared out of the window at the chimney pots. "I don't think that I would call if I were you, Hendle," he said at length.

"Why not?"

"Because this case needs a more careful handling than you are able to give it, my friend. Leave Leigh alone until to-morrow, and I'll come down some time about midday to interview the vicar along with you."

"It's very good of you, Carrington," said the perplexed Squire gratefully. "I don't expect one night will make any difference, as I shall be certain of the bad news soon enough. I'll wait until you can go with me to-morrow to the Vicarage; perhaps, by then, Leigh will have found the will."

"I don't leave the Vicarage until he has found it," said Carrington grimly. "It's too important a document to be left in the hands of a shiftless creature such as Leigh. He is quite capable of taking it to Mallien, if it is in favor of Mallien's grandmother, as he asserts."

Hendle, standing up to go away, shook his head. "I don't think he will go past me," he remarked slowly. "In the first place, he dislikes Mallien because of Mallien's brusque manners, and in the second Mallien refused, out of his present income, to help him to fit out an expedition to Yucatan."

"Central America. Why does the vicar want to go there?"

"Oh, he's been reading some diary of Mallien's father, describing certain researches amongst buried cities in those wilds, and wants to go there and look up things for himself."

"I dare say if you finance this expedition, Leigh will say nothing about the will—that is, if he has already said nothing to anyone," said Carrington.

"He told me that he had not. Save you and I no one knows about Leigh's discovery. It's just as well that Mallien doesn't know," ended Rupert, with a shrug, "or he would tear down the Vicarage, or rob it, to get the testament which would make him a rich man."

"Well, I don't think a weak old buffer like Leigh could put up much fight, Handle. Well, my advice is for you to hold your tongue, and refrain from seeing Leigh until to-morrow afternoon. Then we can tackle him together. Buck up and face the music, old chap," added the barrister, clapping his friend on the back, "after all, the thing may prove to be a false alarm. I don't place much reliance on that dreaming parson."

"Nor do I," answered Rupert, as he took his leave, "but, in this case, I fancy there must be a fire to account for the smoke. Leigh could not have invented a will which does not exist. Well then, good-bye. I shall see you to-morrow."

"At one o'clock or thereabouts; anyhow, before two. Meanwhile, don't see anyone and particularly not Miss Mallien. She is sure to spot your dismals, and if she begins to question you may give yourself away."

Rupert halted on the threshold, hesitating for a while, but finally promised not to see Dorinda.

Then, as there was nothing else to be done, he went to a matinée of a successful play to distract his mind, and returned, as he had arranged, in time for his eight o'clock dinner. After the meal, he spent a very dull evening, reading the newspapers and playing patience. But for his promise to Carrington he would have walked to the cottage to see Dorinda, and he sorely felt the want of her society at this crisis. However, he saw the wisdom of the barrister's advice, not to acquaint her with the trouble until more was ascertained for certain, lest, by arousing Mallien's suspicions, that gentleman might learn too much. And Mallien was very quick as a rule to guess that something was being kept from him.

So Rupert possessed his soul in patience and retired to bed early. After a somewhat restless night, he descended to breakfast to find that ill news travels fast. It was Mrs. Beatson who conveyed this especial information, and she did so with delight, always anxious to pass on any news of any disaster.

"Oh, Mr. Hendle," she cried, bursting into the breakfast room without knocking; "such a terrible thing has happened! Mr. Leigh is dead! Mr. Leigh has been murdered!"

CHAPTER VII

A NINE DAYS' WONDER

The information concerning the vicar's violent death was so extraordinary and so wholly unexpected that Rupert could not believe it to be entirely true. However, Mrs. Beatson's tempestuous announcement spoiled his breakfast, and, leaving the meal unfinished, the Squire hurried down to the village. Here everything was in a state of commotion, as it was rarely that so untoward an event disturbed the placidity of Barship. No one—from the flying rumors Hendle gathered during his progress—appeared to be acquainted with the exact facts of the case. Some said that Mr. Leigh had committed suicide; others, that a burglar, surprised at midnight, had struck the blow; while a few declared that the vicar was only wounded and would recover. But when Hendle reached the untidy house, he learned from the tearful Mrs. Jabber that the information was only too true. Mr. Leigh, with a nasty ragged wound on his right temple, had been found dead in his study at seven o'clock in the morning, and Kensit, the village constable, was already on the premises looking into the matter along with Dr. Tollart. The two, it seemed, had arrived simultaneously, Kensit having picked up the doctor on the road.

"And you could have knocked me down with a feather when them two walked in," wailed Mrs. Jabber, who was all rags and tears; "me expecting to be taken to jail straight off, though being, as you may guess, sir, as innocent as new-born infants. Ten o'clock was the hour as me and Jabber went to bed, as I can take my alfred davit in any court of lawr, and never a sound or a whisper did we hear, both being heavy sleepers. And when I come with a duster and a broom into the library, to clean it for the day, there I sees that blessed man lying on the floor under his writing table bleeding like a pig, face downward. As you may think, sir, I went white, and felt my inwards quaking, as I said to Jabber when we took someat strong later to keep our legs from giving way. I hollered and Jabber come to see if I was in a fit. Then says he, 'This is murder,' and runs out to shriek for the perlice, which is here with Dr. Tollart, hardly sober if you can believe me, sir. And that's the Bible truth of the whole thing, as I'd swear on my mother's corpse, though she's been an angel these many years. And what 'ull happen to me and Jabber," ended the good lady, dissolving in many tears, "is more than I can say, having no gift in prophets."

Considering her prolixity, Mrs. Jabber's account was fairly clear, and the chubby policeman was inclined to believe that she spoke the truth. He informed the Squire that he had already sent to Tarhaven for his Inspector, and that Dr. Tollart was examining the body with a view to learning the exact cause of death.

"Though to be sure, sir, that isn't hard to see," said Kensit, who was of a more chatty disposition than his position warranted. "There's a knock on the head as 'ud kill a navvy, much less a delicate gentleman as we know Mr. Leigh always was. He was struck down by a loaded cane or a bludgeon, unexpected like, if my experience goes for anything."

"But who on earth could have murdered him, Kensit?" asked Rupert, greatly puzzled. "Mr. Leigh was such a harmless man and had no enemies."

"P'raps a burglar, sir," suggested the constable wisely.

"But who would commit a burglary here?" said Rupert, looking round the entrance hall where they were standing. "There is nothing to carry off except books, and no man would risk a rope round his neck for such antique rubbish."

"True enough, Mr. Hendle. And, knowing that he had nothing worth stealing, Mr. Leigh never bothered himself to lock up the house at night. There's no catches to speak of on the windows, and the bolts of the doors ain't up to much. Anyone could walk in and walk out at any time without trouble, as he did."

"Oh. Then you think that the assassin was a man?"

"Well, sir, I don't suppose a female would come along assaulting people with blows on the back of the head. To be sure, there's Miss Sophy Tollart, who is a suffragist," mused the constable; "but Mr. Leigh never argued with her over them votes for women as I've ever heard."

In spite of the seriousness of the case, Hendle could not help smiling. "I think we can acquit Miss Tollart, Kensit," he observed. "The militant suffragist destroys property and not human beings. Ah, here is the doctor. Well?"

Tollart emerged into the hall as the Squire spoke, but did not seem to be over-eager to reply. He was a tall, bulky man, with a large red perspiring face, eyes like poached eggs, and a loose mouth suggestive of the hard drinker. As Mrs. Jabber had hinted, he had already had his morning dram, and his wits seemed to be muddled. Not at all the man, as Rupert thought with some disgust, to examine a murdered fellow-mortal's remains.

"Whew, isn't it hot, Hendle?" he remarked, mopping his streaming face with a dingy handkerchief. "That in there"—he jerked his head toward the study—"will have to be buried pretty smart; it won't keep long. The sooner he's under ground the better."

"He won't be put under ground," said Kensit, smartly. "The Leighs have their family vault, you know, doctor."

"Well! Well, vault or grave, the weather's too hot to keep the thing sweet," was Tollart's unpleasant reply. "Nice business, isn't it, Hendle? I always thought that the old man would be knocked on the head."

"Why?" asked the Squire, and Kensit looked the same question.

"Why!"—Tollart leaned against the pile of books near the wall, as his constant nipping made him shaky on his ponderous legs—"why, because he never locked up the house, and it stands away from the village in quite a lonely fashion. Anyone could break in here, or rather walk in, as Leigh never bothered about bolts and bars."

"There was nothing to guard, Tollart. I don't think it was worth any burglar's while to risk his neck for nothing."

"The man who downed Leigh was of a different opinion," said Tollart grimly.

"Do you think a burglar killed him, sir?" asked Kensit anxiously.

"Who else?"

"But Mrs. Jabber says that there is nothing missing."

"Isn't there? How does she know? Anyhow, his papers and books are all turned topsy-turvy. The burglar had a good hunt for loot, anyhow."

"The room is rather in a mess," observed Kensit thoughtfully.

"It always was in a mess," said Rupert, with a shrug. "When did the death take place, doctor?"

"Judging from the condition of the corpse I should say at eleven o'clock last night, Hendle. Did you see any stranger about the village when you were on your rounds last night, Kensit?"

"Not a soul, sir. But at eleven o'clock," Kensit reflected for a moment, "I was at the other end of the village. But when I passed the Vicarage about ten there was no one to be seen and nothing suspicious visible. The gate was open, as usual, and the door I expect was simply jammed to, as it usually was. Mrs. Jabber saw the vicar last, just before she went to bed with her husband at ten o'clock, and she left him busy at his writing and books as usual. I suppose the blow on the head killed him, sir?"

"Partly it was the blow on the head and partly heart disease," mumbled Tollart, staring at the two men with a glazed eye. "Leigh never was very strong, and I always told him to take care of his heart."

"I never knew it was weak," observed Rupert, "and he could not have thought so himself, as he was contemplating an expedition to Central America."

"Sheer madness," muttered Tollart. "However, he's gone on a longer journey now, Hendle. Kensit, when is your Inspector coming?"

"I expect him here every moment, sir."

"Well, the sooner he comes the better, as that corpse must be screwed down without delay. Have the inquest this afternoon if you can. It will be a mere formality, as the cause of death is apparent enough. There, you won't want me here now. I'll be at home at one if the Inspector from Tarhaven wants me, Kensit. Meanwhile I'm off to get a drink. Thirsty weather," and the doctor stumbled away in a hurry to get some beer.

"I don't think the weather makes much difference to the doctor's thirst, sir," said Kensit disapprovingly, and his chubby face looked severe. "However, it ain't any of my business, Mr. Hendle. You'll excuse me, sir, but I'll go and see that no one enters that library. Nothing must be touched until my Inspector sees the room. You haven't any idea as to who killed Mr. Leigh, sir?"

"Not the least idea," replied Rupert, lingering at the hall door. "I saw the vicar the night before last when he dined with me, and yesterday morning I called to see him on my way to London."

"So Mrs. Jabber said, and she said also, sir, that you said you'd call in the evening."

"I did, but did not," Rupert hesitated, for Kensit was looking at him keenly. "I really hadn't very much to say to him, and intended to call this morning."

"Do you know if he expected visitors, sir?"

"No. He made no mention to me of expecting any."

"Then it was a burglar," declared Kensit, positively.

Hendle shrugged his shoulders. "I don't see what there was to steal," he replied carelessly, and then he went away, after leaving a message that he would like to interview the Tarhaven Inspector when he was at leisure.

There was a crowd round the rickety gate—now closed for the first time for many years—but a policeman, summoned by Kensit from a neighboring village, was on guard, and would not allow anyone to enter. He saluted Rupert as he passed out, and the young man mechanically touched his hat in response. Down the road he came suddenly upon old Titus Ark, who was ruminating against a stone wall, looking more prehistoric than ever. The ancient grunted as the young Squire sauntered along thoughtfully in the blazing sunshine, and raised a gnarled hand to his battered hat. Considering that he was Leigh's bodyguard, who followed him everywhere like a dog, Hendle expected to find the old man tearful with the weakness of age. But Titus was smiling in a way which showed his toothless gums, and piped out an ordinary greeting, quite oblivious of the tremendous event which was disturbing the village.

"Morning, Squoire," said Ark, with his usual grunt. "Fine weather fur they crops I du think. Hor! Hor! Hor!"

Rupert stopped to rebuke this levity. "Don't you know that Mr. Leigh is dead?"

"Oh, no, he bain't dead," said the ancient easily. "A knock on the head don't settle such as he."

"Nonsense, man! Why, the vicar was extremely weak, and a mere tap would settle him. What are you talking about?"

"About Muster Leigh. Hor! Hor! Hor! He ain't dead. I've seen him dead afore, but he nivir come my way fur the berryin', Squoire."

"He'll come your way this time, Titus, I am afraid," replied Rupert, wondering why the old man was so stubborn. He surmised that, as Leigh—according to the doctor—had heart disease, he must have fainted at times in Ark's presence, which would account for the sexton's saying he had seen him dead. "I suppose you don't know who murdered him?"

"He bain't murdered, Squoire."

"Then you don't know who struck him?" said Hendle, amending his question.

"Naw. Muster Leigh, he said good-bye to me last night at six when he left Mussus Pattens, who is my datter. She's taken a turn for the better."

"I'm glad to hear it, Titus. Did Mr. Leigh say if he expected any visitor last night?"

"Naw," said the ancient again. "He niwer told naught to I, Squoire. You can ask him himself when he comes aloive again."

Plainly Ark declined to believe that his lifelong friend was dead, and it seemed useless to impress him with the undoubted fact. He complained that the policeman would not allow him to enter the Vicarage, and that no one would take any notice of his protestations that Leigh was not dead. Rupert, although in a hurry to return to his unfinished breakfast, stayed to persuade Titus to take a more reasonable view of the situation.

"Dr. Tollart says that Mr. Leigh has passed away. Besides the knock on the head he had heart disease, and either the one or the other was enough to kill him."

"Dr. Tollart," grunted Ark stolidly, "he be better wi beer than wi curing folk. I nivir heard tell as Muster Leigh had heart-badness. He be aloive, I tell ee, Squoire."

"Well, Titus, have your own way. But it will be your duty within a couple of days if not less, seeing that the weather is hot, to put our late vicar in his family vault."

"Oh, I'll put him there, Squoire; but he bain't dead fur all that. Hor! Hor! Hor!"

With another shrug Rupert passed on, and returned to The Big House to find Dorinda. She greeted him hastily and appeared to be very dismayed at the dreadful news of the vicar's murder. "Who could have hurt him, Rupert?" she asked, again and again. "He had no enemies. He would not have harmed a fly."

"I'm sure I can't tell you, dear. Kensit seems to think that it was a burglar did the trick."

"But there was nothing in the Vicarage to rob," protested Dorinda.

"Just what I say. However, some burglar from London might have believed that Leigh was a miser and had treasure."

"Has any stranger from London been seen about the village?"

"No. Kensit can't make head nor tail of it," Rupert shook his head and thought for a moment. "Unless some very startling evidence turns up, Dorinda, I don't believe that the truth will ever become known. What does your father say, dear?"

"Nothing. You know father did not care much for Mr. Leigh. He told me that he was sorry, but that Leigh was a fool, or he would have locked up his house regularly every night."

"Your father hasn't much sympathy, Dorinda."

"He never has. You know how badly he thinks of everyone. What is to be done about the murder, Rupert?"

"The Inspector from Tarhaven is coming to-day, and he will arrange for an inquest this afternoon or to-morrow. Upon what evidence is obtainable will depend the next step. I expect the body"—Dorinda quivered and turned pale—"will be buried almost immediately."

"Why. Don't they keep bodies a week?"

"Sometimes. But in this case, Tollart says that the sooner poor Leigh is buried the better. The corpse"—Rupert hesitated—"won't keep."

"Oh, don't"—Dorinda made a wry face—"poor Mr. Leigh. He was such a good man, Rupert. Who inherits his books, which are all he has left?"

"I think there's a distant cousin of sorts, a ship captain. He won't benefit much by Leigh's death. I wonder if the old man made a will."

"Oh, yes. He told me a year ago that he had, but did not mention to whom he had left his library. You are the executor."

"Am I, indeed? That is news to me, as Leigh never asked my permission. However"—Hendle was thinking of the probability of his ancestor's will being among the papers and books—"it is just as well under the circumstances."

"What do you mean by that?"

Hendle tugged at his moustache and replied in an embarrassed fashion, "Oh, nothing, only I can look after things better than a stranger, you know. By the way, Dorinda, I forgot to tell you that Carrington is coming down by the midday train."

"Coming again so soon," said Dorinda, remembering her father's warnings against the barrister, "and why?"

"Only about some business I went up to town about yesterday," answered Rupert confusedly. "Will you walk with me to the station to meet him?"

"No," said the girl promptly. "I don't want to meet Mr. Carrington again. I don't like him overmuch."

"Ah, you've been listening to your father, dear. Mallien likes no one."

"I saw Mr. Carrington myself, Rupert, and I didn't like him. I don't require my father to judge for me."

"What a spitfire you are!" laughed Hendle, putting his arm round her waist.

"Because I want you all to myself, and I think Mr. Carrington is not a good friend for you."

"Jealous."

"Sensible. There, Rupert, don't worry me." She slipped out of his arms, much to his surprise, and he showed his feelings so visibly that she colored. "I am rather out of sorts this morning," she said hurriedly. "Father has been rather trying."

"Never mind, dear; in a month you will be with me forever."

"I hope so," sighed Dorinda, "but somehow this death of the vicar suggests to me the possibility that something will occur to prevent our marriage."

"Oh, nonsense!" Rupert stared. "What could prevent our marriage?"

"It's only a feeling," persisted Dorinda, "and I dare say it is a foolish, silly feeling; but it's here for all that," and she laid her hand on her heart.

Rupert took as much pains to argue away this fancy as he had done to argue away the fancy of Titus Ark. But Dorinda was quite as stubborn in her belief that evil fortune was coming to prevent the marriage, as the sexton was that Leigh was alive. Finally, because Rupert laughed at her, she parted from him rather irritated at the corner, where he branched off to the station road. She would not even look back when her lover went away, and Rupert walked on to meet Carrington with the reflection that women were kittle cattle, as the Scotch say. As a rule, Dorinda was amiable and calm, so it seemed strange that she should be so easily annoyed this morning. But there was a reasonable excuse after all, as Hendle concluded, since the girl, always having been markedly friendly with the vicar, the poor man's violent death naturally shocked and upset her greatly. Moreover, the heartless comments which Mallien the cynic was more than likely to make, assuredly would add to Dorinda's distress. By the time he reached the station, Rupert had explained away to his own satisfaction the unusual emotion of the girl.

True to his promise Carrington arrived by the midday train and hopped out onto the platform as lively as a cricket. In gray flannels, a straw hat and brown shoes, the barrister looked handsome, well-bred and very much alive. The sight of his keen face and intelligent dark eyes comforted Hendle, as he knew that Carrington, if anyone, would be helpful in the matter of the vicar's mysterious murder.

"Here you are and here I am, Hendle," cried the new arrival briskly, as he gave up his ticket and walked out of the station along with the Squire. "I say, old chap, you're worrying considerably over this will business. There's a drawn, tired look on your face, which shows that you haven't slept a wink."

"Well, I didn't have a particularly restful night," admitted the other with a sigh. "And what has happened this morning doesn't help to make me feel any happier, Carrington."

"Eh, what?" the barrister stopped. "Then Leigh has found the will and—"

"Leigh is dead," Hendle informed him abruptly.

"Dead!" Carrington stared. "Dead! What are you talking about?"

"About what has happened," replied the other heavily. "Leigh was found dead in his study this morning."

Carrington looked at Hendle doubtfully. "You're pulling my leg," he said, in a disbelieving tone.

"I don't pull people's legs over such a serious matter. I tell you positively that the vicar is dead. All the village is in commotion."

"Dead!" repeated Carrington once more as they moved on toward Barship. "The unexpected has happened with a vengeance. Well, well, he wasn't young, and looked like a delicate man, who would pop off at any moment."

"This death has nothing to do with delicacy, Carrington. Leigh has been murdered."

"Oh, Lord!" Man of the world as he was, Carrington received a shock. "Poor old chap. Murdered! What a beastly thing to happen! Who murdered him?"

"No one knows. The police are looking into the matter now. He was found dead in his study at seven this morning, and there is a wound on the right temple. So far, the only conclusion arrived at is that some one tried to rob the house, and, being discovered, struck Leigh down."

"I can't see that there was anything in the house worth a burglar committing such a crime for," remarked Carrington, taking off his hat.

"There wasn't. No one in the village would have attempted a burglary, since

Leigh was known to be very poor. Besides, Leigh was too popular for anyone to hurt him. But a stranger—"

"Ah," broke in Carrington swiftly, "a stranger. Has any stranger been seen hovering about the Vicarage?"

"No. Kensit, our village policeman, was on his rounds as usual last night, but declares that he saw no one."

"But some tramp—"

"No tramps have been hanging about the village of late."

Carrington looked puzzled. "It seems to be a mystery. At what time was the poor chap murdered?"

"No one knows. But Dr. Tollart thinks the blow was struck about eleven o'clock last night."

"Has the weapon been found?"

"No!"

"Did that housekeeper hear any noise?"

"No! Nothing was known of the murder until she found her master dead near his writing table. The Inspector has been sent for to Tarhaven and will be here shortly. Indeed, I expect he is here now. He will take charge of the house and look into the matter."

"Humph!" remarked the barrister thoughtfully. "As I said before, it seems to be a mystery. This Inspector will take charge of all Leigh's books and papers, I suppose."

"Yes. Why not?"

"Oh, I am not saying against his handling them. But the will—"

"The will. Yes?"

"Can't you see, Hendle. If this Inspector looks through the papers left by Leigh, which he probably will, he is bound to come across that hundred-year-old testament you mentioned yesterday."

Rupert winced. "I expect he will, unless poor Leigh has so carefully mislaid it that it cannot be found. But what if he does?"

"Well, then all the fat will be on the fire," said Carrington with an air of finality.

"I suppose you mean that the will must be made public. Why not? If it is a legitimate document, Mallien must get the money, and if it isn't, my position remains unchanged. In any case, whether Leigh lived or died, what he discovered would have to be shown all round."

"Quite so. But you didn't want it to be shown all round until you looked into the matter privately along with me," argued Carrington, quickly.

"True enough. I should like to have seen the document before Mallien became aware that it existed. However, as things stand, the will is bound to be found, and Mallien is bound to know. We must thresh out the matter openly straightway, and I shall do my best to avoid trouble."

"I don't see how you can avoid it, Hendle. Mallien is not the man to let a chance of getting a fortune go."

"I am sure he isn't," retorted the Squire positively. "And he is certain to make things as disagreeable for me as possible. But if I surrender the property, should the will prove to be legal, I don't see that he can worry me."

"You will lose everything," warned the barrister, significantly.

"Unfortunately, yes."

"Including Miss Mallien."

"I suppose so," admitted the Squire reluctantly. "Even if she remains true to me, as I am sure she will, I can't ask her to marry me on nothing a year."

There was silence for a few minutes as the two men walked into the village, and it was Carrington who spoke first. "I'm awfully sorry for you, old man."

"I'm rather sorry for myself. However, what must be must be, so there's no more to be said. By the way, Dorinda told me that Leigh had made me his executor. I never knew that he had, until she told me."

"Leigh took your friendship for granted, it seems. Who inherits?"

"I don't know. His sole relative is a sea captain, somewhere in Australia. I have heard him speak of the young fellow—a cousin of sorts—as the last of the Leighs. There isn't much to leave in the way of property."

"So you are executor," murmured Carrington thoughtfully. "In that case, you will have the handling of the papers, and may be able to get possession of the will before the Inspector lays hands on it."

"What good will that do?" asked Hendle, irritably.

"You can suppress the will."

"I shouldn't think of doing such a thing."

"You'll lose all if the will proves to be genuine," Carrington warned him.

"Then I must lose all."

"That's quixotic."

"So you said yesterday. But I mean to be honest." And again there was silence, Carrington secretly considering his friend an honorable ass.

CHAPTER VIII

MALLIEN SPEAKS

Anxious to help Rupert, and, at his friend's request, Carrington remained at The Big House until the inquest was over, and the burial of the murdered man took place. Both he and the Squire could do little save watch the course of events, as neither of them wished to say anything about the missing will, and neither could suggest any reason why the crime should have been committed. And, indeed, the police were equally unable to solve the problem, since the murder, on the face of it, appeared to be purposeless and the assassin could not be discovered. Inspector Lawson, of Tarhaven, did his best to find a clue, but from first to last was unsuccessful. He did not even know where to look for one, and when the inquest was held, had absolutely no evidence to place before the Coroner and jury. Leigh's murderer had come out of the night and had gone into the night; but why he had come to commit so dastardly a crime, and whither he had gone after achieving his aim, it was wholly impossible to say. The affair was unpleasant, mysterious and uncanny.

Pursuant to the opinion of Dr. Tollart, proceedings in connection with the death were hurried on as speedily as possible. The weather was certainly amazingly hot, as for weeks a powerful sun had been blazing in a cloudless blue sky. The gardens glowed with many-colored flowers, but the growing crops were parched for want of rain, and everywhere in the district people were complaining of the shortage of water. Under the circumstances, and because nothing relevant to the assassin could be discovered, Tollart's advice seemed to be very sensible. Therefore the inquest was held at *The Hendle Arms* on the day after Mrs. Jabber had discovered her master's corpse, and on that same afternoon the body was placed in the family vault of the Leighs. The trouble had happened so suddenly, the proceedings had been carried through so swiftly, that everything in connection therewith was over and done with before people had time to wholly realize what had taken place.

With regard to the inquest, that necessary function was dispatched very quickly. There was little to be done and little to be said, as no new details were forthcoming concerning the dreadful event. The jury inspected the body at the Vicarage, and then went on to *The Hendle Arms* to hear what could be said about the matter. Several reporters from London journals were present, but the interest in the case was more local than general, as there was nothing in it likely to cause a sensation. The general opinion was that some burglar had entered the ill-guarded Vicarage, and that the parson had been struck down while trying to capture the thief. But, as nothing was missing from the house, many scouted this idea, and ascribed the death to a deeper cause. But what that cause might be, this minority were unable to say. Nor did the evidence procurable tend to lighten the darkness which shrouded the crime.

Mrs. Jabber, more respectably dressed than usual, and even more voluble, gave her evidence with many tears and sighs. The old woman had been deeply attached to the vicar, and could not understand why he should have met with so terrible and unexpected a death. She deposed to going to bed at ten o'clock as usual, after taking into the study a glass of milk for her master.

"And there I left him, as happy as a trout in a pond," cried Mrs. Jabber, with tears running down her face, "busy with his books as usual; he, enjoying them the more after having been to see Mrs. Patter, as I'm glad to say is getting better, though it's more nor she deserves, her being such a gossip, and—"

Here the witness was checked by the Coroner, on the ground that she was dealing with matters irrelevant to the inquiry. "Did Mr. Leigh expect anyone to visit him on that night?"

"Lord, bless you, no, sir, and if he did, he wouldn't have mentioned it to me."

"You retired at ten o'clock?"

"Me and Jabber, yes, sir, both being tired with the heat and the day's work."

"And you saw nothing of Mr. Leigh until seven the next morning?"

"Not even the nose of him, sir, and I heard no noise, me being a heavy sleeper as Jabber is, although I don't snore, say what he likes."

In fact Mrs. Jabber's statement did nothing to solve the mystery. She admitted that the bolts and bars at the Vicarage were not what they should be, considering the lonely position of the house. "But, Lord bless you, sir, there ain't never been no trouble with thieves and robbers nohow, as there wasn't anything to tempt them."

"Then you don't think that a burglar—"

"No, I don't, sir. There's nothing missing."

Mrs. Jabber stuck to her tale, and what she said was corroborated by her husband, a meek, trembling little man, wholly dominated by his stronger-minded wife. He had gone to bed at ten o'clock; he had heard nothing during the night likely to arouse his suspicions, and the first news he had of the murder was from his wife, when she stumbled on the dead body at seven in the morning. "And then I went and told Kensit all about it," finished Mr. Jabber with a very white face, evidently afraid lest he should be accused of committing the crime.

Tollart, who was just as red-faced, but much more sober than usual, stated that he had been called in by the village constable within an hour after the body had been discovered. Mr. Leigh had been struck on the right temple by some heavy instrument—probably a bludgeon—and the blow, taken in connection with his weak heart, must have caused death instantaneously. The certificate of death was worded to that effect. Leigh was a patient of his, and had never been very strong, added to which, his mode of life had weakened him considerably. On the whole, the shabby, disreputable doctor, knowing that the eyes of his little world were on him, gave his evidence very clearly and resolutely, so that he created a good impression. There was no question as to the cause of death after Tollart's statement, even though his coupling of heart disease and a blow seemed rather muddled. No one in the village had expected Leigh to live to any considerable age, owing to his delicate appearance, so it was quite certain that the violent assault had killed him. It would have been a wonder to many had he survived the blow.

For no very apparent reason Hendle was called, but all that he could say brought nothing to light. He related how Leigh had dined with him, and how he had called at the Vicarage next day while on his way to London. So far as the witness knew, Leigh was in good health and spirits. "The announcement of his death came as a shock to me," finished Rupert.

"Had he any enemies?" questioned the Coroner.

"Not to my knowledge. A more amiable man never existed."

"Do you know anything of his past life?"

"Only that he had been vicar here ever since I was a child, and was devoted to books and to archæology. With the exception of his parishioners, myself and Mr. Mallien and his daughter, I don't think he ever saw anyone. He was wholly wrapped up in his books."

"Then there was nothing in his past life which suggests any reason why this crime should have been committed?"

"Certainly not, so far as I know."

Inspector Lawson and Kensit, the village policeman, gave what sparse evidence they could. The latter declared that while on his rounds on the night of the murder he had met no one and had seen nothing suspicious when he passed the gate of the Vicarage. At the hour when the crime was said by Dr. Tollart to have been committed, witness was on the other side of the village. Lawson deposed that no weapon had been found, that no evidence of any intruder had been discovered.

"I understood that the study was in a state of disorder," said the Coroner.

"I gather from many sources that the study was always in a state of disorder," retorted the Inspector.

Kensit, recalled, said that he did not think that the study was even more untidy than usual. Everything was turned upside down—books and papers, "Just as if some one had been searching for something," declared the witness.

"Then you think that the murderer killed the vicar, and then looked about to find something, which he wished to get, and for the possession of which he committed the crime?"

Kensit hesitated. "I am not prepared to go that far," he remarked, after a pause. "All I can say is that I gained some such impression."

When this speech was made, Rupert glanced at Carrington and Carrington looked at Rupert. The same idea struck them simultaneously, that the murderer might have been searching for the will of John Hendle. But then the existence of that document was known only to the dead man, to the barrister and to the Squire. Rupert had been fast asleep when the crime was committed, and Carrington had been in London, so, of course, neither of the two could have had anything to do with the matter. Still, it seemed strange that the books and papers of the deceased should have been messed up. If search had not been made for the will in question, for what had the mysterious murderer been looking? This question both the young men asked themselves, and asked each other when the inquest was over.

It came to an end very speedily. The Coroner could only direct the attention of the jury to the facts laid before them, and did not offer any opinion, as indeed he could not. The jury brought in a verdict of "Willful murder against some person or persons unknown," which was all that could be done. Then the meeting broke up, the reporters slipped away with their loaded notebooks, grumbling at the dullness of the matter, and the crowd of villagers dispersed to wonder, for the hundreth time, who could have killed their amiable and kindly natured vicar.

"The beast who murdered Leigh could not have been looking for that will."

It was Hendle who spoke, as he walked back to The Big House with Carrington. The barrister shrugged his shoulders and replied, "I had the same idea when that policeman made his statement, and I saw you look at me. I agree with you, although it is strange that the books and papers should have been turned upside down. But only you and I know of—"

"Of course, of course," broke in the Squire quickly, "and, as I was in bed, and you in London, of course we had nothing to do with the matter."

"Did you tell anyone else about the will?"

"No. I never mentioned it to a soul."

"Good. I shouldn't if I were you."

Carrington's tone was so significant that the Squire turned on him in a sharp, inquiring way. "What do you mean?"

"I mean that if anyone knew about the existence of John Hendle's will, and what it meant to you, it is possible that on you suspicion might rest."

"What rubbish!" said Rupert uncomfortably. "I was in bed and asleep at the time the crime was committed."

"How can you prove that?"

Rupert looked surprised. "Why, I saw that the butler locked up as usual, and he knew that I went to bed earlier than usual."

"Quite so. But when all the house was asleep, you might have risen from your bed and have gone through the sleeping village to see Leigh."

"Why should I do that?"

"I don't say you did," persisted Carrington. "I am only suggesting what people would say if the existence of the will were known."

"Hang it, Carrington," fumed the big man, "you don't mean to insinuate that I had anything to do with so cowardly a crime."

"No! No! No! I don't insinuate anything of the sort, as I know that you are incapable of such a thing. But other people have nasty, suspicious minds."

Hendle looked more uncomfortable than ever. "I understand," he murmured, after a pause; "it is just as well to say nothing about the will. I dare say I shall find it among Leigh's papers when his lawyer writes to me about my being the executor."

"And if you do not?"

Rupert shrugged his big shoulders. "Then there's nothing more to be said or done," he remarked with resignation.

"There is this to be said," observed Carrington, thoughtfully, "that if the assassin really was looking for the will, and turned over the books and papers to obtain the reward of his crime, the will is sure to turn up sooner or later."

"I don't follow you," said Hendle, both perturbed and puzzled.

"Think for a moment. That will is of the greatest value to you, and the man who murdered Leigh must have stolen it to—shall we say—blackmail you. When everything has blown over, he will certainly make some attempt to gain the reward he risked his neck for, by taking the will to you or to Mallien."

"If he comes to me I shall hand him over to the police," said Rupert vigorously. "And Mallien, in spite of his misanthropic ways, would do the same. I don't see, however, how anyone can have killed Leigh for the sake of that will, as no one but you and I knew about it."

"True enough. Did you tell Miss Mallien about it?"

"No, I told no one. And if I had told Dorinda—"

"She might have told her father, to whom the will was of importance, seeing that it might possibly place him in possession of four thousand a year."

"Good Lord, Carrington, you don't infer that Mallien murdered the vicar?"

"No, I don't, because I have no grounds to go upon. But if you told Miss—"

"Confound it, man, I didn't. Haven't I been saying for the last half hour that I told no one but you. Even if I had told Dorinda she would never have spoken to her father without my permission. And even if she had done so, her father would never have murdered Leigh to get the will, as he would know very well that I am not the sort of man to conceal such a document."

"H'm! I'm not so sure of that," said Carrington doubtfully. "Mallien is not a particularly scrupulous man, from what I have seen of him. He may judge you by himself."

"I don't care if he did judge me to be a scoundrel," retorted Rupert, "that would not make me one. But aren't we twisting ropes of sand, Carrington? I tell you solemnly that I told no one about John Hendle's will, save you."

"Oh, I'm only suggesting what people might say about you and Mallien, did the existence of the will become known. After all," added Carrington cheerfully, "there may not be any will at all. You have never seen it, and have only the word of a dead man to go upon. It may not exist."

Rupert shook his head seriously. "I think it does exist, and that I shall probably find it among Leigh's papers."

"And if you do?"

"I shall take it to our family lawyers and call in Mallien to talk the matter over."

"It's a risk, considering that Leigh has been murdered."

"I don't see it. Even if anyone was crazy enough to suggest that I killed the poor old man, the mere fact of my producing the will would show that I had no reason to murder him. Pouf!" ended Rupert contemptuously, "it is all froth and foam. Don't talk rubbish and make mountains out of molehills."

Carrington shrugged his shoulders and said no more, since on the face of it he was, as Rupert stated, twisting ropes of sand. No more was said on this particular phase of the case, but during luncheon the young men discussed the matter freely. Naturally, on what had been set forth in the evidence, they could arrive at no conclusion, and went to the funeral of the vicar as much in the dark as anyone in the great crowd that gathered in the churchyard. Mallien was there, but beyond scowling at Carrington, for whom he had little love, and nodding curtly to his cousin, he took no notice of the two men. Titus Ark was there and mumbled every now and then something to the effect that the vicar could not possibly be dead. But no one took notice of so crazy a statement, since the doctor had given the certificate of death. It was known how Ark idolized the parson, and how constantly he had been with Leigh, therefore everyone thought that it was simply the senile weakness of age on the sexton's part, to disbelieve that his only friend was gone. And, finding that no one heeded his protests and mutterings, Titus became stolidly silent, attending to his part of the burial sullenly.

So far as Ark's duties were concerned, he had little to do, not even having had to dig a grave. The family vault in a quiet corner of the churchyard was duly opened, and the coffin was carried down the damp, worn steps. For a few centuries the Leighs had been buried here, as formerly—before the Hendles came on the scene—they had been the Lords of the Manor. Now, save the seafaring cousin, who was on the distaff side, the last of the race had been laid to rest. A neighboring clergyman read the service, which was listened to with reverent attention, and when the door of the vault was closed again, the crowd of mourners slowly dispersed. Judging from the observations made, it was widely believed that the mystery of the death was hidden away with the dead man in that dreary vault.

"I can't see, sir," said Inspector Lawson to Rupert, "how anything is to be discovered. I looked over the poor gentleman's papers, but could find nothing in his past life to suggest that anyone would kill him."

"Yet, according to Kensit, the papers were searched through," hinted Hendle, relieved that the officer made no mention of the lost parchment.

Lawson shrugged his square shoulders. "Oh, these young constables always see more than need be seen," he observed slightly, "they are so eager for promotion you see, sir. My opinion is that some tramp on the prowl walked in at that invitingly open gate on the chance of stealing. Finding some door or window unbolted—he probably tried them on the chance, as I say—he got into the study and, while tumbling over the contents of the room and with the idea of finding something worth taking, was surprised by Mr. Leigh. Naturally, the tramp's first idea would be to escape, and, being prevented, he naturally would strike down the man who strove to detain him."

"You appear to have the case, quite cut and dried," remarked Carrington, smiling.

"It is all theory, I admit," retorted Lawson, rather nettled. "But if you can find a better explanation on what is known, sir, I should be glad to hear it."

"Oh, I dare say that your theory is as good as any other, Inspector. I suppose you will search for more evidence on those lines?"

"Search? In what direction am I to search?"

"Oh, don't ask me," replied the barrister lightly. "I am as much in the dark as you are, Inspector. Still, it will be just as well to order Kensit to keep his weather eye open on the chance of something unexpected turning up."

"I have told Kensit to do so, Mr. Carrington, but I don't hope for any result."

Everyone was of much the same opinion as the worthy official, and his theory was finally accepted by all, even by those who had hinted at a deeper reason for the commission of the crime. A stray tramp, moving from one town to another under cover of night, had probably killed the vicar, so as to escape arrest for burglary. And it might be that he did not even mean to murder Leigh, but only intended to stun him, so as to get away. The heart disease, as much as the blow, was the cause of death, according to Tollart, and the presumed tramp could not have been expected to know that the parson suffered in this way. At all events, the explanation of Lawson seemed likely to prove the sole explanation which would be forthcoming.

Carrington stayed for the night, but his consultations with Rupert led to nothing. Then he took his departure, on the understanding that if Hendle, as Leigh's executor, did find the will, or did not find it, he would call down to Barship again to give his help.

"I don't say that I am rich enough to do so for nothing, Hendle," confessed the barrister frankly, "but I'm not greedy, and you can give me what you consider fair."

"Oh, I don't mind," answered Rupert, rather contemptuously, for he thought that Carrington might have behaved more as a friend and less as a professional adviser. "You shall name your own price, if the will proves illegal, and I am left in possession of the property. Otherwise, you will have to get your fees from the new heir."

"Mallien. H'm! He is too avaricious a man to pay if he can help. I want to work for you and not for him, Hendle. However, I understand the position, and you can depend upon my doing my best to pull you through."

"I shall expect that, if I am to retain your services professionally," said the Squire rather dryly, and then, mindful of the obligations of hospitality, he drove Carrington to the station in his motor to catch the midday express.

Nevertheless, he was disappointed that his old school chum should bring pounds, shillings and pence into the matter. It imported a sordid element into their friendship, and when Rupert reached The Big House again, he came to the conclusion that perhaps Dorinda was not far wrong in her estimate of the lawyer's character; or Mallien either, for Mallien also mistrusted the man. And now it appeared that there were grounds for a certain amount of mistrust, as Hendle ruefully confessed to himself.

In a short time, Leigh's lawyer, having seen the report of the murder, inquest and burial in the newspapers, made his appearance and intimated to Hendle that he was the dead man's executor. Besides his income as a parson, Leigh only had a few hundred pounds invested in Consols, so it was evident that the sea captain in Australia would not benefit overmuch. The solicitor arranged to write to the legatee in Australia, and promised to send some one down to value the books with a view to selling them. Mrs. Jabber remained on at the Vicarage along with her husband pending the arrival of the new parson, who was to be appointed immediately by the Bishop. Rupert, as executor, went to the untidy house, after the solicitor departed for London, to look over all papers belonging to Leigh, and to put affairs shipshape. The lawyer had no time to attend to the matter, since the estate was hardly worthy of his professional attention, and when Hendle explained that certain documents had to be restored to the Muniment Room, and that a search for them would be necessary, the attorney allowed him to attend to the matter wholly by himself. Thus it came about that Rupert found himself three days after the burial digging among the bookish rubbish in the study.

Of course, his chief aim was to find the will, which Leigh had so positively asserted existed. But, although the young man turned over every paper and parchment, hunted through various boxes, and even examined many of the books, on the chance that it might have been slipped into one of them, he was unable to find what he wanted. At the end of three or four hours, and when the afternoon was waning, Hendle began to think that the will was a myth. It probably had never existed save in Leigh's dreamy imagination. On the other hand, it might have existed, and the assassin might have taken it. But this was too fantastical an idea for Hendle to accept for one moment. Seeing that only himself and Carrington knew about the will, whether it was real or fictitious, it was impossible to believe that the crime had been committed for its sake.

By the time five o'clock came, Rupert, working, for the sake of coolness, in his shirt sleeves, was hot and dusty and weary. Looking for a needle in a bundle of hay did not appeal to him as an amusing task, and he was about to abandon the search for the day, when a quick, firm step was heard, and Mallien, looking like a thunder cloud, entered to scowl a greeting.

"Well?" he asked disagreeably, "have you found John Hendle's will?"

CHAPTER IX

A SERIOUS POSITION

Sitting on the floor in a grimy snowdrift of scattered papers, and surrounded by piles of dingy books, Rupert stared at his cousin, scarcely taking in the purport of his words. Mallien appeared to be pleased with the expression of genuine bewilderment on the other man's face, but did not improve the occasion by speaking immediately. Since the afternoon was oppressively hot, he wore a suit of cool white flannel, which made him seem blacker in his hairy looks than ever. In the heavy yellow sunshine streaming through the dusty room, his many jewels twinkled and shot fire; scarf-pin and studs, sleeve links and rings. Near the door, which he had closed, the newcomer leaned, against the many volumes filling the book shelf, with folded arms and crossed legs; an odd, and, as it impressed Hendle, a sinister figure. It was the Squire who spoke next, as he was not entirely sure if he had heard Mallien's astounding question.

"What do you say?" he asked, almost mechanically.

"You heard me right enough," sneered the other.

"John Hendle's will?"

"Ah, I thought so. None so deaf as those who won't hear. Well, have you found it, Rupert?"

"John Hendle's will," repeated the Squire, greatly taken aback by this sudden display of knowledge on the part of his cousin.

"Yes! Don't pretend that I am talking nonsense; you know better."

Hendle gradually collected his scattered thoughts, and rose slowly to his feet. Then, quite in a mechanical way, he took out pipe and tobacco pouch. "I should like to know who told you," he remarked, filling the bowl.

"You shall know—Mrs. Beatson told me."

"And how did she know?"

"As women generally know things they are not meant to learn—by eavesdropping. You understand. She listened to the conversation between you and the parson, when he dined at The Big House, on the evening before his death."

"He did dine with me," admitted Hendle seriously. "And he did tell me about the discovery of the will you mention. But why did Mrs. Beatson listen, since she could not have guessed what he was going to speak about."

"It seems to me, Rupert, that you are asking questions, whereas it is my right to do so. However, to make things clear, I don't mind in the least answering you. Mrs. Beatson explained to me, in excuse for her eavesdropping, that you had told her of your approaching marriage with Dorinda, and she was afraid lest you should turn her out."

"I told her I wouldn't."

"Oh, did you? Then evidently she did not believe you, and hovered round the dining-room and drawing-room, hoping to hear anything you might say to the vicar on the subject. Leigh hinted at some mystery he had to impart to you. Mrs. Beatson heard his remark through the open door of the dining-room and it aroused her curiosity. When you went to the drawing-room, she was outside the window drinking in every word."

"Hum!" said Rupert, lighting his pipe. "I remember that the windows of the drawing-room were open on account of the heat. She stole along the terrace, I presume."

"Yes, and heard every word," repeated Mallien significantly. "In the first instance, you will understand that Mrs. Beatson only hovered round you and the vicar to hear anything connected with her possible dismissal. But, when she grasped the fact about the will, she became aware that she had overheard a secret, which she could turn to her own advantage. For a time she hesitated whether to let you or me buy her silence. Then, thinking that I would get the money, she came and told me all about it."

"Hum!" said Rupert again, and very calmly. "Rather treacherous behavior toward me, considering how kind I treated her."

"Treachery be hanged!" burst out Mallien, leaving the wall and throwing himself onto a convenient pile of books, which afforded him a seat. "She wanted to see me righted."

"She wanted a price for her secret, I think you said."

"Well, and why not?" demanded the hairy little Timon, in a blustering way. "It is only natural that you should wish to keep the secret, and only natural that Mrs. Beatson should try and make money out of telling it to me."

"I suppose it is, with some natures. So you are going to pay her."

"Yes! She's done me a good turn. I'll give her an annuity when I come to live at The Big House."

"You are not there yet," said Rupert, dryly. Now that he knew the worst he was perfectly calm. And he had every right to be since he had done nothing with which to reproach himself.

"I shall be there, when this will comes to light," bullied Mallien fiercely. "Naturally you wish to hide it—"

"There you make a mistake," interrupted the big man leisurely. "As soon as the will is found, I shall take it to our family lawyers, and have it looked into."

"Oh, yes, you say so now, because you can't keep the secret any longer, thanks to Mrs. Beatson," retorted Mallien coarsely.

"I never intended to keep any secret."

"Then why didn't you tell me as soon as Leigh told you?"

"Because I had not seen the will, and so far as that goes, I have never set eyes on it yet. It may be a myth, and it was useless for me to speak about it until I was sure that such a document was in existence."

"It is in existence," insisted Mallien uneasily.

"We have only the vicar's word for it."

"Oh, of course you say that."

"What else can I say? Listen to me, Mallien. Unpleasant as it is for me to lose my property, I am quite willing to surrender it to you without the intervention of the law, if the will proves to be legal. If it doesn't, of course I shall keep my own."

But even this generous and reasonable speech did not appeal to the grasping hearer. "You can do what you like," he replied doggedly; "but if I don't get the property, I shall bring the case before a judge and jury."

"There will be no necessity for you to do so, if the will is legal."

Mallien sneered. "I suppose you'll try and prove that it isn't."

"Certainly," retorted Hendle, angered by this extreme selfishness. "You may be sure that I shall do all I can to protect my own interests. Would you not do the same were you in my position?"

The other shirked a straightforward reply as a selfish man would. "That is neither here nor there," he snapped, "I want my rights."

"You shall have them, if you have any."

"From what Mrs. Beatson told me—"

"Mrs. Beatson knows no more nor no less than I do," interrupted the Squire patiently. "She is aware that Leigh found—or said that he found—a will made by John Hendle one hundred years ago, leaving the property to Eunice Filbert and her descendants. If such is the case, and you are rightfully entitled to take my place, well"— Rupert shrugged his square shoulders, and completed his sentence by waving his hand vaguely to the four corners of the room. Mallien scowled and tried to pick holes.

"Oh, you can be certain that I shall claim my rights to the last farthing," he growled savagely, and rather annoyed by Rupert's reasonable attitude.

"Naturally. That is only fair. I am not the man, as you well know, to keep what does not honestly belong to me. But," added Hendle with emphasis, "the will has yet to be found."

"It must be found," declared Mallien violently.

"That is easier said than done. Leigh seemed to have mislaid, or hidden it, very thoroughly. Inspector Lawson did not come across it, and I can't lay my hands on it nohow. And, remember, even when it is discovered, the legality of it has yet to be proved."

"If it is signed and witnessed properly I inherit," shouted Mallien, doggedly, and objecting, as such an illogical man would, to the mere shadow of a contradiction.

"Don't go too fast," said the Squire dryly. "There is such a thing as the Statute of Limitations."

"Oh, is there? And what deviltry is that?"

"A law which, in most cases, operates against the restoration of property devolving under a lost will, found—as this one has been—after so long a period of time."

"You talk like a book," sneered Mallien, uncomfortably, for here was an obstacle which he did not expect to meet. "And you will take advantage of this infernal Statute?"

"Why not?" demanded Rupert, calmly. "Would you not do the same under the same circumstances?"

"I prefer not to enter into any argument on that point," said Mallien loftily. "It seems to be a silly law. And what about not keeping what isn't your own."

"If the Statute of Limitations acts in my favor, the property would be my own," answered the Squire coolly.

"Hair-splitting!"

"Common sense! And I would not have used such an argument, but for your display of greedy selfishness."

"Me selfish. How dare you!" Mallien fumed and fretted, and made as though he would throw himself on his cousin.

Hendle held out one hand to keep him off. "None of that, Mallien. No violence or it will be the worse for you. If it comes to a physical tussle, it will not be difficult for me to lay you on your back."

Mallien knew this, so tried verbal bullying. "I order you not to address me in that insolent tone."

"Don't be a fool, man. And don't talk about insolence until you learn how to behave yourself. Everyone far and near considers you a most objectionable person."

"Indeed!" Mallien grew livid. "And you?"

"I am of the same opinion," replied Rupert, smoking placidly. "If you were not Dorinda's father, I should have thrashed you ages ago."

"You shall never marry my daughter," gasped the other, panting with rage.

"Dorinda and I can afford to do without your permission. See here, Mallien, don't you think it's time you stopped playing the fool. I said before, and I say again, that if the property is proved to be rightfully yours, as the descendant of Eunice Filbert, I shall not stand in the way. So the best thing you can do is to behave your silly self and help me to search for the will. We can leave the question of my marriage to Dorinda alone just now. Until the will is found, or is proved not to exist, you are well aware that no marriage can take place."

"And if the will is found, and I am put in possession of The Big House, no marriage shall take place," retorted the other, still fuming.

"On the other hand, if the will is found and proves to be illegal? What then will be your attitude?"

"Even then I shall refuse to—"

"Not you," broke in Rupert with a broad smile. "You are too anxious to buy that blue sapphire you were talking about. If you want the five hundred a year that my marriage with Dorinda will put into your pocket, you will have to put your pride in the same receptacle."

"We'll see about that!" snarled Mallien vindictively, but in a more subdued tone, for he did not wish to cross the Rubicon too soon. "The will has yet to be proved illegal."

"The will has yet to be found," answered the Squire, thinking how difficult it was to hammer an idea into the man's obstinate head.

"Ah!" Mallien's tone was significant. "I am quite sure that it never will be found."

Rupert opened his big blue eyes in genuine surprise. "You seem to have changed your opinion," he remarked, after a pause. "Just now you made sure it would be found."

"Bah!" Mallien's pent-up rage burst forth anew. "Do you think that I can't see through your pretended search?"

"Pretended search." Hendle rose slowly and towered above the stout little man like a giant. "Explain what you mean."

"It's easy to see," snapped the other, sulkily. "Lawson could not find the will among the papers of Leigh and you will not find it. And why? Because it is already in your possession, and has been destroyed for all I know."

"Still, I don't understand," said Rupert, and his eyes grew hard as he began to have an inkling of Mallien's meaning. "Leigh did not give the will to me before he died."

"I dare say not. He had his own fish to fry, and would only have given it to you on getting your promise to finance his silly Yucatan expedition. You took the will from his dead body."

Hendle's temper, long held in check, blazed up. He took two steps toward the gad-fly which so irritated him, caught Mallien by the throat and flung him right across the room. "You liar," he said, in a dangerously quiet tone.

"It's true! it's true!" gasped his cousin, struggling into a sitting position amid a pile of tumbled books.

"Do you want your neck twisted?"

"I dare you to do it," shrieked Mallien hysterically. "You daren't add one murder to another."

Rupert sat down suddenly, afraid lest his wrath should carry him too far, and reined in his feelings with a powerful effort. "I think you are a fool, and should be answered according to your folly," he said, with suppressed anger. "What makes you think that I did such a thing?"

His cousin gathered himself together and smoothed his ruffled plumes. But he still remained among the pile of books his fall had scattered, as he did not wish to come within arm's length of Hendle. There he sat and grinned like an ugly little gnome. "Anyone can guess your game," he sneered, venomously. "Leigh told you about the will and said it was here, but—I am quite sure of this—he refused to give it to you, unless you agreed to finance his Yucatan expedition. Of course you refused, and then came here in the dead of night to murder him and get the will. Bah! I can see through your pretence of searching for what is already found."

"You read my character according to your own base thoughts," said Rupert, now quite self-possessed; "and what you say is wholly untrue. Leigh told me about the will, as Mrs. Beatson informed you, and she can bear witness that the vicar declared that he had mislaid the document. I called to see him the next morning, but he was away—as Mrs. Jabber can testify—seeing Mrs. Patter, who was reported to be dying. I then went to Town to consult Carrington—"

"Oh, you have brought that beast into it," sneered Mallien vindictively.

"I consulted him as to what was best to be done, and he advised me not to see the vicar until the next day, and then in his company. Carrington, as you well know, came down by the midday train, for the purpose of seeing Leigh along with me. But by that time Leigh was dead."

"Quite so. And you killed him."

The accusation was so absurd that Rupert merely shrugged his shoulders, and wondered why he had lost his temper with this gad-fly even for a moment. "I think you will find it difficult to prove that," he observed, suavely. "I did not see Leigh on the night he was murdered; I did not even call at the Vicarage, thanks to Carrington's advice. My servants can prove, if you like to question them, that I locked up and retired to bed at ten o'clock."

"Oh, I dare say you did," scoffed Mallien; "but, remember, that Leigh was killed—if Dr. Tollart is to be believed—at eleven. It was easy for you to slip out of The Big House and come along to—"

"I did not." Rupert started to his feet again, but maintained his calmness.

"How can you prove that you did not?"

"How can you prove that I did?" counterquestioned the Squire.

Mallien rose and brushed the dust from his flannels. "I shall leave Lawson to find the proof," he cried, triumphantly. "Oh, yes. Once Lawson knows that the will, which would rob you of your property, exists, it will be easy for him to assign a cause why Leigh should have been murdered. Remember, the papers were all tumbled about, as Kensit can witness. The burglary business is all rubbish. It was to get the will that Leigh was murdered, and you are the culprit."

Hendle did not reply for a moment, for so skillfully had the venomous little man built up the case, that he was quite taken aback. Then he remembered how Carrington had warned him that, if the business of the missing will was known, it was possible some such accusation might be brought. Thanks to Mrs. Beatson's treachery, Mallien had been placed in possession of dangerous facts, and Mallien, sooner than forego the chance of acquiring the Hendle property, was quite prepared to have his cousin handed over to the police. Not only was a strong motive for the murder provided, but Rupert knew that he would have the greatest difficulty in proving an alibi. After ten o'clock, all his own servants and the inhabitants of Barship were in bed, so it was perfectly feasible, on the face of it, that to protect his own interests he might have stolen through the village to commit the crime. Of course, he knew very well that he had not; that any idea of securing the will in this way had never entered his head. Nevertheless, the position was both uncomfortable and dangerous, and, for the moment, he did not know what to say. Mallien noted his cousin's silence, and concluded that guilt prevented his speech.

"You can't deny what I say," he cried viciously.

"I am too much taken aback by your audacity to reply, or to deny," retorted the young man, drawing a deep breath. "Knowing me as you do, can you think me guilty of so cowardly a crime, as to strike down an old man?"

"I think you capable of acting anyhow to retain your own property," answered Mallien cynically.

"You judge me by yourself. You might act so, but I should not. However, it is useless to prolong this talk. I now know that you are an envious and disappointed man, and to get my money you are willing to go to the length of getting me hanged."

"You shouldn't murder people, you know," taunted Mallien, believing that he was now top dog and could have everything his own way.

Rupert passed over the accusation. "I suppose," he remarked, laying a trap for his foe, "that if I hand you over the property, will or no will, you won't say anything to the police?"

Mallien's dark eyes gleamed with greed and triumph, as he had not expected to gain so sudden a victory. Hendle had evidently surrendered without firing a shot. "Yes," he said eagerly. "After all, I don't want to wash dirty family linen in public, and it would be unpleasant for me and for Dorinda to see you in the dock. After all, also, the will leaves everything to me, as the descendant of Eunice Filbert."

"The will has yet to be found; it has yet to be proved legal," said Rupert calmly, "and we are not even certain if this presumed will is not a figment of Leigh's brain."

"Leigh could not have invented such a story," said Mallien doggedly. "And whether he did or not matters little. The property is mine—"

"That has yet to be proved," interpolated Hendle quietly.

"If you don't climb down, it will be proved at the expense of your arrest for the murder," threatened Mallien.

"I see." Rupert's lip curled with contempt. "And if I give you all I have, you will condone a felony?"

"I don't care what beastly terms you use," snapped Mallien uneasily. "You know that it is in my power to have you arrested."

"And in Mrs. Beatson's also."

"Oh, I'll make it worth her while to keep quiet."

"I wonder how Dorinda ever came to have so dishonorable a man for her father," commented Rupert reflectively. "I always knew you to be a bully and an avaricious animal, but I did expect some decency."

"Take care," raged Mallien, growing livid again. "I shall tell the police what I know, if you insult me further."

"It is impossible to insult you. A man who had agreed to hush up what he supposes to be a crime cannot be insulted. He is beyond the pale of decency. I presume, Mallien, that it never occurred to you that if I were weak enough to agree to your blackmailing, that you could be arrested later as an accessory after the fact, always supposing that I am guilty, which I am not."

"Oh, for your own sake you'll hold your tongue," said the other confidently, "and Mrs. Beatson can be squared. I don't think she'll connect the murder and the will, anyhow, as I have done."

"I see. She is not quite so clever as you are. Well, then, if I hand over the property to you straightway, and not bother about finding the will—"

"Which you have already got and destroyed."

"I see. We'll let it go at that. I am guilty, and you will condone my guilt on condition that you get my money?"

"Yes," said Mallien impudently.

"And you will take the risk of being proved an accessory after the fact?"

"Yes! Because I know that you'll hold your tongue for your own sake."

"Of course, you will keep Mrs. Beatson quiet?"

"Certainly. She won't say a word if I give her an annuity; and she is not likely to connect the will and the murder, as I remarked before. Well?"

"Well?" echoed Rupert ironically. "I'm not taking any, thank you."

Mallien's face fell when he found that, in the moment of his fancied triumph, victory was suddenly snatched from his grasp. "You refuse?"

"I do. Go to Inspector Lawson and bring your accusation. I am quite ready to meet it."

"You'll be arrested," threatened Mallien.

"I am quite willing to be arrested. That's better than being in the power of a blackmailer."

"You are mad; you are quite mad."

"You would like me to be, but, as it happens, I am perfectly sane. Meanwhile, until you have me locked up, help me to search for the will."

Mallien could not understand his cousin's attitude. He had insulted him; he had brought a vile accusation against him; yet Rupert coolly refused his greedy terms, and evidently did not mind being in his company. Knowing how he would have cringed and agreed to anything under similar circumstances, Mallien at once sought refuge in a taunt. "I thought you were a man?"

"Obnoxious animals such as you are cannot judge what is a man and what isn't, my friend," retorted Rupert, putting on his coat. "Will you walk along with me toward The Big House and discuss the matter further?"

"No, hang you, I won't."

"As you please. And your denunciation of me to the police?"

Mallien hesitated. "I'll give you a week to think things over."

"Thank you," said Hendle gravely, and, the treaty having been made, the conversation ended with victory for the Squire—a victory won by sheer honesty.

CHAPTER X

DORINDA

Here was a pretty kettle of fish. Hitherto, Rupert had led an easy life, wholly devoid of any great trouble. His mother having died when he was born, and his father while the lad was at school, Hendle had never been brought face to face with any heartbreaking sorrow. But, with the advent of Carrington, as a species of stormy petrel, had come one woe after another. In a remarkably short space of time, Rupert found himself in danger of losing his property, his position, his promised wife, and even his good name, if not his liberty and life. Should the will be found, and should it prove to be legal, Mallien, without the least compunction, would ascend the local throne as the new Squire of Barship, with an income of four thousand a year. And, in that event, there would be every chance that the marriage with Dorinda would never take place. Her father, having all he wanted, would never agree to the match, and, even if the girl remained true—as he knew very well she would—how could he ask her to marry one reduced to the position of a pauper? These things alone were sufficient to drive an ordinary man crazy; but the possibility of being arrested for a crime he had not committed, made Hendle feel that the burden was too great to be borne. He returned to The Big House with his mind in a turmoil, and his head aching with anxious thought.

Aware that Mrs. Beatson had acted treacherously, Rupert's first idea was to call her in and dismiss her straightway with a month's wages. But, on second thoughts, he decided to do nothing until he had consulted with Carrington. Certainly, the barrister, by refusing to help as a friend, had shown himself almost as greedy of gain as Mallien; but Hendle decided that the prospect of a fat fee would make the man more alert to earn it. Carrington, when all was said and done, had a shrewd brain and a great deal of experience connected with the seamy side of life, so he was just the man to handle the problems Fate had so unexpectedly given Rupert to solve. Mallien did not like Carrington, and if Mallien secured the property, Carrington would not even get his costs for taking up the case. Therefore, both as a professional man and as Hendle's friend, the barrister had every reason to work on the side of the Squire. What he would advise in the matter of Mrs. Beatson and her eavesdropping Rupert did not know; but he thought it would be just as well to see what he said. With this idea the Squire made no difference toward his treacherous housekeeper, and concealed his feelings so well that Mrs. Beatson had no idea that her batteries had been unmasked. All the same Hendle saw as little of her as possible, and, beyond giving her necessary orders, did not speak to her.

It must be noted that Mallien's estimate of Mrs. Beatson's brain was a perfectly correct one. She did not in any way connect the conversation about the missing will with the death of the vicar. All she knew was that Mr. Leigh had found an ancient testament which would probably transfer the property to Mallien, as the descendant of John Hendle's granddaughter; and, for this reason, she worshipped the rising sun. Had she guessed that there was any doubt about the legality of the will, or any danger of its not being found, she would have held her tongue until such time as she saw on what side it was best to range herself. But, in the conversation she had overheard, Leigh had seemed so certain that Rupert would lose the property and as certain that his cousin would get it, that Mrs. Beatson had lost no time in reporting the position. Mallien's conduct had justified her action, for he had promised her an annuity whenever he came into his own. And, to gain a certain income, the housekeeper was quite willing to see her kind-hearted young master driven as a pauper from his house.

Some natures are so strangely constituted that they resent kindness, and the more benefactions they receive, the more do they hate the person who bestows them. Mrs. Beatson was a woman of this class, and all Hendle's consideration for many years had only increased the dislike she had felt when she first set eyes on him. Moreover, she detested Dorinda for her beauty and sweetness, and for the certain happiness which the marriage with Rupert would surely give her. Mrs. Beatson knew enough of the girl's unsophisticated nature to be sure that no amount of money would make up to her for the loss of her promised husband. She did not like Dorinda getting a fortune through her father, but that could not be helped, and, after all, the breaking of the engagement would assuredly prevent the girl from enjoying the same. Therefore, the good lady smiled comfortably to herself as she went about her duties, and rejoiced to think, as she put it, in quite a Biblical way, that the pride of the young couple would soon be brought low. She might not have rejoiced so prematurely had she guessed the contents of the after-dinner letter which her master wrote. But she did not and gloried in her fool's paradise. Dorinda would be made miserable; Hendle would be made a pauper; and she, who had brought about these things, would retire on an annuity of two hundred a year for her services, as she thought that Mallien could not possibly give her less.

Meanwhile, after a meal to which he gave little attention, Hendle retired to the snug little library of The Big House and sat down to his desk. After a few moments of reflection, he wrote a long and exhaustive letter to Carrington, setting forth what had taken place in the study of the late vicar. He pointed out that what the barrister had conjectured had actually come to pass, for Mallien, in possession of the secret, now deliberately accused him of the crime. Rupert added that he had been given a week to think over things, and then asked whether it would not be well to dismiss Mrs. Beatson at once, lest she should act in a further treacherous manner. Finally, the young man ended with inviting Carrington to come down and stay at The Big House until everything was put straight, hinting that any fee Carrington liked to demand would be given to him for his services. In a postscript, Rupert significantly added that if Mallien got the property, Carrington would either receive less remuneration, or none at all. Therefore, and this was the end of the letter—it remained for Carrington to say whether he would give his services on these doubtful terms. Having placed the position before the barrister thus fairly and squarely, Hendle slipped the epistle into an envelope, addressed and sealed it, and sent a special messenger to post it in the village. Afterward, as there was no more to be done, he lighted his pipe, and, sitting in one chair with his feet on another, he began to read the morning paper, which he had not yet glanced at, so deeply had he been involved in the direction of his own affairs.

But the young man's brain declined to interest itself in public doings and, before he knew where he was, Rupert found himself thinking of what had happened in connection with Dorinda. Laying the newspaper on his knee, and placing his hands behind his head, he leaned back to think what was best to be done. He sorely needed a sympathetic soul to converse with, and there was no one so fitted to help him as Dorinda. Carrington's request for a fee had placed him in the position of a business man rather than in that of a friend, so there was nothing to be gained in that quarter. But Dorinda always understood and always gave good advice, and always soothed his feelings. Hendle longed for her looks, and touch and words so much, that he very nearly decided to cross the park and visit the cottage. But two considerations caused him to alter his mind, one was that Mallien, now openly hostile, would be present at the interview; the other was, that he could not speak straightly to the girl, seeing that her father had so much to do with the matter. Dorinda knew that her parent was what is known as a hard case, and had not much respect or affection for him, since he did not deserve the first, nor demand the last. All the same, it was impossible, as Hendle felt, for him to tell the girl frankly that her father was little more than a blackmailer. With such a delicate perception of what was right and just as Rupert possessed, such a course of action was not to be thought of, so he subsided again into his chair, whence he had risen, and determined to carry his heavy burden all by himself. And, considering that the young man had no experience of burdens, he carried it well and bravely.

Then Fate, who had interfered so much in his affairs that matters had been brought to this pass, interfered again with a kinder motive. Just as Rupert was wondering how he was to get through the long night without receiving human sympathy, there was a tapping at the right-hand window of the room, which brought him to his feet. In the stillness of the library, the sound was so unexpected and imperative that even Hendle's steady nerves were unstrung for the moment. With an effort he pulled himself together, and went to the window to lift it and see who had made the signal. Through the glass he saw Dorinda standing on the terrace in the luminous summer night, and she nodded smilingly to him when he lifted the sash.

"Why didn't you go to the door?" asked Rupert, leaning out, and more astonished by her unexpected appearance than he would admit.

"I don't want that prying Mrs. Beatson to see me," replied Miss Mallien, advancing toward the window, the sill of which was so low that she could very easily step over it. "I don't want her to know that I am here. Help me in, Rupert. No!" she suddenly stepped back. "Better come out and join me in the garden. I have much to say to you, and I don't want to risk Mrs. Beatson listening at the door."

"You never did like her," said Hendle, vaulting through the open window onto the terrace. "But why do you suspect her of eavesdropping?"

"My father has told me what she told him," rejoined the girl calmly. "It is for that reason that I have come over."

Rupert took her arm, and they descended the shallow steps to the second terrace, and then gained the lawn, which was dry and warm to the feet. For a few minutes the Squire said nothing, but guided her down a narrow path, which wound deviously to a kind of glade, wherein stood an ancient sundial. Near this and against a dense shrubbery stood a low marble seat on which he placed the girl. Then he sat down beside her and, still remaining silent, strove to collect his scattered thoughts. Dorinda did not hurry him into speech by making any further observation. She had said all that was necessary, and the next remark must be made by her lover. So the two sat quietly under the calm beauty of the stars, breathing the cool fragrance of the night, and the myriad odors of the dreaming flowers. There was no moon, yet the light of the dying day, which still lingered, revealed the garden in a kind of warm twilight. It was such an evening as would have inspired Romeo to venture into the magical garden of Juliet; and love-talk was the only language fitted for such an hour and scene. Yet the stern necessities of the hour demanded that this bachelor and maid should talk on more prosaic matters. A sad waste of time and opportunity, to be sure, as both regretfully thought; but there was no help for it, if future peace was to be insured. Only by the two solving the problems which Fate had set, could happiness come.

"I am sorry that your father told you," said Rupert at last.

"Why?" Dorinda turned her thoughtful face toward him, and saw his white shirt-front glimmer in the half-light.

"Because I did not intend to tell you myself."

"Why?" she asked again, and very calmly—even wonderingly.

"Is there any need to worry you?" fenced the young man evasively.

"If you are worried, as you are, it is only fair that I should be worried also, which I am. We are not yet married, dear; all the same, we are as perfectly of one mind as any two people can be. And, if I am to be your wife, I must naturally share your burdens; it is easier for two to bear them than one. You understand?"

Hendle took her hand, which lay lightly on her lap, and pressed it in token of thanks. "I understand that you are a staunch and true woman," he said, in a soft voice, "how you came to have such a father—?"

"Oh, don't let us speak of him," interrupted Dorinda impatiently.

"My dear, we must speak of him, as he is part and parcel of the affairs which we must discuss. Yet, had he not spoken to you, I should have held my peace, although I was sorely tempted to come to you for sympathy no later than a few minutes before you tapped at the window."

"I knew, from what my father said, that you were in trouble, Rupert, and I felt that you needed me. For that reason I flung a cloak over my dinner-dress and came on here. Mrs. Beatson would be very shocked if she knew that I was sitting alone with you in the garden in this hour."

"Mrs. Beatson is the kind of woman who would be shocked, however innocent the thing that startled her might be. So your father told you of our interview in Leigh's study?"

"Yes. That is, he told me about the missing will, and how Mrs. Beatson overheard what poor Mr. Leigh had to say on the matter."

"What else did he tell you?" asked Hendle anxiously.

"My dear," Dorinda's eyes opened widely, "what else was there to tell?"

"Hum!" murmured the Squire doubtfully. "Your father let out just as much as suited him. Let us talk of what he did tell you to begin with; afterward, we can talk of what he did not tell you. Yet"—Rupert tugged at his moustache nervously—"I am not quite sure if I should speak frankly."

"I am," retorted Dorinda, giving his hand a squeeze, "if I am to help you, I must know everything."

"I don't feel quite certain if that is playing the game."

"Is my father playing the game?" questioned the girl, with a shrug.

"No," answered Rupert decidedly, "he isn't. And it is that which makes it so hard for me to be frank. After all, your father is your father, dear, and I have no right to say anything which will lower him in your esteem."

Dorinda laughed rather sadly. "Dear, I have no illusions left about my father," she said, in a low tone, "he has never been a father to me, as you know very well. I have tried my best to respect and love him, but his actions and life are such that I can do neither. Be as open with me as you can, Rupert, for you know that my father will not spare either of us where his own feelings are at stake. Therefore, it only seems fair to me that we should not spare him, more than is necessary, on account of my unfortunate relationship to him."

"Do you really think so, Dorinda?"

"Yes, I do. If my father deserved filial affection, he should have it. But, as he has made no attempt to secure it, how can I give it to him? And remember, you are to be my husband and your interests are mine, even though my father's selfish desires intervene. You have the greatest claim on me."

Rupert heaved a sigh of relief. "I am so glad to hear you say that," he remarked thankfully, "for I badly need some one who can help me and sympathize with me. I thought Carrington would prove to be a pal, but, like everyone else, he is eaten up with greed for money."

"What makes you say that?"

"He said that he would only help me on condition that I paid him."

"Ah-r-r-r," said Dorinda, much disgusted. "I told you that I did not like him, Rupert. He is a bad man."

"Oh, not so bad as that, dear. A little greedy perhaps, but not wholly bad."

"He is a bad man," repeated Dorinda, obstinately. "As my father said, long ago, all he wants is to get money out of you."

"As your father does," said Rupert dryly.

Dorinda looked down at her white shoes and placed them both together before she answered. "I have told you my opinion of my father," she said with a sigh, "so what is the use of going over old ground. But time is passing, Rupert, and there is much to say. I wish to go home soon, lest my father should find out that I have come here. I left him busy in his study with his jewels, so we are safe for half an hour, at least. Come now, what took place in the Vicarage library?"

"What did your father tell you?"

"He said that Mrs. Beatson told him about the will found by Mr. Leigh, and how Mr. Leigh had mislaid it. The will, he declared, left the Hendle property to him entirely."

"I have not yet seen the will," answered Rupert, cautiously, "and, beyond Leigh's word, I don't even know that it exists. But he maintained that it did, as he came across it in the Muniment Room, and took it to the Vicarage to look into. Then he lost it, or mislaid it somehow. As I have access to his papers, as executor, I am trying to find it."

"Does it leave the property to my father?"

"Not directly, I understand," admitted Rupert, quietly, "but Leigh explained that John Hendle, from whom we are both descended, dear, hated his younger son Frederick, who inherited, and loved his son Walter, who was killed at the Battle of Waterloo. In the year when that battle was fought, he made this will, leaving the Hendle property to Walter's daughter, and cutting off Frederick, who represented the younger branch."

"Eunice Hendle was the daughter, my father said."

"Yes. She afterward became Eunice Filbert, as she married a man of that name," explained Rupert laboriously. "Her daughter, Anne Filbert, married Frank Mallien, your father's parent, so, if the will proves to be legal, your father will certainly get the property through his descent on the distaff side."

"And you?" asked Dorinda, apprehensively.

Rupert rested his elbows on his knees, linked his hands loosely together, and looked down at the shadowy turf of the lawn. "I shall lose everything," he stated calmly. "I descend in the male line from Frederick through Henry Hendle and Charles Hendle. And, as Frederick was cut off by his father in favor of Walter's child, Eunice, I am an interloper and a fraud. If this will is found, and can be proved to be legal, Dorinda, I shall not have a penny. As things stand, your father is better off with his five hundred a year than I shall be. It is a very unpleasant position, as it stops our marriage."

"Oh, does it?" cried Dorinda, flaming up, "in what way?"

"Well, in the first place, your father would never agree to your marrying a pauper, and in the second the pauper could scarcely ask you to share his nothing a year."

"Darling,"—Dorinda drew closer to her lover and laid her cheek against his —"I will marry no one but you. I don't care what my father says."

"It is not of your father that I am thinking of, but of my honor," rejoined Rupert, slipping his arm round her waist and holding her tightly to him. "If we got married, how could I support you? I have no trade, and no profession, so the only thing that I could do to keep body and soul together is to enlist. I might emigrate certainly, but then your life as my wife would be as hard and impossible in the backwoods as it would be if you followed the drum along with me."

Dorinda sighed. "You take a very prosaic view of the position."

"In justice to you I must take a prosaic view. Romance is all very well, but without money romance means trouble and sordid cares."

"Yes," sighed the girl again; then added, after a pause. "And if the will is not found?"

"I shall keep my own," answered Rupert firmly. "It's no use my being a silly fool, and giving up what isn't proved not to be mine. But I am looking for the will, Dorinda, and if it comes to light, I shall hand it over to the family lawyers to be adjusted. And, of course, you may be certain that I shall take advantage of everything likely to prevent my losing The Big House and the income."

"That is quite right," said Dorinda, in a tone of satisfaction, patting her lover's hand consolingly. "I daresay my father will fight, but if you have right on your side, you will be sure to win. Money would do my father no good, as he would only waste it in collecting jewels, whereas you make good use of your income. After all the will may not exist. Mr. Leigh may have dreamed that there was such a document."

"He seemed to be very positive that it did exist, dear," said Rupert, with a shrug, "and, although Leigh was a bit of a dreamer, I don't think he would have or could have made up such a fairy tale as this. For my part, I believe that there *is* such a testament, and that it will come to light sooner or later. I shall make use of the Statute of Limitations, and of any flaw in the will to keep the property, but if everything is legal and shipshape, I shall hand over what I have to your father. As an honest man I can do no less."

"It's very hard on you, dear."

"It is," admitted Rupert quietly; "but I may have to bear harder things."

Dorinda stared. "I don't see anything harder to bear."

"The loss of liberty and, perhaps, of life—"

"Rupert, what are you talking about?"

"Ah!" Rupert rose and stretched himself. "Your father did not tell you all that we spoke about in the Vicarage study. You don't know what he proposes to do, Dorinda, and I don't know if I ought to tell you."

"You must! you must!" She sprang up and laid her two hands on his shoulders with a grasp of which he did not think she was capable. "I share all your troubles—all your sorrows, all—all."

Hendle caught her hands, and holding them to his heart looked into her eyes dimly seen in the light. "Your father declares that I murdered Leigh to get the will," he said quietly; "don't scream."

"I am not going to scream," replied Dorinda, looking aside and speaking rather rapidly. "What on earth makes my father say such a ridiculous thing? On the face of it, such an accusation is absurd."

"Your father doesn't seem to think so, dear. And if Inspector Lawson learned what was at stake with regard to this will, he would not think so either. Remember that I had every reason to steal it, even at the cost of a life."

"What rubbish," declared the girl, vehemently. "You would never, never, never—"

"No," said Rupert positively, and his heart leaped when she defended him. "I would never save my property at the cost of a crime, however small or however necessary. You know, Dorinda, that I would let everything go rather than lose my honor and my good name. Your father thinks otherwise, so he is determined to get my money and my position, and my good name into the bargain."

"I can't believe it, I can't! I can't!" gasped the girl, overwhelmed. "My father may be selfish, but he wouldn't surely—"

"But he has. He accuses me of committing the crime, and has given me one week to think over the matter. If I come to his terms, he will shut up Mrs. Beatson's possible chatter and will hold his own tongue."

"Did he offer you safety on those terms?"

"He did, and I refused them."

Dorinda flung her arms round his neck and her lips sought his. "I knew you would; I knew you would. Oh! don't say anything more, Rupert. I am glad you told me, as I now know where I stand—where you stand. We have a week to think over things, and in that week much may happen. God will never permit such an injustice. Cheer up, dearest"—she kissed him again—"it will all come out right; it will all come out right."

"I hope so," said Rupert, doubtfully, and adjusting the cloak on her shoulders. "But what will you say to your father?"

"I don't know, I can't say, I must think. Meanwhile, see me home, Rupert."

Thus abruptly she ended the interview, and the Squire escorted her to within sight of the cottage. But he did not enter.

CHAPTER XI

CARRINGTON'S ADVICE

The details given by Rupert of the conversation which had taken place in the Vicarage study shocked Dorinda profoundly. It was natural enough that her father, informed of an existing will which would give him an estate, should try and gain possession of it, so as to secure what he believed to be his rights. Dorinda did not blame him for taking up so reasonable a position; but she was horrified to think that he should accuse an innocent man of committing the crime. It was wholly impossible that Mallien could believe Rupert to be guilty. He had known the Squire intimately for twenty-five and more years, therefore he was well aware how strictly honorable Rupert was in every way. Moreover, Hendle had always treated his cousin with consistent kindness, having again and again given him sums of money, large and small, which had never been repaid. Even if Rupert were guilty, it was cowardly of Mallien to threaten; but, seeing that Rupert was innocent—and Dorinda was well assured in her own mind that her father knew him to be so—the attack was cowardly in the extreme. If the girl had little affection for her father before, she had still less for him now.

What troubled her throughout the night was the question of speaking, or of not speaking, frankly to her father. He had withheld from her the more serious portion of his interview with Rupert, and Dorinda was strongly inclined, not only to intimate that she knew about the accusation, but to tell her father how strongly she disapproved of his conduct. More than this, she wished to state that she was on the side of her lover. Dorinda was straightforward herself; and greatly desired that Mallien should be straightforward also. To bring such rectitude into being, plain speaking was necessary. Yet the girl hesitated to broach the subject, knowing only too well her father's temper, his tricky nature and his unscrupulous greed. But at breakfast, her hesitation to make trouble was ended by Mallien himself, as he began to speak furiously the moment she laid her hand on the coffee-pot.

"This is a nice thing, Dorinda," he raged, without returning her morning greeting. "You went out last night and did not return until after nine; in fact, it was nearer ten. Don't deny it. You slipped out when I was busy in my study, but I came to ask you something and found you had gone out. What do you mean by such conduct?"

Dorinda lifted her eyebrows. "I am not aware that there is anything strange about my conduct. I have been out late before. I am quite capable of looking after myself, I assure you, father."

"I don't think so," retorted Mallien, bristling with anger; "and I don't like such underhand conduct."

"I never behave in an underhand way," returned Dorinda, her color rising and her eyes flashing. "You know that quite well."

"You slipped out last night and slipped in, without telling me."

"There was no need to tell you."

"There was. Don't contradict me. If your conduct was not underhand, why did you not come and say good-night to me in my study as usual?"

"Because I could not," said Dorinda coldly, and looking straight at her angry parent. "What Rupert told me about you disgusted me too much."

"Rupert!" Mallien rose and pushed back his chair noisily. "You went to see that—that—that scoundrel?"

Dorinda rose in her turn. "He is not a scoundrel."

"He is, I tell you, and I forbid you to see him again."

"As I am engaged to my cousin, I shall see him when and where I please," said the girl deliberately. "Don't try me too far, father, or you will be sorry for it. I am not in the best of tempers this morning."

"You—you—minx!" gasped the angry man, choking with rage. "How dare you address me in that way?"

"And how dare you accuse Rupert of murdering Mr. Leigh," she retorted boldly.

Mallien's wrath suddenly died away, and he dropped back into his chair with an uneasy look. "Who says that I accuse—"

"Rupert himself told me. I saw him last night, to hear what he had to say about this missing will, and he told me what you did not tell me."

"He's a mean hound to put my daughter against me!" shouted Mallien.

"Please"—Dorinda flung up her hand—"I am not deaf. Rupert did not wish to tell me. I made him speak out, as I saw that he was hiding something. If you were as honorable and scrupulous as Rupert, father, you would not need to get into these rages with me, as I don't deserve them. And it's no use your behaving in this way. I can hold my own, as you well know, and I intend to do so. We may as well understand one another."

"I am your father; you owe me respect."

"How can I give you what you don't deserve? You *are* my father, and God help me that I should have such a one."

"If you talk to me in this way," snarled Mallien, blustering, "I shall turn you out of doors neck and crop. What will you do then?"

"Marry Rupert," rejoined the girl promptly.

"A ruined man," sneered the other.

"He is not ruined yet; he never may be ruined. That will has yet to be found; it has yet to be proved legal, and you may be sure that Rupert will take all the advantage he can, to keep what he has."

"I see. You are fighting against your father."

"I fight on the side of right. If the property is yours, Rupert is willing to hand it over; if it is his, he has every right to keep it. But you have no right," cried Dorinda, striking the table passionately, "to accuse an innocent man of committing such a cowardly crime."

"You are talking nonsense," said Mallien, doggedly and folded his arms. "He is guilty."

"He is not. No one knows that better than you."

Mallien cringed at that last sentence, and his dark face grew strangely pale as he avoided his daughter's steady blue eyes. "I don't know why you should say that," he muttered.

"What else can I say when you have known Rupert for so many years?" was the passionate reply. "Has he ever behaved otherwise than honorably? Is he the man, father, to kill a weakling like poor Mr. Leigh, for money which he cares very little about? You know better."

Mallien recovered his self-possession during his daughter's speech and shook his shoulders as he laughed harshly. "I know that the will stands between Rupert and absolute poverty," he retorted obstinately; "and if a man has to make a choice—"

"A man like Rupert would chose poverty rather than crime," interrupted Dorinda imperiously. "What reason have you to believe that Rupert would do such a wicked thing?"

"My knowledge of human nature—"

"Oh, is that all?" There was an expression of relief in Dorinda's voice as she interrupted him again. "So your evidence is purely circumstantial?"

"Yes!" admitted Mallien sullenly, and feeling that Dorinda was too strong for him to deal with. "All the same, a very powerful case can be built up against the fellow. The will has disappeared in the nick of time, and Rupert had every reason to make it disappear."

"You seem to forget that no one but Mr. Leigh has seen the will," said Dorinda crisply; "it may not exist."

"It does exist," stormed Mallien violently, "and it leaves the property to me as the descendant of Eunice Filbert."

"That is what Mr. Leigh said, but he may have imagined the whole thing. He was always a dreamer, you know. Anyhow, father, I don't see much use in your threatening Rupert with shadows."

"I don't think that Inspector Lawson will think that they are shadows," said Mallien significantly.

"Don't you?" replied Dorinda, with a lightness which she was far from feeling. "Well, then, I do. Before the police can arrest Rupert, they must first prove that the document, for the sake of which the crime is supposed to have been committed, is in existence. Then they will have to prove that Rupert was at the Vicarage on the night, and at the time when Mr. Leigh was struck down. I don't think it will be easy to do what you say."

"I have no wish for Rupert to be arrested," said Mallien restlessly. "All he has to do is to give up the property and I'll hold my tongue."

"There is nothing for you to hold your tongue about," said Dorinda sharply, "as what you say is purely theoretical. As to the property, you certainly shall not have it unless the will is found and the property is proved to be yours. I am on Rupert's side, remember, and I shall do my best to make him hold on to his own."

"You go against your father?"

"Oh!" she cried impatiently, "you said that before, and I answered you. Yes, I do go against my father, and I have every reason to. I am not going to countenance a robbery which would give you money you are better without."

"Better without?" demanded Mallien indignantly. "What do you mean?"

"What I say," said Dorinda tartly. "Rupert makes good use of his fortune in helping the poor, and in keeping up the church. You would only waste it in buying jewels for your own satisfaction."

"I won't be spoken to like this."

"It is your own fault that I am so frank. If what I say doesn't please you, I can easily go to London to see my old schoolmistress and ask her to get me a position as a nursery governess."

"You wouldn't do that?"

"Yes, I would, and you know that I would. I should like to respect you and to love you, father, but I cannot. Your last action, in threatening to denounce an innocent man, widens the gulf between us. If you dare to go to Inspector Lawson, I shall go out as a governess until such time as Rupert is ready to marry me. Now you know exactly what I mean."

Mallien did know, and was well aware that she would act precisely as she declared she would. It was no use to storm and bluster and try to reduce her to tears, as Dorinda was not a tearful woman. She knew how to hold her own and intended to hold it. Mallien, having tried rage, was reduced to attempting pathos, which he did very badly. "My own daughter! my own daughter!" he murmured sadly. "It's heartbreaking."

"It's pretty uncomfortable, I grant you," answered Dorinda, with a queer smile, "for me as for you. But as you have made the position entirely yourself, I don't see what you have to complain of. But now that we understand one another, let us call a truce."

"Very good. I will overlook your unfilial behavior and try to forget this conversation. All the same," cried Mallien, blazing up again, "I intend to get my rights."

"Certainly. And if the will is found, you shall have them."

This was cold comfort to Mallien, who doubted if the will ever would be found. Leigh might have made a mistake, and there might be no will in existence, in which case, by making an enemy of Rupert, he would be worse off than he was at present. He thought that until the truth came to light, it would be just as well to temporize, and let things stand as they were. Therefore, as an outward sign of reconciliation, he dropped a cold kiss on his daughter's white brow, and retreated to his study. Dorinda, left alone in the little dining-room, had no desire to eat any breakfast, as the struggle to secure Rupert's safety had exhausted her greatly. She hastily drank a cup of coffee, then wrote a note to her lover, saying that he need not be afraid of the intervention of the police, and relating in detail the conversation just ended. Having sent this by hand to The Big House, the girl went about her daily duties, resolutely cheerful. Only by assuming a bold front could she combat the great trouble which threatened to overwhelm her and her lover. When the worst came to the worst, there would be time enough to think of further defense. But Dorinda believed that further defense would not be required.

Rupert was very well satisfied when he received Dorinda's note, as he had winced at the idea of Inspector Lawson intervening. He, of course, had been very certain that there was no chance of his being arrested, owing to the fact that the will could not be proved to exist. Still, Lawson was ambitious of promotion and obstinate in his own opinion, therefore, if Mallien had told his story, there might have been a chance of scandal. However, Dorinda having reduced her father to neutrality, the only thing that remained to do was to find the will. Rupert intended to search again among the papers at the Vicarage; but could not do so until the afternoon, as Carrington had sent a wire saying he would be down by the midday express. The Squire intended to meet him at the station, and talk to him on the way home, since he was anxious to know what was the best way to deal with the treacherous Mrs. Beatson. Knowing that she was a spy and an enemy, Rupert could hardly bear to see her about the house. However, he tolerated her presence until he heard what Carrington had to say.

By this time, all excitement had died out of the village, as the crime had been so thoroughly discussed that there was no more to be said about the matter. In their stolid bovine way, the rustics accepted the positive fact that their late spiritual adviser was dead and buried—accepted, also, the evident truth that the murderer would never be caught and punished. This being the case, they dismissed the past, and looked eagerly forward to the future when the new incumbent would arrive. It was reported that a vicar had already been appointed by the Bishop and that he had a family, and would make the Vicarage a much more lively place than it had been in Mr. Leigh's time. Oh, there was plenty to talk about and *The Hendle Arms* was filled with conversational yokels from morning until evening.

On the way to the station, Rupert stumbled across Titus Ark, who grinned in a toothless manner, touched his shabby hat, and shuffled along in a manner surprisingly spry for a man of eighty-odd years of age. Hendle stopped to give him a sixpence for snuff, to which the ancient was much addicted.

"You miss Mr. Leigh, Titus," he said, pityingly, for the old man was a lonely figure in the midst of the new generation.

"Hor! Hor! Hor!" croaked the aged sexton. "Why should I miss him Squoire when he bain't dead?"

"Why, Titus, you buried him—that is, you helped to place the body in the family vault. Poor Mr. Leigh could not have been buried alive."

"Who said as he was alive, Squoire? I never did."

"You say that he isn't dead."

"No more he be."

"Then he must be alive."

"No, he bain't. Hor! Hor! Hor! Crack that nut, Squoire!" and the ancient shuffled along the dry dusty road, chuckling to himself.

Hendle shrugged his shoulders, wondering if it would be necessary to lock up Titus in a lunatic asylum. He appeared to be quite crazy, and talked in so confused and contradictory a manner that no meaning could be extracted from his speech. Evidently his brain was far gone in decay, and although so far he had kept his legs, he would shortly be bedridden. Ark's office as sexton was a sinecure, as his grandson, an active young fellow, dug the graves, and attended to funeral details. The activities of Titus were confined to appearing in the churchyard and telling what he knew about the deceased. On the whole, the old creature was harmless enough, so Rupert banished from his mind the idea of shutting him up, satisfied that, so long as his grandson looked after him, he could be permitted to be at large. Ark's incomprehensible talk reminded Hendle of Wordsworth's poem—"We Are Seven." No more than the child therein could Titus understand what death meant. And this was strange, considering that he was an old and accomplished sexton.

However, Rupert had more important things with which to employ his mind than in thinking about the babble of the ancient. He forgot all about Ark when he came in sight of the station, the more readily when he saw Carrington on the lookout for him. The train had arrived early, and the barrister was waiting for his friend's arrival. After greetings, Carrington linked his arm within that of his old school-friend, and they sauntered leisurely toward The Big House.

"That was a strange letter you wrote me, Hendle," said Carrington, when the two settled into their stride. "I could scarcely believe it."

"Why not? I wrote plainly enough."

"Oh, yes. But I never thought that my idea of risk to you would ever become an established fact so soon. It's queer that Mrs. Beatson should have listened on that particular night to that particular conversation."

"Well, you see, she got it into her head that I intended to dismiss her when I married Dorinda, and so kept her ears open to hear if I spoke to the vicar about my intention. As a matter of fact, I had no idea of turning her away."

"*Then*, you had not. But now?"

"She must go," said Rupert shortly. "I can't have a spy at my elbow."

"Have you said anything to her?"

"No! She is quite in the dark as to her treachery having been discovered."

Carrington thought for a few moments. "If Mallien goes to the police, she will then learn that you know how she has behaved."

"Mallien is not going to the police," said Rupert, quietly.

"But I thought you said in your letter that he had given you one week to—"

"Yes, yes," interrupted the younger man, "I did say so, and such was the case when I wrote. But circumstances have changed since then, thanks to Dorinda."

"Miss Mallien? What has she to do with the matter?"

"A great deal. Last night she came over, as her father had told her about the will. I was forced to tell her that Mallien threatened to accuse me of the murder."

"Oh! Oh!" said Carrington significantly. "So Mallien did not tell her that?"

"No. He was ashamed to, I suppose, as he is well aware that I am innocent. But this morning he had a row with Dorinda about her engagement to me, and she stood up for me, bless her. What she said, or what he said, I don't know, but Dorinda sent over a note this morning saying that her father had changed his mind about speaking to Lawson."

Carrington heaved a sigh of relief. "That makes things easier, anyhow. We can take our own time to work out the case. Have you found the will?"

"No. I haven't seen a sign of it. I intend to look again this afternoon, and you can assist me if you care to."

"Oh, yes. Four hands are better than two, and two searchers better than one,

Hendle. And if the will isn't found?"

"Well, I suppose things will remain as they are."

"Don't you make any mistake, Hendle," replied the barrister shrewdly. "Mallien won't stop until he gets that will."

"I don't mind. In fact, I told him that he could help me look for it."

Carrington frowned. "I hope I won't be brought into contact with him. He's such a rude beast."

"Well, after our quarrel of yesterday. I don't think he'll put in an appearance," said Hendle consolingly. "Anyhow, whether he does or not matters little. Our business is to find the will, and thus knock Mallien's possible accusation on the head."

"As you please, what must be, must be. Miss Mallien is a charming girl, but if marriage with her meant a father-in-law like that boor I should cry off."

"Ah, you are not in love, you see," said Rupert calmly; "besides, when we are married, we will see very little of Mallien. I am bribing him with five hundred a year to make himself scarce. As he doesn't care a cent for his daughter, he will probably agree to clear out."

"Not before he has had a try to get the whole of your money," said Carrington dryly. "The man is a shark, and a sponge, and a greedy animal."

"Why call him names, Carrington? He is Dorinda's father after all, so it is best to leave him alone."

"He won't leave you alone," retorted the other. "I wonder you can be so calm over the matter, Hendle."

Rupert cast a side-look of surprise at the flushed dark face of his companion. "I am quite innocent, so why shouldn't I be calm?"

"Hum!" growled the barrister. "Innocent men have been hanged before now."

"Well, this innocent man won't be hanged, Carrington. No one can prove that I was near the Vicarage on that night."

"Probably not. But you had every motive to go there and get the will, seeing that it may render you a pauper."

"If I am to be a pauper I must become a pauper," replied Rupert coolly; "but I certainly would never attempt to save myself from poverty by murdering an old man who was my friend."

"Well, you see, people will talk as Mallien has talked," said the barrister with a shrug. "You and I alone knew about the will. I was in town, so no one can say a word about me. But you, near at hand, and—"

"What is the use of talking rubbish?" interrupted Rupert sharply. "I never was near the place on that night, and if people talk, well, they must just talk, as I am perfectly innocent. Besides, you forget that Mallien knew about the will."

"Only after the murder, as Mrs. Beatson probably did not tell him beforehand."

"I don't suppose she did. Hum!" Rupert stopped and looked down at his neat brown boots and gaiters. "Queer that I never thought of asking Mallien when she did tell him. I'll ask him next time we meet. Just now we can cross out Mallien as knowing. But Mrs. Beatson—"

"Exactly," interrupted Carrington gravely; "it occurs to me that she knows more about the matter than she chooses to say."

"But you don't mean to infer that she killed the vicar?"

"Why not? She knew about the will and guessed that if she could get hold of it she could make you squeal."

"At the risk of being accused of murdering Leigh."

Carrington nodded. "Perhaps. But then she may think that you would hold your tongue about that if she gave you the will."

Hendle walked on sharply. "I don't believe a word of what you say," he cried, looking much worried. "Mrs. Beatson has behaved treacherously, but I don't think for one moment that she would kill the vicar."

"Perhaps not," said Carrington soothingly. "Well, then, let us say nothing to her, but watch. If she is guilty, she is bound to betray herself. The main thing is not to let her suspect that you have found out her treachery."

Hendle took off his cap and let the balmy air play on his hot head. "It is very unpleasant," he said in a vexed tone.

"Very," assented the barrister cordially; "but for your own sake—"

"Well, well, do what you like, Carrington. The case is in your hands."

CHAPTER XII

ON THE TRACK

Generally speaking, it seemed as though Mallien's prophecy of Carrington picking Rupert's pockets was likely to come true. Owing to circumstances, the barrister had found a perfectly legitimate way of getting money from his friend, and intended to take every advantage of the opportunity. He explained to Hendle that it would be necessary for him to remain at The Big House until all these crooked affairs were straightened out, and that, his time being valuable, he would require a handsome fee for his services. The Squire professed himself quite willing that things should be so arranged, but he was scarcely so dense as Carrington believed him to be. He saw that the visitor was anxious to make money, and concluded that perhaps it was best to settle matters on this coldly legal basis. The cut-and-dried situation was thus perfectly understood by both men, and they got on very amicably together. On the surface everything was as it should be.

But below the surface, things were scarcely so pleasant. Rupert's susceptibilities for Carrington, dating from Rugby days, had received a shock. He had looked to find in the barrister an intimate friend, only to discover that he was a hard business man. Had Carrington looked into matters without stipulating for a fee, and had behaved as a chum, Hendle would have gladly dealt handsomely with him, knowing that he was not particularly successful in his profession. But the Squire, with the memory of his school hero-worship in his mind, was dismayed to find that his former idol had feet of clay, and that Carrington was quite willing to use him as a means to an end. Rupert was by no means sentimental, yet he felt anxious for sympathy in his present unpleasant position. That sympathy should be sold, as the barrister was selling it, chilled his ardent nature, and made him less confidential with his school-friend than otherwise he would have been. Everything seemed to be for sale, and nothing appeared to be given as a gift. Mallien, Mrs. Beatson, Carrington, all had an eye to the main chance; and even the late vicar had hinted in a veiled way that the will would be given up if his Yucatan expedition was financed. It seemed to Rupert that his only true friend was Dorinda, who loved him for himself, and not for what she could get out of him. And Dorinda was nearer and dearer than a friend, since she was to be his wife. Hendle, who was deeply religious in his unobtrusive way, silently thanked God that he had one staunch comrade. And such Dorinda was, therefore their marriage would certainly be happier, when founded upon so solid a foundation, than if it were a mere romantic passion.

For the next three days, the two men paid daily visits to the Vicarage and hunted high and low for the missing will. They examined every paper; they opened every book; they looked through the pockets of old clothes, and turned out every cupboard. Rupert expected that Mallien, being so keen about his rights, would search also; but the day after Carrington's arrival, he went up to London, and remained absent for some time. Apparently he disliked coming into contact with the sharp-tongued barrister, and probably would not return until his enemy took his departure. Carrington, of course, was not Mallien's enemy, as he had no reason to be, but Mallien in his odd misanthropic way regarded him as such. He therefore would not have been pleased had he learned that on the third day of his absence, Dorinda entertained the two men at dinner.

Miss Mallien did not like Carrington any more than did her father, but for the sake of helping Rupert, she extended the hand of hospitality. In fact she gave quite a little dinner-party, as Kit Beatson and Miss Tollart were also present. The master of the house always objected to these small entertainments, as they cost money; but Dorinda paid no attention to his objections, as she claimed a reasonable right to amuse herself. Nevertheless, she considered her father's feelings so far as only to ask her neighbors to luncheon, afternoon tea and dinner when he was absent. Yet, notwithstanding this concession, there was always trouble when Mallien returned; and, since Carrington had been invited, it was probable that, on this occasion, there would be a royal row. Dorinda did not mind, as she was used to rows. The only way in which she could make her situation bearable was by standing up for herself and defying her father in small matters. If she did not do so, he would bully her still more, for every inch she gave meant several ells with him. Her mild entertainments were therefore useful in preserving her independence, and in coloring a somewhat drab existence.

With the assistance of the small servant, Miss Mallien had prepared a simple but appetizing meal, which was done full justice to by the quartette of guests. Afterward, they sat in the tiny drawing-room, and enjoyed a real old English evening of the Albert Period type, including games and music. Carrington had brought some jig-saw puzzles from London, and when the excitement of putting tricky pictures together palled, music supplied new pleasure. Sophy Tollart, who had been well-trained, rendered scraps of very up-to-date harmony, which began anyhow and ended nowhere. Kit sang sentimental ballads in a pleasant uncultivated tenor, and Dorinda delighted her hearers with old time songs such as "Kathleen Mavourneen" and "Robin Adair." Finally, as the evening waned, the company gathered near the open window to chat about this and that and the other thing. Sophy recounted her experience as a militant suffragist; Kit informed everyone of what progress the motor industry was making, and, of course, the coming of the new vicar supplied interesting conversation. It was Miss Tollart who introduced the topic.

"He will arrive in a fortnight," she explained, bending her black brows in quite a tragic way, "and has a family of four girls. I hope to interest them all in the movement."

"Votes for Women?" asked Carrington, who found Sophy very amusing, since she knew little and asserted much.

"Of course. What other Movement is there?"

"Well, you see, Miss Tollart, Women's Rebellion isn't the only pebble on the beach. Humanity has other interests also."

"Then it shouldn't have," retorted Sophy daringly. "Until women have votes, the world will never be put right."

"Things have gone on very well so far," ventured Rupert, only to be crushed.

"How can you say so, Mr. Hendle, when there's nothing but war and bankruptcy, and silly football matches, and smart society, and—"

"Sophy! Sophy! that's enough to go on with," cried Dorinda, smiling. "Don't give us too much to think about."

"You never think at all, Dorinda. You are fainthearted about our votes."

"I don't think you'll get them by destroying property and having hunger strikes," replied Dorinda, with a shrug. "What do you say, Kit?"

Kit blushed and wriggled, for Sophy's eye was on him. "I don't say anything you know. I never do. The motor business takes up all my attention." Then he hurriedly changed the subject, lest his lady-love should fall foul of him for his shirking. "I hope Sophy will gain her ends easier in Australia."

"I'm not going to Australia, Kit. I told you that and I told your mother."

"Mrs. Beatson," said Carrington, pricking up his ears. "Does she want you to go to Australia, Miss Tollart?"

"She wants to go herself."

"That's news to me," observed Hendle, with a start.

"It's news to all of us," put in Kit, dismally. "The worst of mother is that you never know what she'll be up to next. The other day she came to me and said that she soon hoped to inherit an annuity of two hundred a year and intended to go to Australia. She wants Sophy and me to come with her."

Hendle, Dorinda and Carrington exchanged glances. "Who is leaving this annuity to your mother?" asked Rupert, guessing the source of the windfall.

"She didn't say," replied Kit, "some old aunt, I fancy. But I don't want to go with mother. She and Sophy never get on well together."

"How can we when she wants everyone to bow down to her?" said Miss Tollart, who hated Mrs. Beatson thoroughly. "I'm not of the bowing-down sort. And when I marry, I want my house to myself."

"Natural enough," observed Carrington, who was listening eagerly. "And Mrs. Beatson wants you all to live together on her annuity?"

"Not exactly that," said Kit reluctantly. "She won't keep us, but hopes that in Australia I shall make more money out of motors."

"She may hope," said Sophy positively; "and, if she is disappointed, she will have to be. You are not going to Australia, Kit. My father needs my care, and I can't leave him."

It seemed to Carrington that between Kit's mother and his future wife's father, the poor young fellow was in a most uncomfortable position. However, for obvious reasons, connected with Sophy, he did not say so and contented himself with the remark that he thought Dr. Tollart very clever. "When I came down here first, I called in to get a cure for toothache and he gave me one which acted like a charm."

Sophy, who seemed to have a deep affection for her disreputable parent, colored with pleasure as she rose to go. "Father has his faults, but he is a very clever man," she said emphatically; "but for his failing he would be in Harley Street as a Specialist."

"Great men have more room for faults than small men," quoted Carrington. "Don't look angry, Miss Tollart; I really mean what I say. Your father is clever."

"I'm glad to hear that some one does him justice," said the girl bitterly, and looking more womanly as she spoke. "Usually everyone is against him. But Kit will help me to keep him straight when we are married. Mrs. Beatson would drive him crazy."

"Sophy! Sophy! She is my mother," expostulated Kit, blushing.

"I know that," snapped Miss Tollart tartly. "It is the only thing I have against you as my husband. But so long as she lives at a distance—well, it's no use talking. Dorinda, I'm going now."

She went out to put on her hat and cloak, while Kit stood irresolutely by the door he had just opened, looking so downcast that Hendle clapped him on the back. "Cheer up, old boy; it will be all right," he said, feeling profoundly sorry for the lad since Mrs. Beatson was decidedly a very disagreeable mother. And then Carrington put a question.

"When does your mother expect her annuity?"

"She says she may get it at any time," replied Kit, rather stiffly, as he did not see why a stranger like the barrister should interfere; "but I know very little about it. All she told me was that she was to get two hundred a year and would leave Mr. Hendle to go to Australia."

"Oh, I shall place no obstacle in her path," observed Rupert somewhat grimly. "After all, as I soon marry Miss Mallien, there will be no need for me to have a housekeeper."

It was at this moment and before Carrington could ask further questions, which he very much wished to do, that Sophy returned. Evidently she had been crying, for her eyes were red, but her emotions were quite under control and, after taking leave of her hostess and the two men, she went away with Kit. They seemed to be rather a forlorn young couple. Dorinda remarked as much when she returned to the drawing-room after seeing them to the door.

"What else can you expect," asked Carrington coolly, "when they are connected with a drunkard like Tollart and a shrew like Mrs. Beatson? So she intends to go to Australia, does she? I don't want to hurt your feelings, Miss Mallien, but I see your father's finger in this."

"Say as little about my father as is possible," answered Dorinda, with a rich color flushing her fair cheeks. Little as she respected her shady parent she did not intend to discuss him with a stranger whom she disliked.

Carrington was diplomatic enough to skate away from the thin ice. "Rupert and I have taken all the papers and clothes and odds and ends of Leigh to The Big House," he remarked; "and there they can stay until we hear from the Australian sea-captain who inherits. The London lawyer has written him."

"And the will?"

"We have not found it yet."

"I don't think we ever will find it," commented Hendle soberly. "I have searched the Vicarage from cellar to attic without success. I really believe, Dorinda, that, after all, Leigh was dreaming, and that the will doesn't exist."

"Either that," said Carrington deliberately, "or Mrs. Beatson made away with Leigh and stole it."

"I can't believe that," protested Dorinda, turning pale. "I told you so before when you first broached the idea, Mr. Carrington. She is not a nice woman, but I don't think she would commit a murder."

"There is nothing Mrs. Beatson would not do, if she were assured that her crime would remain undiscovered," insisted the barrister grimly. "After all, if

Mrs. Beatson didn't kill Leigh, who did? Rupert and I and the housekeeper knew of the will and of its value. As I was in town I am innocent, and we know, Miss Mallien, that Rupert is not the man to commit such a crime. There only remains Mrs. Beatson, who told your father, when she made all things safe."

Dorinda started, and looked searchingly at the barrister. "How do you mean?"

Carrington smiled meaningly. "I believe that Mrs. Beatson murdered Leigh and now has the will. She intends to sell it to your father for this annuity."

Dorinda grew red and her eyes grew bright. "How dare you say such a thing to me, Mr. Carrington? In the first place, my father would never condone a crime even to gain a fortune; in the second, the moment Mrs. Beatson offered to sell him the will, he would know her to be guilty."

"Yes, of course," replied Carrington soothingly, "and naturally would hand her over to the police. It was only the idea of the annuity which suggested the idea to me, and maybe it is far-fetched. I apologize, Miss Mallien."

Dorinda bowed silently. She did not like the ironical tone in which the barrister spoke, as she felt convinced that he still held to his preposterous idea. What is more, in her own mind, she did not consider that the idea was so preposterous as she declared. Her father had been prepared to hush up the matter when he believed Rupert to be guilty, so it was not improbable that he would make terms with Mrs. Beatson, provided he secured the will. Still, the girl did not intend to let Carrington know what she thought, and therefore stood up for her absent parent. "I don't believe that Mrs. Beatson is guilty of such wicked conduct," she repeated, after a pause. "What grounds have you to say such a thing?"

"Well," murmured Carrington with a shrug. "No very good grounds, I admit. But Mrs. Beatson knew about the will before Leigh was murdered, and I firmly believe that he was got rid of for the sake of the will. This suggestion of an annuity hints that she has the will and is trying to dispose of it at a price. Perhaps Hendle—"

"She has said nothing to me," interrupted Rupert quickly, "and, after all, Carrington, you have watched her for the last few days without seeing anything suspicious."

"Mrs. Beatson is a sly creature, who will not give herself away easily," returned the barrister dryly. "I shall continue to watch her. There's ten o'clock, Hendle," he added, as the mellow tones of the church bell floated through the warm night. "We must not keep Miss Mallien from her beauty sleep."

Dorinda did not suggest that they should remain, although she would have liked to speak privately with her lover. But while Carrington was at his elbow, that was impossible, and she did not wish to talk freely in the presence of a man she mistrusted. The two young men said good-night to their hostess and went away, leaving Dorinda in anything but a happy frame of mind. What had been suggested about her father trading with the housekeeper worried her considerably. There might or might not be some truth in the idea. She tried to dismiss it from her mind; but it would not be dismissed, and troubled her far into the small hours of the morning.

Meanwhile, Rupert and his friend sauntered leisurely homeward. It was so hot that they did not wear coats over their evening suit, and so dry underfoot that they walked to and from the cottage in shoes. The sky was radiant with innumerable stars, and although there was no moon, there was ample light in which to see surrounding objects. Through the shadowy world, warm and peaceful, the young men wandered, taking their way across the fields, as the high-road was so dusty and hard. For a time neither spoke, for each was busy with his own thoughts, which had to do with the case. Finally, Carrington broke the silence, and spoke soft, as though he feared listeners.

"I did not press my point, Hendle," he remarked significantly, "as the little I did say rather offended Miss Mallien."

"You were rather libellous about her father, you know, Carrington."

"If the saying, that the greater the truth the greater the libel is true, I certainly was," retorted the barrister, "for what I said I hold to."

"That Mrs. Beatson is the guilty person?"

"Yes. And that she is trading with Mallien to give him what he wants."

"The will?"

"Of course. I am as certain of that fact as I am that I live. She has the will, and she intends to deliver it to him—if she hasn't done so already—on condition that he gives her the two hundred a year annuity, which she told her son comes from a mythical aunt."

"Well," said Rupert, after a pause, "since Mallien was willing to come to terms with me, I see no reason why he should not come to terms with Mrs. Beatson, always provided that she is guilty."

"She is," insisted Carrington bluntly. "It is no use my giving you my reasons again, I think."

"If things are as you say I don't see how Mrs. Beatson's part of the business can be concealed. The will is of no use to Mallien unless he makes it public.

And if he does, he will have to explain how he became possessed of it. I suppose his confession of the deal with Mrs. Beatson would bring him into trouble as an accessory-after-the-fact?"

"It would, and I am wondering how Mallien intends to make himself safe on that score. There is only one thing to be done, Hendle. We must wait until Mallien produces the will. Then we can move."

"It's an infernal messy business altogether," growled the big man, restlessly; "and I wish we were all well out of it. I don't want Mallien to get into any trouble for Dorinda's sake."

"I think you can be pretty certain that Mallien will look after his own precious skin," said the barrister dryly; "and if—hush!—not a word." He dropped his voice to a whisper. "Who's that?"

"What?" Rupert looked round, as Carrington caught his arm, and pulled him off the footpath into a clump of hazels.

"Don't speak," whispered Carrington with his mouth close to Rupert's ear; "and button your coat as well as you can over your shirt-front. The white may betray us." He acted on his own advice, and kept Hendle well behind the shelter of the leafy trees. "Now watch."

Hendle did so with all his eyes, straining his sight through the shadowy night, and by this time had seen the reason of Carrington's action and caution. The two men had reached the red brick wall which ran round the park, and saw that the postern gate through which they intended to pass was open. A tall dark figure in flowing robes was slipping out, and when Carrington pulled his friend into shelter behind the hazels, the woman—for such it was—closed the postern stealthily. After a glance to right and left, she walked swiftly along the footpath, going in the direction whence the watchers had come. As she swept past the hazel clump, Rupert nearly uttered an exclamation, for, in spite of the black-silk hood pulled well over her head and face, he was absolutely certain that this night walker was none other than his respectable housekeeper. What she was doing outside the house at this time of night and whither she was going he could not conjecture. But Carrington could, and when the woman passed away into the shadows, he whispered an exultant explanation.

"It's Mrs. Beatson, Hendle. She's going to look for the will. Quick! let us follow; but take care she doesn't see us."

"The will!" breathed Rupert, cautiously, as they stole out on the trail. "What do you mean?"

"She has hidden the will somewhere, I am sure, and now is going to get it. We will catch her red-handed if we are careful. What luck!"

"But it's impossible, and—"

"Don't talk," interrupted Carrington, in a savage whisper. "Do you want to give the show away? It's a wonderful chance of learning the truth. Come."

Hendle silently agreed with his companion, although he found it hard to believe that Mrs. Beatson was such a conspirator. Whether her night excursion had to do with the missing will or not, he could not be sure; but it was evident that she was bent upon some shady business, into which he should inquire, as her master. The adventure appealed to him as a welcome break in his monotonous existence, and he felt his nerves thrill, as with Carrington he followed cautiously. In the half-light they saw the black figure of the woman climb the stile at the end of the meadow and enter a spinney, which belted the high road. By the time they reached this, and emerged on to the travelled thoroughfare, Mrs. Beatson had vanished. Carrington bent to run, but halted a moment to whisper.

"If there is any truth in my belief, she has gone to the Vicarage. There, if anywhere, she has hidden the will in the jungle."

Hendle nodded without reply, and the two men sped swiftly along the road until they came to the bend. They were just in time to see Mrs. Beatson vanish through the rickety gate, which, as usual, was standing wide open. Carrington stopped, dodged, stooped, then crossed the road to run alongside the hedge until he halted just outside the gate. Peering round the corner with Rupert breathing hard beside him, the barrister saw that Mrs. Beatson carried a lantern, which she had just lighted, for it gleamed like a star in the darkness of the tall trees.

"We can wait here," whispered Carrington, delaying Rupert, who wanted to enter the grounds. "She will come back this way. We may attract her attention if we make any noise in that jungle."

This was good advice which Rupert was sensible enough to take. Keeping well within the shadow of the hedge, and looking up the avenue, they waited for the woman's return. They had put their collars up and had buttoned their dress coats over the shining expanse of shirt-front, so there was no gleam of white to betray them, as they crouched, two dark figures, in the dry ditch under the hedge. With beating hearts they waited anxiously, taking a peep every now and then. Mrs. Beatson was a long time absent—Hendle judged about a quarter of an hour. Then, unexpectedly, she appeared running swiftly down the grass-grown avenue with her lantern swinging in her hand. At the gate and within touch, she waited to extinguish the light, but before doing so set it on the ground to look at a rustling parchment by its gleam. The moment she stooped with the document, Carrington's arm shot out and it was snatched away. With a shriek Mrs. Beatson straightened herself to face her master and his guest. She had, indeed, been caught red-handed.

CHAPTER XIII

CONFESSION

Paralyzed by extreme fright, Mrs. Beatson stood as motionless as a stone image, staring blankly at her captors with open mouth and unwinking eyes. Her face was whiter than the dingy parchment of which she had been deprived, and her breath came and went in short quick gasps, which echoed audibly through the still night. Rupert looked at her for a moment and then turned away his head; his manhood was shamed by the silent agony of the miserable creature. Carrington, more hardened by experience, stooped to the light, and read, "This is the Last Will and Testament of John Hendle," in vividly black Latin lettering. That was enough to assure him of the truth, and, rolling up the parchment, he turned sternly on the panic-struck woman.

"You are a clever fool, Mrs. Beatson," he remarked quietly—"clever in getting the will and hiding it so skillfully; but a fool to examine so compromising a document here, when the village policeman may pass at any moment."

The word "policeman" galvanized Mrs. Beatson into life and action. With a final gasp she suddenly became, as it seemed, conscious of her peril, and bolted. Down the road and across the road she sped, and was in the spinney before the two men could grasp the situation. For a single moment they stared after the flying figure, then simultaneously started in pursuit. With terror-winged feet the housekeeper fled as swiftly as the wind, and it was not until the brick wall, encircling the park, again loomed through the shadows that they caught up to her. Instinctively, like a homing pigeon, she made for the only place where she thought she would be safe. Much, as Carrington grimly thought, after the fashion of a child, who believes himself to be free from danger when smuggled between the blankets. It was while she was fumbling with the lock of the postern that he laid a detaining hand on her shoulder. With a terrified cry she dropped on her knees.

"Mercy! Mercy! I am innocent—innocent," she wailed, and hugged his legs in a frenzy of fear.

"Here, get up!" said the barrister, roughly pulling her to her feet. "Come inside and explain yourself."

"There's nothing to explain," cried Mrs. Beatson, suddenly defiant; "and you are not my master."

"I am more than your master; I am the man who has found you out," stated Carrington, in a hard tone, and pushing open the postern. "Walk in, I tell you."

"Gently, Carrington, gently," said Rupert, sorry for the shaking woman, who was desperate enough to say anything or do anything. "We can deal with this matter reasonably. Take my arm, Mrs. Beatson, and come to the house. You can no doubt give us an explanation."

"I shan't give it to him," muttered the housekeeper, trying to control her shattering emotions. "What has he got to do with me, I should like to know? You are always a gentleman, Mr. Hendle, and I wish you a better friend. Spying and prying, watching and following. Call yourself a man, do you? Ha! Ha! call yourself a man? God help the woman who marries you, say I."

Neither of the two made any reply to this aimless speech, and babbling incoherently, Mrs. Beatson was led by Hendle to the house. Fortunately none of the servants were in the entrance-hall, and when Rupert opened the door with his latch-key, Mrs. Beatson swept in toward the drawing-room, which was lighted up. Carrington and his friend followed close behind, to find her seated in an armchair, fanning her heated face with the hood which she had removed. Her color had returned and her self-possession, so that she eyed the pair defiantly. Her attentions were mostly directed toward Carrington, and if a look could have slain him, he would have dropped dead there and then.

"Come now," said the barrister, when the door was closed and the trio were alone, "what have you got to say to all this?"

"I shan't answer you," snapped Mrs. Beatson viciously. "You aren't going to bully me."

"I think you had better answer," said Hendle, sternly. "This is not the time to play the fool."

"Are you against me also, sir?"

"I am advising you for your good. As to being against you, what attitude do you expect me to assume toward you, seeing how treacherously you have behaved, Mrs. Beatson?"

"Treacherously?"

"Yes! You listened to a conversation not meant for your ears and reported the same to Mr. Mallien."

"Did he tell you so?"

"There was no need for him to tell Mr. Hendle," said Carrington pointedly. "The mere fact that Mr. Mallien knows about this will proclaims your guilt."

"Guilt! Guilt!" repeated the housekeeper violently. "I shall thank you, sir, not to use that word in connection with me."

"I shall use it. Don't be a fool, woman! You knew about this will before Mr. Leigh was murdered, and you killed him to get it."

"It's a lie!"

"Then how do you explain your possession of the will?"

"What is your supposition?" demanded Mrs. Beatson, more like a judge than a criminal.

"If you will have it," returned the barrister, smoothly. "I believe you murdered the vicar to get the will, and having found it, buried the same in that jungle. Then you made your terms with Mr. Mallien, and he agreed to give you an annuity of two hundred a year, if you passed the will along to him. When you thought that all was safe, you went to dig the will up again, and here it is."

Carrington pulled the soiled parchment from his pocket, where he had placed it for safety, doubled up into a packet, and shook it in her face. Mrs. Beatson changed from red to white, and from white to red, but maintained a scornful look. "You are talking nonsense," she said briefly.

"Perhaps," put in Hendle quietly, "and we wait for you to talk sense."

"I shall say nothing," said the woman, obstinately.

"In that case I shall send for Kensit and give you in charge."

"You would not do that, Mr. Hendle."

"Indeed, I shall do it within ten minutes if you do not speak out."

"I can—I can—exonerate—exonerate myself," stuttered Mrs. Beatson, her dry lips scarcely able to form the words.

"You had better do so to us," advised Carrington agreeably.

"And if I don't?" she snarled, turning on him.

"Then Inspector Lawson shall examine you."

"What do I care when I know that I am innocent?"

"Well,"—Carrington shrugged his shoulders—"it's your own affair. Ring the bell, Hendle, and send one of the servants down for Kensit."

"No, don't!" cried Mrs. Beatson, when she saw her master walk toward the fireplace to touch the ivory button. "I can explain."

Hendle nodded and returned to his seat, while Carrington replaced the will in his pocket and waited for the confession. Mrs. Beatson wiped her face and glared at the two like a tigress at bay. Only the knowledge that she was driven into a corner made her speak out. "I overheard your conversation with Mr. Leigh, sir," she said to her master and ignoring Carrington. "Oh, I didn't mean to, you know. I only listened as I thought you intended to discharge me when you married Miss Mallien, and fancied you might explain yourself on that point to the vicar."

"I understand. But why did you report the conversation to my cousin?"

Mrs. Beatson looked down sullenly. "You don't know what it is to be poor," she muttered irrelevantly. "I am born a lady, and through the fault of a spendthrift husband I am reduced to act as your housekeeper. It is only natural that I should try and improve my position, so when I learned about a will which would give your property to Mr. Mallien, I thought it wise to make money by speaking about it to him."

"Why not to me in the first instance?"

"Because you are too honest," burst out the woman, raising her pale eyes. "If you got the will you would have made its contents public, even though, as Mr. Leigh stated, you would lose all. For that reason I had no hold on you and would never have got money from you. By telling Mr. Mallien I managed to extract a promise from him that when he came into the property he would give me an annuity."

"Of two hundred a year?" inquired Carrington.

"We did not mention any sum," retorted Mrs. Beatson, "but that was the amount I intended to ask."

"And the amount which you told your son a mythical aunt was leaving you."

"I had to give my son some reason for being possessed of the annuity."

"Hum!" said Carrington with a shrug. "You haven't got the annuity yet, and now you never will have."

"I am not so sure of that. After all, if I hadn't told, Mr. Carrington, the cousin of my master would never have known of his good fortune."

"Then the will really does leave the property to Eunice Filbert?" questioned Rupert nervously.

"I don't know. I have not read the will."

"Come now," said Carrington contemptuously, "you don't expect us to believe that. You must have read the will before you buried it."

"I didn't bury it."

The barrister heaved a weary sigh and glanced at Rupert as if to invite his attention to the way in which the woman was lying. "I don't know why you are wasting our time in this fashion," said Carrington sharply. "Why can't you speak straightforwardly? Twisting and turning won't help you now. You are in a corner, and however you may fight you will not get out of it. Be frank, Mrs. Beatson, and tell us how you killed the vicar."

Mrs. Beatson rose white-faced and trembling, holding on to the back of the chair as she replied. "I did not kill the vicar," she insisted. "I would not do such a thing. I haven't the nerve, and I'm honest enough as people go. Only the sudden temptation to make money easily made me tell Mr. Mallien about the will. But I did no more. I wasn't near the vicarage, and no one was more astonished than I was when I heard of the murder."

"Listen to me," said Carrington, making a sign to Rupert that he should hold his tongue and leave the examination to him. "The police could not find out any reason why the vicar should have been killed, because they knew nothing about this will. Kensit unconsciously hinted at the truth when he said that the papers and books in the vicarage study were all in disorder, as if some search had been made. I believe that such a search was made, and by you, for this will, after you murdered the poor man."

"It's a lie!" screamed Mrs. Beatson savagely. "How dare you sit there and tell lies about me?"

"If it is a lie," said Carrington, quite unmoved by her sudden fury, "how comes it that the will is in your possession?"

"I dug it up."

"And how did you know the spot where it was buried?"

"The letter told me."

"The letter!" Rupert looked up surprised. "What letter?"

Mrs. Beatson fumbled in her breast, and pulling out a torn envelope threw it across the room into Hendle's lap. "I got that this morning," she declared in sullen tones, "and acted as it advised. As there is no name to it, I don't know who wrote it. Don't let Mr. Carrington get it; I trust you, sir, not him."

Rupert picked up the envelope and examined it, while the barrister looked over his shoulder. It was directed to "Mrs. Beatson, The Big House, Barship, Essex," and had evidently, judging from the postmark, been sent through the General Post Office of the metropolis. Having ascertained this, the young man took out a double sheet of tolerably good notepaper, upon which in a backward sloping hand probably disguised, were written a few lines, to which no signature was appended. These intimated abruptly that the will of John Hendle was to be found buried at the foot of the sundial in the vicarage garden, and that Mrs. Beatson could find it by searching. While the two men read and reread this anonymous letter, the housekeeper went rambling on.

"I intended at first to keep it, and show Mr. Mallien when he returned. But then I thought—not trusting him—that if I had the will I could hold it until he gave me a deed making safe the annuity I wanted. For that reason I took advantage of your dining at the cottage, Mr. Hendle, to go and get it. I knew that the sundial was hidden among the grasses and shrubs of the vicarage garden, so there was no difficulty in finding the place mentioned. I did not think that you would return early from the dinner, and so left the thing until it was too late. I dug up the will easily, as it was only a little way under ground and the earth was piled loosely over it. Then I came out and stopped at the gate to make sure that it was the will I had found."

"A silly thing to do, seeing that Kensit on his rounds might have caught you," said Carrington, returning to his seat. "Now how much of this tale are we to believe?"

"The whole of it," retorted Mrs. Beatson, distinctly amazed. "It's the truth."

"Hum!" said Carrington reflectively, "it may be; but did you not send that letter from yourself to yourself?"

"Me!" Mrs. Beatson's voice leaped an octave.

"Hush! hush!" said Hendle, hurriedly glancing at the door. "You'll bring in the servants. I need hardly tell you that it is best to thresh out this matter among the three of us."

Thus warned, the housekeeper sank her voice, and took refuge in angry tears, always a woman's last resource. "I'm so tired of being insulted," she sobbed loudly. "Ever since you came across me, Mr. Hendle, that friend of yours has been taking away my character."

"I rather think you have taken it away yourself by behaving so treacherously to me," said Rupert grimly. "However, I don't agree with Mr. Carrington that you sent that letter to yourself from yourself."

"How could I," sobbed Mrs. Beatson, "when I haven't been near London? And I'm not a conspirator. It's a shame blaming me for trying to help myself. Why can't you leave me alone? Two men on to one woman. You ought to go on your knees and beg my pardon."

This amazing view of the case extorted a contemptuous smile from Carrington. He had much experience in his profession of the fair sex, and knew the marvellous way in which women extricated themselves from difficulties which would overwhelm a mere man. Logic, as he was well aware, formed no part of the feminine nature. "I shan't try to argue with you," he said mildly, "for you would be sure to get the better of me. But you have behaved very badly to Mr. Hendle."

"No, I haven't. I had a right to look after myself."

"Not at his expense. He has always treated you kindly and—"

"Well, why shouldn't he?" demanded Mrs. Beatson, rolling up her handkerchief into a damp ball and dabbing her red eyes. "I have always done my duty, I hope, and at a small salary, too. I could get a better place any day."

"Then I advise you to look out for one," said Rupert, astonished at this ingratitude. "You certainly shan't stay here."

"What?" Mrs. Beatson gasped and stared.

"Well, why should you when you can be happier elsewhere?"

"I didn't say that I would. And if you discharge me—as I knew you would when you talked of marrying Miss Mallien—I shall ask for one year's wages and a letter saying how thoroughly I attended to my duties."

"I had no idea of discharging you until I discovered your treachery," protested Hendle sharply. "It's your own fault and—"

"Mrs. Beatson's future can be settled later," interrupted Carrington at this point of the argument. "Just now she must answer me some questions."

"I shan't!" raged the woman, furious at her humiliating position. "It's all your fault that I have lost my—"

"If you don't answer," interrupted the barrister again, "I shall hand you over to Kensit to be taken to Lawson at Tarhaven."

"You wouldn't dare. Mr. Hendle wouldn't let you."

"Oh, yes, I should," said Rupert sternly. "I'm not going to play fast and loose with the law."

Mrs. Beatson's sour face became gray and pinched. "I know nothing about the matter, more than I have told you," she cried, greatly terrified at the prospect of being locked up. "I told Mr. Mallien about the will, and I dug it up when I got that letter."

"When did you tell Mr. Mallien?" asked Rupert, remembering how he had intended to put this question before and had not.

"On the day after I overheard the conversation," whimpered the housekeeper, very much subdued.

"When I was in London?"

"Yes. I went in the afternoon to the cottage. Miss Mallien had gone to tea with Miss Tollart, and I saw Mr. Mallien. He told me to hold my tongue and he would speak to you about the matter. Also he said that if he got the property he would give me an annuity."

"Did you tell him before the crime was committed?" asked Carrington.

"Am I not saying so?" shrieked Mrs. Beatson, virulently. "I told him on the very afternoon of the next day, and you know quite well that it was at eleven o'clock of the same night that Mr. Leigh was murdered. And no one was more astonished than I was."

"Had you any idea who murdered him?"

"No. How should I have any idea?"

"Have you any idea now?"

"No, I haven't, unless it was the person who sent that letter?"

"Who sent it?"

Mrs. Beatson stamped. "What a fool your are, Mr. Carrington! You have the letter and know as much about the matter as I do."

The barrister thought for a few moments, then turned his back on the angry woman to address Rupert. "Do you think she is speaking the truth, Hendle?"

"Yes, I do."

"Of course you do," cried the housekeeper, looking viciously at the pair. "I am not accustomed to having my word doubted."

"Hold your tongue, or it will be the worse for you," said Carrington sharply. "You have behaved very badly and ought to be locked up. All the same, I advise Mr. Hendle to leave matters as they are for a day or so, until we examine this will and make inquiries as to who sent this letter."

"That letter is mine!" cried Mrs. Beatson, stretching out her hand.

Rupert put it into his pocket. "It will go to the police if you don't hold your peace," he threatened, for strong measures were necessary in dealing with such a woman. "I agree with Mr. Carrington. Go away and say nothing about anything, not even to Mr. Mallien. Do you hear?"

"What are you going to do?"

"Never mind. You know what *you* have to do." Rupert walked to the door and opened it. "Now go to bed."

Mrs. Beatson tossed her head and moved toward the door. She greatly wished to continue the conversation and defend herself, but a glance at Hendle's stern face made her change her mind. Never had she seen her good-tempered master so angry and so decided. Foolishly as she had talked, the woman was well aware that her position was a critical one, therefore she refrained from making bad worse. "I'm going and I'll say nothing," she snarled; "but when you are turned out of this house—"

"Please," said Rupert, nodding toward the hall.

"Beast!" said Mrs. Beatson under her breath lest the servants should hear, "both of you, beasts!" and she sailed out of the room triumphantly, having secured the last word, and so soothed her angry mind.

Hendle closed the door and returned to Carrington. "Take out the will and let us have a look at it," he said in a weary voice.

"Won't you wait until to-morrow?" asked Carrington, glancing at him. "This row has upset you."

"No. I want to see the will now. It may disappear again."

Carrington took out the crumpled parchment from his pocket. "Look after it yourself, then, and you can be certain that it is safe."

"All right. But let us look at it together. Move that lamp nearer."

Carrington did so, and Hendle spread out the rustling sheets—three or four of them, as the will was tolerably long. It was written, as wills of the early nineteenth century usually were, on parchment in a clear, scholarly hand, the writing being excellently engrossed and excellently preserved. The parchment itself was soiled and dog-eared, blotched here and there with coffee-brown stains: but it had suffered little damage during its hundred years' imprisonment in the muniment chest. With Carrington seated beside him the Squire slowly read the faded brown writing, and gradually made himself master of the contents. When he came to the signature of the testator and the names of the two witnesses, he drew a long breath and looked at the barrister in frank dismay.

"It seems quite legal," he said in a despairing voice.

"Quite," agreed Carrington. "So far I can't see anything wrong."

"And John Hendle by this"—Rupert struck the parchment—"leaves all his property, with the exception of sundry legacies to people now dead and buried, to Eunice Hendle, afterward Eunice Filbert, and her heirs. Yes. Leigh said as much. Frederick would have been disinherited had this will been produced in the year 1815. I wonder how it got lost."

"Frederick may have—"

"No, he didn't," interrupted the barrister sharply. "Frederick knew nothing about it, or he would have put it into the fire. I expect John Hendle made it—or rather his solicitor did—and then threw it into the chest where it was overlooked. Queer that the solicitor didn't mention it when the old man died."

"Perhaps he did," said Rupert sadly. "We know nothing of what took place at Hendle's death, save that Frederick inherited and that there was no question of Eunice coming into the property. But the same is left to her and her descendants; so Mallien, as her sole representative, inherits."

"Will you dispute the will?" asked Carrington anxiously.

"No," said Rupert, putting the document into his pocket; "it seems fair enough, and I must act honorably. When Mallien returns I shall give it to him —or rather I shall take it to our family lawyer along with Mallien."

"And lose the property?"

"My honor," said the young man gravely, "is dearer to me than money."

CHAPTER XIV

A CLUE

Needless to say, as it had been agreed to keep the discovery secret for the present, Hendle did not discharge Mrs. Beatson forthwith. Such an action, justifiable though it would have been, might lead to awkward questions being asked, and Carrington, for obvious reasons, advised caution. As things now stood the housekeeper would keep silent for her own sake, so the next day she went about her usual duties as if nothing had happened. None of the servants knew about her excursion, as it was supposed she had remained in her own room, according to her usual custom. So far as the outside world was concerned everything was safe, and the two men had time to look into matters at their leisure. It made Rupert's gorge rise to have the treacherous woman under his roof, but until he was assured of the truth of the will, he did not dare to get rid of her. Driven to bay, Mrs. Beatson being a woman, who would wreck continents for a whim, would ruin herself and everyone else in a whirlwind of rage. Being left alone, she nursed her disappointed anger in secret.

Rupert's expressed intention was to take the will up to London and show it to the family lawyer, who would be able to explain matters. He had intended to do this the very next day, but Carrington dissuaded him from being too impulsive. It was no use for the Squire to burn his boats too soon, said the astute barrister, and to make public the document would be to burn his boats with a vengeance.

"I think you should take time and turn the matter over in your mind," observed Carrington artfully. "It is just as well to be cautious."

"I don't see what I gain by waiting," argued the Squire. "The most honest thing to do is to take the will to the lawyers. I shall have to do that sooner or later, you know."

"Will you?" questioned Carrington significantly.

"Of course. What do you take me for?"

If Carrington had spoken his mind, he would have answered that he took the young man for a superfine fool. To throw away a fine position, a fine house, and a fine income out of sheer honesty, was not Carrington's notion of common sense. But then the barrister's notions of right and wrong had become somewhat warped by a struggling life. A penniless man is always more unscrupulous in dealing with money matters than one who has never been poor, and it seemed to Carrington that his friend's self-sacrificing honor was the result of ignorance. Had Hendle lived from hand to mouth, he would not be so ready to surrender his possessions. Moreover Carrington wanted to pick Rupert's pockets, as Mallien surmised he would. This was the real reason why he urged Hendle not to strip himself of his wealth. But such urging had to be done delicately, for the Squire was by no means a man to be handled easily. With this in his mind the barrister replied carefully, and did not translate his real thoughts into words.

"I take you for one of the best fellows in the world," he said warmly; "but there is such a thing as overdoing honesty, you know."

"I don't know," retorted the other positively. "One must be one thing or the other. There can be no tampering with honor."

"Of course not. I should never suggest such a thing. However, I do suggest that you should wait for a day or so before seeing your lawyer."

"Why?"

"You forget that the will is mixed up with a crime. If your lawyers decide that Mallien must have the money, the matter is bound to be made public. In that case it will become known to Lawson that Leigh possessed the will. I leave you to guess what complications will ensue."

Hendle tugged at his brown moustache moodily. "It's an infernally difficult business," he said after a pause. "What do you suggest?"

Carrington, rejoicing that he had succeeded thus far, had his answer ready. "I suggest that you wait for a few days, and meanwhile come with me to the vicarage."

"What for?"

"To look at the sundial, and see where the will was buried."

"What good will that do?"

"One never knows," said Carrington sententiously.

"Who do you think buried the will?"

"The man who murdered Leigh to get it."

"And his name?"

"Pouf! Ask me another. How do I know?"

"Mrs. Beatson?"

"Well, why not she as well as another? She had much to gain by possessing the will, and the will was in her possession last night. But for the chance of our stumbling across her when she went to unearth it, we would never have known that."

"I can't think that Mrs. Beatson, bad as she is, would commit a murder," mused the Squire reflectively. "After all, if she had the will on the night Leigh was got rid of, and committed the crime, why should she bury it?"

"My dear fellow, that is where the woman's artfulness comes in," said Carrington quickly. "She had to give some reason for possessing the will. By hiding it in a hole, and then writing to herself that anonymous letter saying where it was to be found, she does away with all suspicion against her."

"Not in your mind apparently," said Hendle, dryly.

"Of course not. But a long course of criminal law has opened my eyes to the habits of the animals. I may be unduly suspicious, I grant you, still the fact remains that the story Mrs. Beatson told us last night is too thin. Granting that the woman is innocent, why should the real criminal tell her where to find that which he risked his life to obtain?"

"It does seem strange. And yet—"

"Oh, you are full of scruples, Hendle!" cried the barrister pettishly. "What is Mrs. Beatson to you that you should defend her so warmly?"

"She is a woman, and I have a great respect for women."

Carrington made a grimace. "You answer like a raw boy. My experience of the sex has not led me to respect any single one."

"Yet you know Dorinda?"

"There speaks the lover. Well then, I do respect her, if that concession will satisfy your chivalrous ideas. But I don't believe this cock-and-bull story of Mrs. Beatson, and I certainly don't respect her."

"Neither do I. All the same, I credit her story."

Carrington shrugged his shoulders at this persistent optimism. "Then let us agree to consider her innocent until we prove her to be guilty. But you must see that if you interview your lawyers to-day, within the week a whole avalanche of troubles will descend on your thick head."

"Well," replied the Squire, wavering, "I shall wait for a few days, as you advise. I wonder what Dorinda will say?"

"Don't tell her," said the barrister quickly, for it was difficult enough for him to deal with one honest person without tackling a second. "She will tell her father about the discovered will if you do."

"I don't care if she does. Mallien has to know some time, since he is so deeply concerned in the matter."

"Hendle," said Carrington seriously, "you are a child. Don't say a word to Mallien, or to his daughter, who might tell him, until you have seen your lawyers. That's common sense."

On reflection Rupert was obliged to confess that it was, since his cousin would certainly make trouble straightway. It would be best to have the opinion of the lawyers beforehand, so that the situation might be adjusted so far as possible before the probable inheritor came into the matter. Of course he knew that Dorinda would tell her father nothing if asked to keep silent, but to so ask would be to lay another burden on her. Mallien was suspicious, brooding and pertinacious. If he thought that she was keeping anything from him, he certainly would never rest until he learned what it was.

"I shall not tell Dorinda until I have seen the lawyers," said Rupert.

"And you will see them—?"

"In two or three days. Now let us go out for a walk—to the vicarage if you like. I can't stay indoors worrying over things which at present I cannot remedy. Come!"

"Won't it be better for us to have another look at the will before we go?"

"I don't think so. I know the will by heart, and have locked it safely away, Carrington. It disinherits Frederick, from whom I am descended, legally enough; and if the lawyers are of the same opinion with their larger knowledge, why then my cousin must enter into his own."

"There is the Statute of Limitations, you know," hinted Carrington pointedly.

"I shall take advantage of that and of anything else if I can do so consistently with my honor. But what is the use of arguing?" said Hendle with a burst of bitterness, for the position pained him greatly. "We can do nothing just now. Let us go for a walk."

Carrington was too politic to press the matter further, as he saw how the Squire winced. But he had by no means given up the hope of inducing Hendle to refrain from publishing the possible loss of his estates, and intended to talk about the affair when the young man was more off his guard. Now with diplomatic skill bred from years of experience of shady doings, he put on his straw hat and sauntered out of doors along with his host, talking of many matters which had nothing to do with the burning question of the disputed inheritance. But as they walked down the avenue Carrington spoke of a matter which really interested him. And that was of a qualm he felt when passing under the spreading branches of the oaks. He had felt that qualm before when he had first visited Barship, and in the same place.

"I'm walking over my grave again," he muttered uneasily, and although he would not confess to superstition, the coincidence struck him as disagreeable.

"What's that?" asked Rupert absently. He had been busy with his own painful thoughts and had not paid much attention to his companion's light nothings.

"You know the saying that when one shivers, or has what the Scotch call a grue, one is walking over one's grave. Well, I had some such uncanny feeling in this very avenue when I came to see you first, and now, hang it all, I have it again. I don't like it."

Hendle, now more attentive, laughed. "A lawyer and superstitious?"

"Oh, bosh! I am not in the least superstitious. But there are some things which are hard to explain. It's gone!" Carrington wiped his perspiring face and looked round with an air of relief.

"What's gone?"

"That feeling of walking over my own grave."

"Rubbish!" said Hendle, who was much too stolid to believe in such things. "I expect it was only a sudden chill."

"I dare say, although it is odd that I should get a chill in this blazing sunshine," muttered the barrister, who was more impressed than he cared to admit. "But there are more things in heaven and earth—"

"What a well-worn quotation! You need bucking up. Come into the inn and we will each have a tankard."

"I don't like drinking in the morning."

"Nor do I. I never do. But all this worry has knocked me out of time and you aren't feeling up to the mark. Come along. Mrs. Pansey has known me all the days of my life and is distinctly a good sort. I often look in and have a chat."

"As an Olympian descending among mortals," said Carrington smiling, for by this time his odd feeling had passed away.

Mrs. Pansey, who was a rosy-faced, stout old dame, received her landlord with respectful joy, and soon supplied them with tankards of cool beer acceptable to the thirst on a hot day. Carrington noted how popular Rupert was with the villagers, who came and went, passed and repassed, each with a curtsey, or a touch of the forelock. And Hendle greeted one and all by name with kindly inquiries and genial smiles. A feeling of envy stirred the barrister's selfish heart, but he cynically consoled himself with the reflection that very soon Rupert would be ousted in favor of Mallien. Out of sheer annoyance with this favorite of Fortune, he would have liked to see such a toppling down, but nevertheless, for the gaining of his own ends, he was determined to prevent such a change of landlords. Meanwhile, he listened to the incessant chatter of Mrs. Pansey, which was mostly concerned with the new vicar.

"Such a nice gentleman they say he is," she observed, beaming, "and will be here in a fortnight lodging with Mrs. Jones while the Vicarage is being put to rights. His family come later. Have you seen him, sir?"

"No," answered Rupert promptly; "but my friend and I are now on our way to the Vicarage to see what's doing. We may meet him there."

"I don't think so, sir. He came yesterday to set the men to work and won't come to-day. The workmen are painting and papering the house and digging up the garden and making a nice place of it. Mrs. Jabber remains on as caretaker until the family arrive. She'd like to stay on altogether, but Lord bless you, sir, what would the vicar do with such a slut? He's a much more particular gentleman than Mr. Leigh, I do hear."

Hendle put an end to the landlady's babble by finishing his beer and departing, although the commonplace gossip had distracted his worrying mind for a few moments. As Carrington crossed the square beside his host he ventured a remark.

"Let us hurry on, Hendle, and have a look at the hole by the sundial before the workmen turn up the ground."

"What good will that do?" snapped the Squire sharply.

"One never knows. It is just as well to look round. Who knows but what the assassin may not have left some clue?"

Hendle stared. "What clue could he, or would he, possibly leave?"

Carrington laughed. "Oh, it's only an idea—a silly one, maybe. But I have an idea that we will stumble upon some clue."

"You and your ideas, Carrington. First your walking over your confounded grave business and now the chance of picking up some impossible clue. It's all imagination."

The barrister laughed again, but said no more. Hendle was less amiable than usual, which was scarcely to be wondered at considering what was in his mind. He walked fast enough toward their destination, as if he wished to rid himself of disagreeable thoughts by swift movement. Shortly they came to the rickety gate, and passed up the grass-grown avenue, dank and unwholesome, and not to be warmed even by the blazing summer sun. The surroundings were the same, but the place had lost its uncanny isolating atmosphere, and there was a stir of life in house and grounds, which showed that the place was waking up. Many men were moving in and out of the open doors; there was the noise of conversation and cheerful whistling, and scaffolding was being erected against the ivy-draped walls. Even in the jungle two gardeners were at work cutting down the tall tangled forest of weeds, and opening out the spaces between the trees. Most of the men employed were strangers, but some of the village workers had been pressed into service and these greeted the Squire and his friend respectfully. Hendle nodded absently in return, then strolled through the bare house, watching the ancient paper being stripped off the walls, and the replacing of mouldering boards. Afterward he and Carrington walked into the jungle and, at the far end of a winding path, found the lichen-covered sundial, half buried among luxuriant weeds. It had not yet been disturbed.

"I say, Hendle," remarked Carrington, as they crushed the lush grasses under foot, "this dial is pretty well hidden in this jungle."

"Yes?"

"I gather from that," continued the barrister musingly, "that it would not be easy to find."

Rupert nodded. "Not unless a person knew where to find it," he answered.

"Exactly. Well then, if the assassin of Leigh was a stranger, he would never have buried the will in a place of which he knew nothing."

"You infer that the assassin of Leigh was not a stranger?"

"I do. And that makes me believe still more that Mrs. Beatson is the guilty person. She knew where to find the sundial in this tangle of greenery and in the darkness of night. Therefore she must have—"

"Oh, let us give her the benefit of the doubt," retorted the Squire, cutting short this theorizing and walking forward to peer among the weeds. "I say, here is the hole—not a very deep one."

It certainly was but a shallow hole. The earth had simply been scraped away for a few inches, the document deposited and the loose mold heaped up in a kind of miniature mound. At least the two presumed so as Mrs. Beatson had swept aside a small quantity of earth when uncovering the parchment. There was nothing much to see, and after staring for a moment or so, Hendle turned away moodily. Scarcely had he done so when Carrington touched him on the shoulder, and drew his attention to a small object which glittered in the long grass near the edge of the hole.

"What's that?" he asked, pointing with his finger.

Rupert said nothing, but stooped and picked up the object. "Why," he said, in a tone of surprise, "it's the jewel which Mallien wears on his watch chain."

The barrister exclaimed also, as he stared at the gleam in Hendle's hand. It certainly was the opal in the matrix, to which Mallien had drawn his attention at their first meeting. Such a distinctive ornament was not easily forgotten. After a look and an exclamation he drew back and pondered.

"Surely Mallien never—"

"Nonsense! Nonsense!" interrupted the Squire sharply. "What can Mallien have to do with the matter?"

"That is what I am trying to think out," said Carrington dryly. "You must admit that it is strange."

"What is strange?" asked Rupert, determined not to commit himself.

"Finding this ornament here, near where the will was hidden. If we had found it on the high road now—"

"Yes! Yes! It is odd, I admit," interrupted the Squire again; "but that does not prove Mallien's implication in this sorry business."

"It proves that he was here in this secluded spot at one time or another, since he lost the opal among those grasses."

"Mallien may have wandered round the garden as we are doing."

"We came deliberately here because the will was found in this place by Mrs. Beatson. But what took Mallien to the sundial?"

Rupert slipped the ornament into his waistcoat pocket. "You will find it difficult to fasten the guilt of the crime on Mallien," he said dryly.

"You say that because the man is Miss Mallien's father and you wish to shield her," returned the barrister coolly. "All the same, if Lawson, for instance, knew the circumstances, he would build up a very pretty case against our disagreeable friend."

"As how?"

"Mallien knew about the will before Leigh was murdered, as you know from the story of Mrs. Beatson. The will meant much to him, so it is just possible that he came to the Vicarage to get it from Leigh. Failing to get it given to him freely, he struck—"

"No! No! I can't believe that."

"What else can you believe when the ornament, which we both know belongs to Mallien, is found on the edge of the hole where the will was buried?"

"Mallien may be able to explain."

"Oh, undoubtedly. And the more precisely he explains the less I shall believe his explanation. He has missed this ornament, you may be sure, long ago, and has had plenty of time to make up a story accounting for the loss. However, whether he is guilty or innocent, the finding of this opal in the matrix will settle him."

"In what way?"

"Hang it, Hendle, you are slow in the uptake," cried Carrington exasperated. "Why, a child could understand. All you have to do is to go to Mallien and threaten to show this jewel to Lawson, calling me as a witness, and accusing him of murdering the vicar. Then he'll climb down and you won't need to consider him with regard to the fortune."

Rupert said nothing for the moment, but turned on his heel and forced his way through the tangled path back to the rickety gate. When he and the barrister were well on the road home, he spoke again and very dryly.

"It seems to me, Carrington, that you regard me as a man who will do anything for money. I think I told you that my honor was dearer to me than money. I intend to give up the property to Mallien, if it is legally his, even if it leaves me, as it will, a pauper. The finding of this jewel will make no difference. You understand?"

"Yes. But if the man is guilty he should be punished."

"We can't be sure if he is guilty."

Carrington laughed grimly. "It seems to me that what we have discovered is an excellent proof of his guilt when taken in connection with the known facts of the case."

"I don't want to think about it."

"But you must. For the sake of justice, if not for your own sake. Confound it, Hendle, take advantage of the chance which Providence has placed in your hands to save your skin. Only you and I and Mrs. Beatson know about the will being discovered; only you and I know about this jewel which brings Mallien perilously near the gallows. For your sake I shall hold my tongue, and you can have this Timon on toast."

"There is something in that, Carrington. But I can't expect you to hold your tongue for nothing."

"Oh, my terms won't be exorbitant. And, of course," added the barrister, making light of his knavery, "as a poor man I must make hay while the sun shines."

"Oh, that is your opinion, is it?" asked Rupert dryly, and, on receiving a smiling nod, walked on rapidly in silence. He had laid a trap for Carrington and the man had fallen into it. He was little more than a blackmailer, who was prepared to make use of his power to enrich himself. To prevent such a thing Rupert temporized, although he could scarcely stop himself from catching Carrington by the throat and hurling him into the ditch. "You must give me time to think over the matter," said Hendle at last.

"Oh, there's no hurry. We are both on the same string, you know. We can make Mallien squeal now."

"Yes," assented Rupert, wondering that the man should think him capable of such baseness, "we can make him squeal!"

CHAPTER XV

CIRCUMSTANTIAL EVIDENCE

Rupert felt very uncomfortable. It was bad enough to have Mrs. Beatson in the house, when he knew how treacherous she was; but it was worse to entertain Carrington as his guest. The barrister undoubtedly was determined to make money at the cost of honor. And what was more, he would probably gain his ends, unless the truth came to light. And the truth required to adjust matters was to learn beyond question what was the name of the individual who had murdered the vicar. If, indeed, Mallien was the culprit, Rupert felt that he was in Carrington's power. It was impossible to allow that truth to come to Lawson's ears, as then Mallien would be arrested and there would be a public scandal. Yet if Carrington, who knew all details, were not bribed largely to keep silence, it seemed likely that he would denounce the miserable man. Of course, as yet, Hendle could not be certain that his cousin had committed the crime; but circumstances were against him, and if the police took up the matter, ruin would stare Mallien in the face. For Dorinda's sake such publicity was not to be thought of for one moment.

Hendle had no love for his cousin, who was as disagreeable and selfish a mortal as ever existed. He was capable of the most unscrupulous conduct to feed his egotism, but Rupert thought—and with some degree of truth—that the very egotism in question would prevent the man from risking his neck. Yet, even if he were innocent, as Rupert tried hard to believe for Dorinda's sake, the evidence against him was very strong. Mallien, thanks to Mrs. Beatson, knew all about the will before Leigh's death; the discovery of the ornament, near the sundial, proved that he had been where the will was buried. Also possession of the will meant a fortune to Mallien, and the sole reason for which the vicar could have been murdered was for the criminal to obtain possession of the parchment. Indeed, it was very certain that if Inspector Lawson became possessed of these facts, he would not have the slightest compunction in arresting Mallien, and in doing his best to have him hanged. The evidence was certainly purely circumstantial, but so strong that Rupert felt convinced both judge and jury would accept it as positive truth. And, failing Mrs. Beatson, whom the Squire did not believe to be guilty, it really looked as though Mallien with his greedy nature and bad temper had struck the fatal blow. Never was a man in such a dilemma.

Carrington, afraid of losing his chance, remained at The Big House, and kept a strict watch on Mrs. Beatson and on Mallien himself. That gentleman had returned from London in the best of spirits, having managed to pick up a most wonderful ruby for a small price. Hendle had been under the impression that when so much was at stake his cousin would abandon his hobby to prosecute a search for the will and push on as rapidly as possible his claim to the property. But Mallien never came near the place, and, according to Dorinda, was wholly taken up with arranging his collection of gems in a new set of cabinets. This abstinence from action at such a critical period argued fear on the man's part lest dangerous information should come to light, if he made himself too conspicuous. More and more Rupert became convinced that his cousin was the guilty person, and he did not know very well how to act. He could not talk to Dorinda, as what he had to say was too terrible, and he was unable to converse freely with Carrington, since he now mistrusted him so greatly. Of course, Carrington never guessed that such was the case, as Rupert kept a careful guard over his words and actions, so that the barrister believed that his friend was quite willing to act in the dishonorable way suggested.

And what Carrington did suggest was that Rupert should inform Mallien of what had been discovered, and then threaten to denounce him to the police if he did not surrender all claim to the property. Then the will could be thrown into the fire, Mrs. Beatson could be sent to Australia with a sum of money, to close her mouth, and all would end up with the marriage of Hendle and Dorinda. For this suggestion, and for services rendered in connection therewith, Carrington plainly stated that he required the sum of five thousand pounds. After beating round the bush for some time during the next two days Carrington informed Hendle frankly of his scheme and of the amount he expected for its carrying out. Then Rupert forgot his caution and told his old school friend in the most indignant way what he thought of him.

The two men were walking in the park one morning when the explosion took place. Rupert, as usual, was unable to remain in the house quietly, since his very painful thoughts did not permit him to take an interest in anything. He was on his legs from morning until night, and the barrister, for obvious reasons, since he wished to poison his mind, always hung round him with suggestions of what should be done to hush the matter up. On this particular morning he did more than suggest, as he was growing weary of Hendle's sluggish reluctance to deal with the matter. Therefore, he put his proposal into plain words and mentioned his price. Rupert lost his temper and, wheeling on him in a fury, knocked him down. Carrington was so amazed and startled by this sudden rebellion on the part of a sheep that he remained on the grass tongue-tied, staring up at the big man who stood by, furiously angry.

"I—I—I think—you must be—be mad," stuttered the barrister.

"No, I am not mad, you villain!" said Hendle, between his teeth. "You think that I am as big a scoundrel as you are. I am not, and now you know it."

Carrington pulled himself together and rose stiffly, tenderly feeling his left eye, which was growing black. "I'll make you pay for this," he said savagely, and turned a threatening face on Hendle.

"You can do what you like. I am not afraid of you," retorted the Squire indifferently; "and, as this trouble has taken place, there will be no need for you to return to my house. You can go away and your luggage will be sent down to the station."

"You can send it to *The Hendle Arms*," said Carrington, making up his mind swiftly as to his best course of action. "I don't intend to leave this place until I get what I want."

"You won't get five thousand pounds anyhow, or five thousand pence, I can tell you," said Hendle, with his usually kind eyes growing hard.

"Not from you perhaps, since you are such a fool. But Mallien—"

"Mallien can defend himself. What he does has nothing to do with me."

"It has a lot to do with Dor—"

"If you mention that name I shall knock you down again!" shouted the Squire.

Carrington was wise enough to take the hint, being a coward at heart as all bullies are. "I should like to know why you knocked me down at all?" he complained, in sulky tones.

"I did so, because you are little else than a blackmailer."

"How dare you use that word to me!" cried Carrington, black with rage, and he would have struck his quondam friend but that he knew from experience that he would get the worst of it in any struggle which might ensue.

"What other word applies to your conduct?" demanded Hendle fiercely. "As my old school chum I have treated you well, and have shown you every hospitality, as you know very well. And how do you repay me? By threatening to make things hot for me if I don't buy your silence with a large sum of money."

"I didn't threaten to make things hot for you," protested Carrington, snarling like a disappointed dog. "I only suggested that you should hush up the matter of the murder and the will—"

"Yes, and pay you to hold your tongue. What else is that but blackmail? If I was dishonorable enough to agree to your terms, your request for money would only be the first of many."

"I swear that I would ask no more."

"All blackmailers say that, until they get their victims in their toils by the first payment. Then they show themselves in their true colors. I wonder you are not ashamed, Carrington, to behave so basely."

"I am not behaving basely," cried the barrister furiously. "I am poor, I admit, and I want money. But all I proposed was to your own advantage."

"So that you might get a hold over me by persuading me to hush up a felony and so take every penny I possess."

"That you possess," sneered Carrington, recklessly throwing off the mask, now no longer a protection. "Why, Mallien should have your money."

"And Mallien shall get it when the will is looked into by the lawyers. I take it to them to-morrow. You know that I am honorable."

"I know that you are a fool," snarled the baffled man; "and if you strip yourself of your property to give it to Mallien, it will be all the better for me. I shall go to him and say what I know."

"You are villain enough for anything. Go, if you choose."

"But, Hendle," said Carrington, almost unable to grasp the fact that relations between him and Rupert had so suddenly changed for the worse, "what does all this mean? I have said little more this morning than I said to you before and only now do you object."

Rupert, who was going away, stopped to face his enemy. "I objected all along, as you might have seen if you had not been blinded by your own wickedness, Carrington. Every word you said made me loathe you more and more. The sole idea you had was to get money out of me. I thought you were a gentleman and my friend, whereas you are a villain and a blackmailer."

"Go on! go on!" said Carrington, becoming very white and breathing very hard. "I shall make you pay for every insult."

"It is impossible to insult you," retorted the Squire contemptuously. "Such a worm as you are doesn't feel insults. As to making me pay, you have no hold over me, and you know it."

"I can take away your property by telling Mallien of the will being found."

"I shall tell him myself, so you needn't trouble."

"I can tell Lawson about Mallien's guilt."

"Oh, as to that, you can't prove that he is guilty," said Hendle coolly; "and, as you won't kill your goose with the golden eggs, you will say nothing to Lawson, if Mallien buys your silence. Come along, I've had enough of this. You can go away and do your worst. And if you don't go straight away, I shall make a public scandal, by kicking you out of the gate."

"You are nothing more than a bully. You know that I am not strong enough to fight you," said Carrington furiously, but very wisely moving in the direction of the gate.

"Quite so. But if I were a bully, I should thrash the life out of you for daring to insult me with base proposals as you have done. You have got off very lightly, considering all things. Now march and hold your d—d tongue."

Carrington had to do as he was bidden, for the big man looked at him in a quiet, imperious way, which meant trouble. With a would-be dignified step the baffled villain walked over the grass toward the distant gate without opening his mouth. As he passed out into the road he turned for one moment to make a last threat. Rupert guessed, from the malevolent expression on his face, that he was about to refer to Dorinda and made a quick step toward him. Carrington winced and cringed, shut his mouth, and sped down the road at a remarkably quick pace. He had been turned out of his paradise, where he had expected to live in clover for the rest of his life with Hendle under his thumb, and he knew that the closed gate divided him forever from his old school friend. Therefore, did he curse, not himself, but Hendle, for being such a fool. Carrington was far too egotistic to lay the blame on his own shoulders, as he invariably believed his methods to be perfect.

However, having lost his chance of obtaining money from Rupert, it only remained for him to get it somewhere else. Naturally, Mallien was the first person he thought of, since that gentleman, by inheriting the property, would have the wherewithal to pay. Carrington intended to remain the night at *The Hendle Arms*—to which place his portmanteau was sent during the afternoon—and next day to return to London. He would much rather have stayed on to attend to his nefarious business, but his position was bound to be disagreeable, when the villagers learned that he had been turned out of the Squire's house, so it was best to leave the place. But in the meantime he hoped to bring Mallien to his knees.

With this idea he wrote a short peremptory note to the man asking him to come to the inn at eight o'clock for an interview concerning his safety, and this he sent up by hand to the cottage. On the reply would depend what attitude he would take up toward Dorinda's father. If Mallien refused to come, such refusal would hint that he was strong enough to fight; but if he came in answer to so insolent a message, his arrival assuredly would show that he was afraid of what might come out. Therefore, when a curt line or so was brought to the barrister saying that Mr. Mallien would be at the inn as requested, Carrington felt that he had won the first move of the game. The man was afraid, and it would be as well to take advantage of his fear. Also seeing what had been discovered, it was difficult to understand how Mallien could save himself.

Mrs. Pansey was somewhat surprised when the Squire's guest took up his quarters for the night in her house, and wondered what could be the reason. Carrington, afraid of making bad worse, did not give her any, but simply stated that he would eat and sleep there before leaving for London by the eight o'clock train in the morning. He engaged a sitting-room and a bedroom, and enjoyed a very good dinner shortly before Mallien put in an appearance. That gentleman swaggered into the stuffy little room in his usual truculent manner, carelessly dressed in gray flannels, because the evening was hot, and glittering with jewels after his usual fashion.

"What the dickens do you mean by writing to me as you have done?" blustered the visitor when the door was closed.

"As you have come, I dare say you can guess," retorted Carrington, coolly. He had been bullied by Rupert, who was strong enough to thrash him, but he did not intend to be dominated by Mallien, who was weaker. Also, Hendle being honest and Mallien a rogue, the barrister felt less at a disadvantage. He was certain that his visitor was not one who would hesitate to accept terms, however shady, so long as his purpose was served.

"I can't guess," growled Mallien, sitting down aggressively, "and I demand an explanation. What do you want?"

"Five thousand pounds," said Carrington, thinking it was useless to beat about the bush with a brother knave.

"What for?"

"For certain information which will be of service to you."

"Oh, if you mean the will, Carrington, I'm not going to pay something for nothing," retorted Mallien, viciously. "I know that sooner or later the will is certain to be found, and when it is, Hendle is not the man to dispute possession of what is rightfully mine."

"The will has been found and is in Hendle's possession," said Carrington with a keen look.

Mallien stared and changed color. "And he never told me. Here!" He started to his feet. "Let me pass. I'm off to see Rupert, and get the will."

"Unfortunately, he won't give it to you."

"Won't give it to me?"

"No. He intends to take it to London to-morrow and place it in the hands of your family lawyers."

"Oh, well"—Mallien sat down again—"that will be all right. Once it is in their hands, they will see that I have my rights. Have you seen the will, may I ask?"

"Yes. It leaves the property to Eunice Filbert and her descendants."

"Ha!" Mallien expanded his chest, in a gratified manner. "Then I get the property. That's all right. Where was the will found?"

"Where you buried it."

The man jumped up once more, spluttering and angry. "What the devil do you mean, sir?"

"I mean this: that you murdered Leigh and stole the will and buried it under the sundial in the Vicarage garden. That is the information for which I ask five thousand pounds to be paid when you come into your property."

Mallien staggered against the wall with outspread hands. "You are mad to accuse me of—of—"

"Of murdering the vicar. No, I am not mad; but you will be if you refuse me the money. Only for five thousand pounds will I hold my tongue."

"You have nothing to hold it about," stormed Mallien, savagely.

"Oh, yes, I have. Sit down and listen."

"I won't." Mallien made for the door.

"Very good. Then go, and to-morrow you will be arrested before noon. I shall go straight to Tarhaven in the morning to explain things to Inspector Lawson. For your own safety you had much better let me explain them to you."

Mallien hesitated, then returned to his seat. "You are talking rubbish," he said, pulling his beard in an embarrassed manner. "I have nothing to do with the murder. I wouldn't have come here had I guessed you would talk to me in this way."

Carrington, now master of the situation, laughed. "The way in which my letter was worded compelled you to come."

"It's a lie."

"Then why are you here? You who hate me—you who are a bully," taunted the barrister. "There is the door. Walk out of it, if you dare!"

"Less talk!" cried Mallien, savagely. "Go on and explain on what grounds you dare to accuse me."

"Oh, very good. Now you are talking sense;" and Carrington related the adventure which had to do with the discovery of the buried will by Mrs. Beatson and the subsequent passing of the document into Hendle's hands. "He has it at the present moment," continued the barrister, "and intends, as I said, to take it to the solicitors to-morrow. If the property is yours, as I think it is, you will be done full justice to, as Hendle is not the man to keep what does not belong to him."

"Rupert's a fool, but honest enough," said Mallien shortly, and looking very much relieved. "Well, and what has all this to do with your infernal insolence in asking me for five thousand pounds? By your own showing there will be no trouble about my getting what is mine."

"I have told you why I ask for the money," retorted Carrington, tartly. "Don't make me repeat again and again what you already know."

"What is that?" demanded Mallien, willfully blind.

"You murdered Leigh, if you will have it."

"I did not murder Leigh. I had no reason to do so."

"Oh, yes, you had. You wanted the will, and remember that Kensit declared--"

"Oh, about the disordered papers," struck in Mallien, wiping his face. "What evidence is that, when everyone knows that Leigh kept his study like a pigsty. The papers were no more in disorder than usual."

"Sufficiently upset for the policeman to think that a search had been made."

"The Coroner and jury thought nothing of his evidence in that respect," said Mallien, with an uneasy sneer.

"Because the existence of the will was not known," replied Carrington, meaningly. "Once it is known, a strong motive is supplied for the killing of Leigh."

"Rupert had as much reason to murder Leigh as I had.".

"I don't agree with you, since he is so scrupulously honest. If the money is yours, you will have it, so why should Hendle murder a man to get what in the end would not benefit him? Now, you—"

"I tell you, Carrington, I did not touch the man!" vociferated Mallien.

"Bosh! You struck him down and got the will and buried it under the sundial, as you know. Then you made use of Mrs. Beatson to avert suspicion from yourself by sending the anonymous letter telling where it was."

"I didn't send the letter," insisted Mallien, looking gray and worn.

"You did. You were in Town for a few days, and while you were away, the housekeeper got the letter. Since you had promised her an annuity of two hundred a year, you knew very well that she would give the will to you rather than to Hendle. It was a very clever scheme, Mallien."

"You are talking rubbish!" cried the man in consternation, for he saw how strong was the evidence against him. "How can you prove that I was at the Vicarage on that night?"

"Where is your opal in the matrix?" asked Carrington, glancing at Mallien's watch chain significantly.

"I—I—I—lost it," hesitated the other.

"You did, and Hendle found it in my presence near the sundial; on the very verge of the hole wherein you buried the will."

The listener made an inarticulate noise and clutched his hair. "It's fate, it's fate!" he muttered. "Everything is against me, yet I am innocent."

"Prove that you are so," said Carrington, leaning back in his chair indolently smiling.

Mallien hesitated, then seeing that the barrister knew so much, rushed into an explanation, which he would not have made to a less well-informed person. It was as if a dam had broken, so volubly did the words come tumbling out. Carrington listened attentively.

"I *was* at the Vicarage on that night," confessed the visitor swiftly. "After Mrs. Beatson told me I thought that I would get the will from Leigh, since I was not sure if Rupert would act straightforwardly."

"Knowing Hendle as you do, why did you think that?"

"The most honest of men might hesitate before stripping himself of all his wealth," retorted Mallien sharply. "However, that is not to the point. I made up my mind to go and then I changed it again. I went to bed determined to go in the morning, but, unable to sleep, I decided to visit the vicar on that night. I rose and, putting on my clothes, went out. As I left my cottage, I heard the church clock chime eleven."

"Oh!" sneered Carrington, remembering the hour of the murder, "then you did not commit the crime?"

"No, I didn't," snarled Mallien viciously. "I got to the Vicarage and, in the darkness of the avenue, I stumbled against a man."

"Who was he?"

"I don't know. I clutched him by the throat and we struggled. Then he got away and probably wrenched the opal ornament from my watch chain. I missed it the next day, and surmised that I had lost it in the wrestling match. After the man fled I went to the house and peered into the study through the window. I saw Leigh lying apparently dead on the floor, and was seized with fright, lest I should be accused of killing him. I saw my position in a moment, as you may guess."

"You should have given the alarm," said Carrington, quietly.

"Oh, should I?" sneered the other. "You would have done so under the same circumstances, wouldn't you?"

"Perhaps," returned the barrister ambiguously. "I quite see that you were in a very awkward position."

"Of course I was. If the fact of the will came to light, I might have been accused of killing Leigh to get it."

"Which you did," insisted Carrington, "in spite of this cock-and-bull story."

"Hang you!" shouted Mallien fiercely, and clenching his fists. "I tell you I did not. Things happened as I say, and I ran back to my cottage determined to hold my tongue, and let things take their course. That is why I have made no move about the will. The man I struggled with in the avenue was the criminal, and got my opal."

"How then did Hendle and I find the opal near the sundial?"

"I don't know," returned Mallien moodily. "If you tell the police, I can only repeat the story I am repeating now."

"I don't want to tell the police," said Carrington mildly. "My terms—"

"I know all about your infernal terms, just as I know that I am in a fix. I am innocent, but it is difficult for me to defend myself against the circumstantial evidence."

"Then agree to my terms, and I'll hold my tongue."

"What's the use? Rupert knows as much as you do."

"Hendle won't speak because of your daughter."

"That is true," Mallien hesitated; then burst out, "you must give me time to make up my mind."

"I'll give you a week," said Carrington readily, for he did not wish to press the man too hardly. "But no hanky-panky, remember. I hold you in the hollow of my hand."

"If I had murdered Leigh," said Mallien, deliberately, "I should murder you, in the hope of saving myself. As it is, I shall take a week to consider your terms!" and the man, with a snarl, went out abruptly.

CHAPTER XVI

A NEW WITNESS

The Squire was relieved when he turned Carrington out of his house, as he felt how impossible it was to live under the same roof with such a scoundrel. He was still more relieved on hearing that the man had gone to London by an early train, and hoped that prudence would keep him at a safe distance from Barship. As yet he knew nothing of his late friend's interview with Mallien, nor did Mallien appear at The Big House to report the conversation. But

Hendle had an uneasy feeling that the barrister would not hold his tongue, unless well paid to do so; and undoubtedly he knew many things, the revelation of which would prove highly unpleasant. If Carrington went to Inspector Lawson with his story, Mallien might be arrested and the disgrace would break Dorinda's heart. Therefore, for the girl's sake, it was necessary to make some move, but what action could be taken Rupert did not very clearly see. He passed an uncomfortable morning turning things over in his mind, and rather regretted the impetuosity which had led him to deal so sharply with a dangerous man. However, he consoled himself with the proverb that what was done could not be undone.

Of one thing Hendle was sure, that Carrington would only tell the police what he knew, when all chance of getting money to hold his tongue was at an end. He would certainly wait until Mallien was placed in possession of the property before taking any steps, and this being the case, Rupert felt convinced that no sudden scandal would disturb the present position of affairs. The man who gains time gains everything, and Rupert, mindful of the saying, determined to make the best use of his time. He was in no hurry, and began to think of what could be done to adjust matters. At first—as he had told Carrington—he intended to see the family solicitors about the will; but, on second thoughts, he decided to interview Mallien beforehand. The moment that John Hendle's will was placed in other hands to be dealt with, a certain amount of publicity would assuredly ensue. In that case, Mallien might find himself in an awkward position, although Rupert could not bring himself to believe that his cousin was guilty of so brutal a murder. Nevertheless, the circumstantial evidence was undeniably strong. On the whole the Squire decided that it would be wise to interview Mallien before handing the document to the lawyers, and, unless the man could exonerate himself fully, it seemed dangerous to hand it over at all. There would be little sense in Mallien gaining a fortune, if the necessary steps to place him in possession of it could only be taken at the risk of liberty and perhaps of life. The position was extremely difficult, unpleasant and puzzling, and Hendle scarcely knew what was best to be done. Finally he concluded to give the matter careful consideration for twenty-four hours before acting.

So far, Hendle's intentions were sensible, considering the awkward position in which he was placed. But he was no diplomatist, and, having stirred up Carrington to hostility, proceeded indiscreetly to deal in a somewhat abrupt manner with Mrs. Beatson. Having got rid of one shady person he wished to get rid of the other. Already he had stated that he would send her away, but Mrs. Beatson had never believed that he would act immediately on his determination. She was, therefore, greatly dismayed when he summoned her into the library after luncheon, and intimated that she was to go.

"Why should I go?" demanded the woman with the air of a martyr. "My duties—?"

"I say nothing about your duties. But I can't have a person under my roof who listens to conversations not meant for her ears."

"Then you shouldn't have secrets!" cried Mrs. Beatson furiously. "And I didn't listen intentionally. You know that."

"You shouldn't have listened at all," said Rupert coldly, and bracing himself to meet trouble, which she had every intention of making.

"What, not to protect myself when you thought of turning me out?"

"There was no protection needed on that score," said the Squire politely. "I had no intention of turning you out."

"Then why am I turned out now?" demanded the housekeeper in a most exasperatingly illogical way.

"Because of your behavior, and I don't think that there is any need to explain further. To-day is Saturday; you must leave on Monday."

"Oh, very well, sir. With a year's wages, mind."

"Oh, no. I shall give you three months' wages, and you may consider yourself lucky that I give you any at all."

"I shall go to law."

Rupert shook his head reprovingly. "I shouldn't if I were you. Your dealings with that will won't bear looking into."

"I have done nothing wrong," said Mrs. Beatson, becoming tearful.

"Ah! your ideas of morality differ from mine. I am not going to argue the point," said Rupert, pointing to the door. "You can go now."

"I shall tell all I know about the will," threatened the woman desperately.

"As you please. But in two days the will goes to my lawyers, and if Mr. Mallien inherits, he will become the owner of this place. You have no hold over me there, Mrs. Beatson."

"I believe you murdered Mr. Leigh yourself."

"The wish is father to the thought," replied Hendle dryly.

"Well then, if you didn't, that horrid Mr. Carrington did."

"Why do you say that?"

"Why did you turn him out of the place yesterday?" retorted the housekeeper.

"For a very good and sufficient reason, which doesn't concern you."

Baffled by her master's calmness, the woman walked defiantly toward the door, anxious to hurt him, yet unable to do so. "When Mr. Mallien gets the money he will never allow you to marry his daughter," she said spitefully.

Rupert raised his eyebrows, but made no reply. He was unwilling to take her by the shoulders and thrust her out of the room, so all he could do was to remain silent until her venom exhausted itself. As is usually the case when a man deals with a woman, the weakness of Mrs. Beatson was her strength.

"You will be a pauper without a penny," railed the housekeeper.

Rupert still said nothing, but turned toward the fireplace to pick up his pipe. Mrs. Beatson, finding that he supplied no fuel for her anger, had no more to say, and retired fuming with temper. Her master lighted his pipe and sat down to consider once more how he could best deal with the situation. He was faintly nervous, as it occurred to him that perhaps it would have been better to deal less boldly with the housekeeper and the barrister. But on second thoughts he decided that he was acting straightforwardly, and that it had been just as well to take the bull by the horns.

Mrs. Beatson went to her room, put on her best clothes and sallied forth bent upon the Samson-like intention of pulling the roof down on her own head. She was in such a rage that she did not mind being hurt personally so long as Rupert suffered. Doubtless when her doings recoiled on herself she would be sorry that she had acted like a fool; but at the present moment she did not consider the consequence. All she wanted was to hurt some one and to make things unpleasant all round. Rupert she hated for discharging her. Carrington she loathed because he had brought—as she considered—her shady doings to light, and Dorinda, because she was engaged to Hendle. She even hated Mallien, although he had never harmed her, but did not contemplate hurting him, since she hoped to receive the annuity. How she intended to make things uncomfortable she did not very well know, but she commenced operations by walking toward her son's lodgings in the village. She would tell him everything, and leave him to deal with her insulted honor. That Kit might agree with the Squire in reprobating her eavesdropping never struck her for a single moment. She was in much too great a rage to be reasonable.

Kit was not at home, and his landlady said that he had gone to luncheon at Dr. Tollart's. Mrs. Beatson snorted when she heard this, as she did not wish Kit to marry the girl, and objected to his keeping company with her. Still bent upon relieving her mind of its burden, she made for the doctor's house, which was at the far end of the village, and speedily arrived at the front door. The servants informed her that Dr. Tollart was absent on his rounds, but would be back soon. Meanwhile, Miss Tollart was within along with Mr. Christopher Beatson. The servant, having a feminine sympathy with the lovers, did not ask this marplot to step in; but Mrs. Beatson brushed her aside like a fly and stalked into the drawing-room, where she heard gay voices.

"I went to your lodgings and learned that you were here, Kit," said Mrs. Beatson, grimly, "philandering as usual, instead of earning your livelihood."

The young couple rose in dismay at the sight of this uncomfortable woman, who was always like a stormy petrel. Sophy was the first to recover herself, and immediately took up arms on behalf of Kit. "It's Saturday," she said coolly, "and if Kit works all the week, he has a right to one holiday, I suppose, during the seven days."

Mrs. Beatson sat down and glared. "How do you expect me to welcome you as a daughter-in-law when you behave toward me in this impertinent manner?"

"I don't mean to be impertinent," said Sophy, sorry for the agonized expression on her lover's face; "but you are so unreasonable."

"Unreasonable!" shrieked the visitor. "It is other people who are unreasonable, if you only knew all."

"Knew all what?" asked Kit nervously.

"I've been insulted and discharged. Me, a lady born and bred and—"

"Discharged!" echoed Sophy, interrupting. "Do you mean to say that you have left The Big House?"

"I leave on Monday," said Mrs. Beatson, getting out her handkerchief and beginning to sob. "Oh, the insults that I have received! Mr. Hendle must be thrashed, and I have come to ask my son to thrash him."

"Me!" Kit bounced out of his seat in dismay. "Why, Mr. Hendle is my best friend, and I owe everything to him."

"That's right. Go against your mother," wailed Mrs. Beatson. "You are just like your father, who was always a coward and a bully."

"Kit is neither," said Sophy indignantly. "Little as I think of men who won't give us the vote, I think a great deal of Kit."

"Bother your votes!" cried Mrs. Beatson, suddenly recovering her composure, as it was evident that tears did not help her. "All your goings-on are silly."

"Silly! Well, I like that, when we are trying to vindicate the cause of—"

"Oh, Sophy, don't make a row!" interrupted Kit, who saw how the two glared at one another. "Let us hear what mother has to say."

"I have a great deal to say," said Mrs. Beatson savagely, "and if you young people will only hold your tongues, as young people should in the presence of older and wiser—"

"Older certainly, but not wiser," pertly said Miss Tollart.

"For my sake, Sophy," implored Kit, seeing that his mother was stiffening for a royal row. "I want to hear why Mr. Hendle has discharged—"

The word was enough to recall Mrs. Beatson to a memory of her wrongs and she proceeded volubly to discourse about the same. Yet even as she began it occurred to her that it would be as well to bind the young couple to secrecy for the present, as Hendle's hint about the law lingered uncomfortably in her mind. After all, a judge and jury might be silly enough to condemn her behavior. "What I have to tell you both, you must keep to yourselves," she said solemnly, and looked to see if the door was closed. "It's a matter of life and death."

Kit looked scared at this exordium, and even Sophy, bold as she was, began to feel nervous. She knew what a reckless person her future mother-in-law was, and wondered what she had been doing to justify so grave a request.

"Neither Kit nor I will say anything," she promised, catching at her lover's hand for comfort. "I hope it's nothing very serious."

"It isn't," said Mrs. Beatson, ironically, "unless you consider the death of Mr. Leigh serious."

"What?" Kit jumped up with his face as white as chalk.

"Don't," said his mother irritably, "you get on my nerves, and they're bad enough as it is." She paused, then continued, rather pleased with the sensation she was making. "I know a great deal about the murder."

"Oh!" Miss Tollart's eyes grew large and round, and became filled with curiosity. "Have you any idea as to who murdered Mr. Leigh?"

"I have. But what I am about to tell you, keep to yourselves."

"We have promised that," snapped Sophy, for all this mysterious talk was irritating her greatly. "What is it you know?"

"I must begin at the beginning," said Mrs. Beatson solemnly, and taking every advantage of the situation; "and when my son knows all, I shall expect my son to defend my honor."

"Against Mr. Hendle?" asked Kit nervously.

"He has behaved like a brute!" cried Mrs. Beatson, flaming up. "But bad as he is, he is not so bad as that nasty Mr. Carrington."

"The lawyer," said Sophy, curiously. "What has he to do with it?"

"If you will only let me speak, I shall explain," said Mrs. Beatson, in a dignified manner.

"Go on, mother," said her son impatiently. "Don't keep us on tenterhooks."

Mrs. Beatson frowned severely, but, not seeing her way to an answer, began to relate her grievance. It was characteristic of her profound belief in her own rectitude that she told everything, plainly and baldly, never thinking that her listeners would condemn what she had done. From the moment when the Squire had informed her of his intention to marry Miss Mallien forthwith, down to the interview which had just taken place, the housekeeper detailed all that had happened, concealing nothing, but exaggerating a great deal. Naturally she made herself out to be a martyr, and was greatly annoyed when she brought her story to an end, to see disgust written on Sophy's face and dismay on the face of her son. "What do you both mean by glaring at me in that way?" she demanded, after waiting for comments, which were not made as speedily as she expected.

"I don't think that you have behaved at all well," said Sophy bluntly, seeing that Kit was speechless.

"What do you mean by that?" demanded Mrs. Beatson bristling. "Impertinence."

"Mother," struck in the young man quietly, and recovering his speech, "if this matter is to be discussed we may as well discuss it reasonably."

"I ask for nothing better. Haven't I been disgracefully treated?"

"No," said Kit, pulling himself together and becoming both manly and heroic; "you had no business to listen to Mr. Hendle and Mr. Leigh; you had no business to tell Mr. Mallien what you overheard; and you had no business to meddle with that will."

"Hear! Hear!" said Sophy, clapping her hands. "I agree with Kit. And, as you have behaved so badly to Mr. Hendle, I don't see what he could do but send you away."

After a speechless pause Mrs. Beatson appealed to her son. "Kit, will you sit there and hear me insulted?"

"Sophy doesn't mean to insult you, mother," said Kit quietly, and looking as white as he was determined. "You must be reasonable."

"I am reasonable!" cried his mother violently. "There never was such an unreasonable person as you are. My own son turns against me," wailed the exasperating woman, again taking out her handkerchief to sob—"my own son, and I nursed him as a baby."

Kit and Sophy looked at each other helplessly, wholly undecided how to deal with this impossible woman. Mrs. Beatson only saw things in her own way and expected everyone else to see them as she concluded they should be seen. She had no common sense; she had no logic, she had no control over her temper, and when anyone disagreed with her, she made herself objectionable in every way. Miss Tollart, face to face with this unreasonable feminine nature, heaved a sigh.

"Well, I don't wonder that we don't get the vote," she mourned. "We aren't in the least ready for it."

"Hush, Sophy!" said Kit, touching her hand. "We must understand more about the matter. It can't be allowed to rest here."

"You promised to hold your tongue!" shrieked Mrs. Beatson, rather scared by the look on her son's face.

"I shall do so, so far as is consistent with my honor," retorted Kit bluntly; "and I'm not going to allow Mr. Hendle to get into trouble. He has been a good friend to you, mother, and a good friend to me. If you had a spark of gratitude toward him, you would never have behaved as you have done."

"How dare you speak to me in that way?"

"Because the time is past when you could play the tyrant."

"Tyrant! Tyrant! This to your mother, who bore you."

"I don't wish to be disrespectful, mother, but you are so unreasonable that you compel me to be so. It is all very well so far as things are between ourselves; but in this story which you have told serious matters are concerned. Your share in them is not honorable."

"I can do what I like," said Mrs. Beatson in a more subdued tone, for the attitude taken up by her son impressed her unpleasantly. He was no longer a boy to be bullied, but a man to be conciliated.

"No, you can't do what you like when your doings bring you into trouble with the law," insisted Kit, and Sophy nodded her approbation, which was odd considering how she dared authority as a suffragist. But in her own way she was as unreasonable as Mrs. Beatson, although she would never have admitted as much, and would have been indignant at the mere suggestion.

"I won't get into trouble with the law," said Mrs. Beatson rather nervously.

"That all depends upon what steps the police take."

"The police know nothing," said the housekeeper hastily.

"But the police will know, mother. I don't think so honorable a gentleman as Mr. Hendle will allow things to remain as they are. He is innocent—"

"Is he? He had every reason to kill Mr. Leigh because of the will, which is likely to leave him a pauper."

"I say he is innocent!" shouted Kit, stamping, and the expression on his face was such as to reduce his mother to frightened silence. "Nothing will ever make me believe that Mr. Hendle would act in such a wicked way."

"Then it's Mr. Mallien," whimpered Mrs. Beatson.

"No," said Sophy quickly, "Mr. Mallien knows well enough that Mr. Hendle will act honorably about the will. He would not risk his neck to get a document which he knew Mr. Hendle would not dispute if it is legal."

"Well," said the housekeeper, still bent upon accusing someone, "I shouldn't be surprised if that nasty Mr. Carrington is guilty. Mr. Hendle went up the very next day after the conversation with Mr. Leigh to consult him. Mr. Carrington might have killed Mr. Leigh to get the will, so that he could make Mr. Hendle give him money for it."

"I quite believe that Mr. Carrington did try to get money," said Kit, after a pause, "as he had a quarrel with Mr. Hendle yesterday."

"How do you know that?"

"Someone told Mrs. Pansey that angry words passed between Mr. Hendle and Mr. Carrington at the gate of the Park. And Mr. Carrington slept last night at the inn before going to London this morning."

"They did have a quarrel," admitted the housekeeper, "at least, I suppose so, as Mr. Carrington did not stay at The Big House last night. But we don't know if the quarrel was over money as the price of the will. Mr. Carrington was in Town on the night Mr. Leigh was murdered, so he can have nothing to do with it."

Sophy jumped up and clapped hands. "He was not in Town on that night," she cried, with her eyes blazing with excitement. "Father came down by the eight o'clock train on that night and Mr. Carrington came also. Father saw him on the Liverpool Street station and afterward on the Barship platform."

Kit turned on the girl sharply. "Sophy, are you certain?"

"Yes, I am. You can ask father yourself."

"But Dr. Tollart doesn't know Mr. Carrington," remarked Mrs. Beatson anxiously.

"Yes, he does. When Mr. Carrington came down here first he called to see father about an aching tooth. He came to this very house. Father did not take much notice of Mr. Carrington on that night, as he thought he was just coming down to see Mr. Hendle. He never connected Mr. Carrington with the murder. But now, now,"—Sophy clapped her hands again, so excited did she feel—"from what you say, Mrs. Beatson, I shouldn't be at all surprised to hear that Mr. Carrington was guilty."

"We can't be certain of that," said Kit quickly.

"I am certain," said Mrs. Beatson, rising, "and I'll tell Inspector Lawson what you have told me, just to pay that Carrington out for his poking and prying."

"I shouldn't if I were you, mother," remarked Kit dryly. "If you can make things hot for Mr. Carrington, he can make things disagreeable for you. Better let Mr. Hendle know first, and allow him to attend to the matter. After all, mother," said Kit, with a shrug, "we are assuming a great deal. Mr. Carrington may be quite innocent, and his quarrel with Mr. Hendle may have nothing to do with the will."

"I believe he is guilty," said Mrs. Beatson viciously, and said it because she wished to think so.

"So do I," put in Sophy, earnestly. "Still, Mrs. Beatson, I wouldn't go to see Inspector Lawson if I were you. You might be arrested as an accessory after the fact, you know."

"Me!" Mrs. Beatson grew white and tottered. "I have nothing to do with—oh, Kit, Kit, do you think—do you think—"

"I think you are quite safe, so long as you hold your tongue and allow Mr. Hendle to look into things."

"Oh, I shall not say a word!" groaned Mrs. Beatson, now thoroughly frightened for her own skin, "and you and Sophy will keep silent for my sake."

"I shall tell Mr. Hendle," said Kit, firmly. "I must."

"And I shall tell Dorinda," chimed in Miss Tollart. "She is engaged to Mr. Hendle, and they can talk it over together. Union is strength, as I know from our votes for women troubles, and if Mr. Carrington intends to accuse Mr. Mallien, or Mr. Hendle, he will find himself in the wrong box. They can call father as a witness if the case comes into court."

"A new witness," declared Kit eagerly, "and one who will put the saddle on the right horse. The mere presence of Mr. Carrington in Barship on that night shows that he has something to do with the matter."

"We can't be sure," murmured Mrs. Beatson weakly, for by this time she was becoming dreadfully nervous about her share in the proceedings.

"We'll soon make sure when Mr. Hendle questions Mr. Carrington as to his doings in Barship on that night," said Kit decidedly. "Now go, mother, and hold your tongue. It's dangerous to speak."

"I'll hold my tongue," promised Mrs. Beatson, and tottered away weakly.

CHAPTER XVII

DIFFICULTIES

Kit owed a great deal to Hendle, and was never backward in admitting that the Squire was his benefactor. When Mrs. Beatson first took service at The Big House, the boy was at school, but she explained to her employer that she could no longer pay fees for his education. Rupert, approving of the bright, intelligent lad, thereupon arranged for the rounding off of his scholastic career, and afterwards paid for his training as an engineer. It was due to the Squire that Kit occupied the excellent position he did in the exploitation and sale of motors. Also it must be stated that young Beatson took every advantage of his opportunities, earning the esteem and approval of all with whom he came into contact. With the Squire's aid and his own brains there was every chance that Kit would succeed in life more than most.

Naturally the boy was deeply grateful to Hendle for his consistent kindness; but he also adored him as an athlete, who possessed all those out-of-door qualities which youths most admire in their seniors. It therefore distressed him greatly when his mother came with her tale of woe. Kit, loyal to the core, would not admit for one instant that his benefactor was in the wrong, especially as he knew only too well what a trying woman the Squire had to deal with. As a parent, Kit had always found Mrs. Beatson uncomfortable, since she invariably used her authority to force him into agreement with herself, however unreasonable her ideas might be. Like many another mother, Mrs. Beatson would not recognize that her son was grown up and had a right to have his own opinions. He was to obey her in all things and do what he was told. Kit thought otherwise, and, as the views of the two clashed, there was always a certain amount of friction between them. Having regard to his mother's aggressive personality, it was extremely hard for young Beatson to obey the fifth commandment.

Rupert knew the boy's difficulties in the adjustment of his filial duties and greatly sympathized with him. Therefore he was by no means surprised when Kit made his appearance at The Big House early on Sunday afternoon. It was to be expected that Mrs. Beatson would tell her son about her dismissal, but when Hendle heard what his visitor had to say he was surprised to hear that the woman had been so frank in her explanation. He made Kit sit down and repeat his story of the interview, then walked up and down the library much perplexed, for the boy, being the son of the woman who had been discharged, it was by no means easy to talk to him. And Rupert was so kind-hearted that it was a positive pain for him to say a word against anyone. Yet what could he say in condonation of Mrs. Beatson's extraordinary behavior? Kit saw the worried look on his hero's face and felt worried himself in consequence. Therefore did he try to smooth matters.

"Of course, sir, I know that my mother is rather unreasonable," he remarked, in a low voice, twisting and turning his straw hat. "I don't quite agree with her views, you know."

Rupert gave the boy an approving glance, as he quite understood how unpleasant was his position. "Your mother has had much trouble in her life, and perhaps her nature is rather warped. What would you like me to do?"

Kit reflected, then spoke up straightly with a flush on his face. "I think it would be better for you to allow mother to go away for a holiday instead of dismissing her at once. While she is away, she can give you notice and can look for another place. In this way her pride will be saved."

"Why should her pride be saved?" asked the Squire hastily and bluntly.

"How can I answer that question, Mr. Hendle?"

"Of course not. I beg your pardon, Kit. I should not have asked it. What you say is very reasonable, and I have every wish to make things easy for your mother. She shall take a holiday, and can leave when she has found a better place."

Kit shook his young head. "She'll never find a better place, sir, or a better friend," he said sadly. "You have been good to her, and more than good to me. I wish mother could see things as I see them, but—but—"

"There! there!" Rupert clapped him on the back. "I know how you feel and what you wish to say. Even if your mother does leave me, Kit, that need make no difference to our friendship."

"It certainly will not," said the young fellow emphatically. "I don't think mother has acted well; nor does Sophy."

"Your mother certainly was very explicit, Kit. I wonder she did not make out a better case for herself."

"Well, you see, Mr. Hendle, mother never thinks that she does wrong. It is a very difficult thing for me to say, since I am her son, but I quite understand why you want her to go. I suggest that she should take a holiday, and that she should give you notice on the plea of finding another place, both to save her pride and to shut people's mouths."

"You think they will gossip—that your mother will talk?"

"I don't think that mother will talk, Mr. Hendle: she is much too frightened to do so, as she knows that she has not acted well. Sophy and I told her so, and gradually she came to see that she had made a mistake. But if you send her away people will ask the reason."

Rupert nodded and straddling on the hearth-rug put his hands behind his back. "And I can't give any reason other than the true one. It is impossible to give that, since it involves danger to other people. I am glad that you persuaded your mother to hold her tongue, Kit, and it is a great relief for me to know that you and Miss Tollart are acting so discreetly."

"We want to help you, sir."

"I don't see how either of you can do that, Kit."

"Why not? We know the story of—"

"From your mother's point of view you know the story," interrupted the Squire hastily, "but she does not know all."

"There is a will, which may disinherit you, I suppose, Mr. Hendle?"

"Oh, yes. The will of John Hendle, leaving everything to the elder branch of the family, represented by Mr. Mallien. I intend to take it to my lawyers to-morrow, after I have seen my cousin."

"Why not surrender the property to your cousin, sir, without taking the will to the lawyers?" questioned Kit shrewdly.

Rupert shook his head. "I wish everything to be done openly."

"But seeing what is involved, Mr. Hendle, isn't there some danger of a scandal if any public statement is made?"

"There is. All the same, if I gave up the property and sneaked away, people would talk, and the truth might come out in a crooked way. I wish it to come out in a straight way, and so intend to act as I say."

"Will you lose everything, sir?"

"I think so, if the will is proved to be legal. Then, Kit, I shall have to come to ask you to get me a situation in that factory of yours."

The boy was greatly distressed. "Oh, Mr. Hendle, don't talk like that. It is wicked to think that a kind-hearted man like you should lose your property. I don't think Mr. Mallien will make such a good use of the money."

"That is his affair, Kit," replied Hendle, with a sigh. "But you may be sure that I shall do all I can do to keep the property. There is a certain Statute of Limitations which may help me. Perhaps Mr. Mallien and I can arrange to divide the money. But what is the use of talking?" Rupert threw himself despondently into a chair. "You can't help me."

"Not so far as regards the property, Mr. Hendle," said Kit earnestly; "but I may be able to help you to clear up the mystery of the murder."

Rupert sat up and stared. "What?"

"Oh, I don't say that I know anything for certain, sir, but I have my suspicions, you know."

"Oh, have you? Who is it you suspect?"

"I shall tell you when you relate to me all details unknown to my mother." Hendle rose again restlessly, and walking up and down, thought deeply. When he paused again before Kit, he had made up his mind to be frank. "I know you are my friend," he said earnestly, "and I know that you are honest and true."

"I am all that," rejoined Beatson emphatically, "especially when there is anything to be done for you, sir. I shall never forget your kindness to me. Anything you say will go no further than Sophy."

"Why Sophy?" asked Rupert suspiciously.

"Because she knows so much that she may as well know all. And her suspicions point in the direction that mine do. She is now with Miss Mallien--"

Rupert uttered an ejaculation. "Not reporting the conversation with your mother, I hope," he said hastily.

"Yes," answered Kit bluntly; "it is better for Sophy to speak to Miss Mallien than to Mr. Mallien."

"Does she—do you—suspect my cousin?"

"No! But Sophy will explain when she brings Miss Mallien here. We arranged to meet here shortly, Mr. Hendle"; and Kit glanced at his watch. "I dare say the two ladies will be here in an hour."

"I didn't want Miss Mallien to know anything," said Hendle, frowning.

"It is absolutely necessary that she should know," said Beatson calmly; "and as she loves you, sir, and is going to marry you, she should know all. I'm always in the habit of telling Sophy my troubles, and she gives me the best of advice. Every woman is not so unreasonable as my mother, Mr. Hendle."

Anxious as he was, Rupert could not help smiling.

"I trust not," he said at length, and sat down quietly. "Well, Kit, you are more shrewd than I gave you credit for being. Perhaps you can help me, after all. Let us take advantage of the hour before the ladies arrive to go into the matter."

"You must be quite frank with me, sir, you know."

"That is only fair. Yes. I shall be quite frank. Take a cigarette, Kit, and listen carefully to what I have to say."

Shortly Rupert had his pipe and Kit a cigarette. The door and windows being closed, Hendle felt quite secure, as it was unlikely that Mrs. Beatson would indulge in eavesdropping again, seeing what a severe lesson she had received. Hendle related slowly all that had happened, and supplied details missing in the story of Mrs. Beatson. He ended with a short sketch of his present position, and the difficulty he found in deciding what action to take. Kit was so interested in what was said that he allowed his cigarette to go out, and when the story was ended stared tongue-tied at the Squire. Rupert laughed at the expression on the boy's face.

"You seem as perplexed as I am," he remarked with a shrug.

"I don't think that I am perplexed," said Kit slowly and relighting his cigarette; "only I am astonished that you have not spotted the right man who murdered the vicar."

"Things are too muddled for me to spot anyone," replied Hendle dryly. "My cousin accuses me; Mr. Carrington accuses your mother."

"It is ridiculous for you or my mother to be accused," said Kit quietly. "My mother hasn't the pluck to kill a fly in spite of her tempers, and you—-"

Kit laughed. "What bosh! I'd as soon believe Sophy was guilty."

"Well, only your mother and I and my cousin knew about the will before—-"

"Mr. Carrington knew."

"Oh, yes. But he was in town on the night Leigh was killed, so—-"

"He was not in town," interrupted Kit sharply. "He was in Barship."

Hendle dropped his pipe and stared. "Are you sure of what you are saying?"

"You can ask Dr. Tollart if you doubt me."

"Dr. Tollart!" echoed Hendle, much surprised. "What does he know?"

"He came down on the evening when the vicar was murdered, and saw Mr. Carrington both on the Liverpool Street platform and on the Barship platform."

"Did he speak to him?"

"No. He told Sophy that Mr. Carrington had come down, but that he had traveled in another carriage. After all," went on Beatson thoughtfully, "there was no reason why the doctor should speak. He had only seen Mr. Carrington once when he called on him to get a cure for his toothache."

"Yes. I remember he went to see the doctor when he first came," replied Rupert mechanically. "I was in the church with Miss Mallien, and Carrington, on his way back to The Big House, looked in about his tooth on Tollart." He paused, then continued: "What train was it?"

"The one which leaves Liverpool Street at eight."

"That arrives here at a quarter past nine," said Hendle meditatively.

"Yes, and as the vicar was murdered at eleven, Mr. Carrington had plenty of time to make his plans."

"I can't believe that Carrington is the assassin," muttered Hendle, in dismay, for he dreaded lest he should prove the accusation to be true. "Did Dr. Tollart connect Carrington with the murder?"

"No. If he had, he would have spoken out. He took little notice of Mr. Carrington, thinking he was coming down on a visit to you. And as Mr. Carrington was with you the next day, of course the doctor believed that it was as he had thought."

"Yes, I see. But Carrington did not come on that night. He came by the midday train next day."

"The doctor didn't know that," said Kit, nodding; "in fact, he thought no more about the matter after he told Sophy, and he only told her as a piece of gossip, you understand."

"Yes! yes! I see that, as Carrington was with me the next day, his presence in the eight o'clock train on the previous night would arouse no suspicion in Tollart's mind. Still, his being at Barship on that night doesn't mean that he killed the vicar."

"Well," said Kit, with a wisdom beyond his years, "I rather think that it is very good evidence against him. You had told him about the will, and he knew what it meant to you. What he said when you kicked him out the other day shows that he wants a large sum of money. He intended perhaps to stun the vicar and get the will, so as to make his terms with you; but the vicar, having heart disease, died straightway. For that reason Mr. Carrington buried the will, and sent an anonymous letter to my mother."

"But Mr. Carrington did not know where the sundial was. How, then, could he find it in the nighttime, hidden as it was among the bushes?"

"Oh, I can't explain everything," said Beatson frankly; "but you must admit, sir, that it is odd Mr. Carrington should have been in Barship on the night of the murder, without saying a word to you. If his intentions had been innocent, he would have come for the night to you."

"True enough, Kit. I wonder where he did spend the night?"

Kit shrugged his shoulders. "You will have to ask him that. I really believe that he is the guilty person."

"But what about that opal in the matrix which belongs to my cousin? It was found by me on the verge of the hole where the will was buried."

"Did you find it?"

"Well, no. It was Carrington who pointed it out glittering among the grasses. I merely picked it up."

"Well," said Kit, with a judicial air, "the person who loses generally manages to find. How do you know that Mr. Carrington didn't drop the opal there when your back was turned?"

"You are very rapidly weaving a rope for the man's neck," observed Hendle dryly. "After all, we are taking a great deal for granted."

"Well, sir, all you have to do is to ask Mr. Carrington to explain."

"Humph! That will be awkward, considering we are declared enemies. However, we shall see. I think it will be best to speak to my cousin first."

Kit agreed with this suggestion and then held his tongue. He had said all that he could say, and having placed the Squire on his guard, there was nothing more to be done. Rupert himself did not pursue the conversation further, but walked up and down, musing over what he had heard. For quite five minutes there was silence, and then Dorinda made her appearance, followed by Miss Tollart. The girl looked very pale and anxious.

"What does all this mean, Rupert?" she asked nervously.

"All what?"

"Sophy has told me a strange story," said Dorinda, taking a seat, "and I suppose Kit has told it to you also."

Hendle nodded. "Yes. I know that Carrington was in Barship on the night when Leigh was murdered—unless, of course, Dr. Tollart has made a mistake."

"My father made no mistake," struck in Sophy, flushing, for she guessed that the Squire was hinting at the doctor's infirmity. "He was quite sober when he came home on that night. I was waiting up for him. He mentioned in quite a casual way that Mr. Carrington had traveled down by the same train, and neither of us thought anything more about the matter, even when we heard next morning about the murder. We thought that Mr. Carrington had come down to see you, Squire, and he certainly was with you the next day."

"He was," admitted Rupert quietly, "and his being with me made you believe that what you thought was true. Is it not so?"

"In a way. But the real truth is that neither my father nor myself thought anything at all about the matter. Only Mrs. Beatson's hint that Mr. Carrington might possibly be guilty made me remember."

"Do you think that the man is guilty?" asked Rupert quickly.

Sophy bent her dark brows in a frown and reflected. "I couldn't go into a witness box and swear that he committed the murder," she observed; "but he came down to Barship on that night, and if he did not stay with you, Mr. Hendle, he must have had some strong reason to keep his visit a secret."

"Your father can swear to this visit?"

"Yes. I asked him again if he remembered Mr. Carrington coming down, and he said that he could. Of course," added Sophy significantly, "I had to ask the question in a way not likely to arouse my father's suspicions as to why it was asked. It is no use letting him know too much, as he might talk. But if necessary he can prove what he told me."

Dorinda shivered. "I never liked Mr. Carrington," she observed. "All the same, I can't believe that he murdered Mr. Leigh."

"Some one must have murdered him," said Kit, a trifle dryly; "and why not Mr. Carrington, rather than your father, or the Squire? For my part, going by what Mr. Hendle has told me, I believe Mr. Carrington is guilty."

"How are we going to prove him to be guilty?"

"Well," said Rupert doubtfully, "I see no way save asking him to explain why he came down to Barship on that night. Unless he gives a reasonable excuse, he will be in danger of being arrested."

"But, Rupert, in that case my father will be in danger."

"How so?"

"Don't you know that Mr. Carrington sent for my father the other day, and had an interview with him at *The Hendle Arms?*"

"No. What did he wish to see your father about?"

"He threatened to accuse him of committing the crime, so as to gain possession of the will. I don't know exactly what passed," went on Dorinda anxiously, "as my father told me little. All he really said was that he was in danger of being arrested, because Mr. Carrington could give evidence against him, which would be difficult to disprove."

"But your father surely did not admit that he was guilty, Dorinda?"

"Certainly not," cried the girl, flushing indignantly. "How can you suggest such a thing? But as Mr. Carrington wants money he is ready to say anything or do anything likely to force my father into paying him to hold his tongue."

Rupert smiled grimly. "Carrington knows that your father has not sufficient money to pay him what he wants."

"What does he want?" asked Sophy, looking up.

"Five thousand pounds was the price he demanded from me," said Hendle, "and I don't think he'll take a penny less from Mr. Mallien. But in order to get the money Carrington will have to wait until my cousin is in possession of my property. Until then you can be sure, Dorinda, that he will take no steps to make things uncomfortable."

"No, I think you are right," murmured Miss Mallien, greatly relieved. "But what is best to be done?"

"I have already made up my mind. In the first place I shall see your father and learn exactly what took place at this interview. Afterwards we can have a talk with Carrington. Then he will—"

"Oh, let the will alone until we learn the truth about this murder," urged Dorinda anxiously. "To clear my father from all chance of being accused is the first thing to be done. See my father, Rupert; perhaps he will be more frank with you than he was with me."

"He must be frank if he wants to save himself," said Sophy bluntly. "Don't worry, Dorinda. My opinion is that we should give Mr. Carrington plenty of rope with which to hang himself. When he is fully committed, then we can turn the tables on him by saying what we know of his presence in Barship on the night of the murder. There's nothing to be afraid of."

"I'm not exactly afraid," said Dorinda slowly, "but the suspense is very trying, with Mr. Carrington working in the dark."

"We'll force him to come out into the open, Miss Mallien," said Kit resolutely; "then he will have to defend himself, and won't have time to accuse other people. He shan't have everything his own way, anyhow."

"Hear! hear!" cried Sophy, clapping her hands. "You're a brick, Kit. For my part I believe that Mr. Carrington has only to be faced boldly to bring him to his knees."

Rupert shook his head. "He can do some damage before he is forced to take up that position."

"What does it matter, so long as the damage won't be lasting?" said Dorinda impatiently. "I am certain that my father is innocent."

"And so am I," finished Hendle with a shrug; "so there only remains Carrington as the possible criminal. Well, we shall see. Anyhow, as he won't move until my cousin is in possession of the property, we have ample time to arrange what is best to be done. Meantime let us keep what we know to ourselves."

"But what about Mrs. Beatson?" hesitated Sophy, glancing at Kit.

"Mrs. Beatson," said Rupert, grimly polite, "is going away for a holiday, and if she hears of a better situation she will not return here."

"I'm glad of that, Squire!" and Sophy, guessing the plan which was to save the housekeeper's pride, felt greatly relieved. Little as she liked her future mother-in-law, she did not wish to see her disgraced. "And now I think Kit had better take me home."

"But I have more to say," began Kit anxiously, only to be silenced by Sophy.

"No, you haven't," she declared imperiously, and marched him to the door. "You have given the Squire quite enough to think about"; then she sank her voice to scold: "Don't be a fool. They want to be alone!"

"Oh!" murmured Kit, "I see"; and he submitted to be led away.

CHAPTER XVIII

SETTING A TRAP

Mallien, by telling his daughter a half truth instead of the whole truth, had made her very nervous, and although she asked for a more detailed explanation he had refused to give it to her. Dorinda was therefore much relieved when Sophy conducted her to The Big House and hidden matters were made more plain. When in possession of facts she quickly recognized that the position of her father was highly dangerous, should Carrington speak to the police. But the girl agreed with Rupert that he would not do so, until all chance of getting money for his silence had disappeared. Even if Mallien was willing, such money could not be obtained until the property passed from the Squire to his cousin, so if Rupert refused to give up the same, Carrington would be forced to wait. It was not likely that he would kill the goose with the golden eggs by speaking prematurely.

And there was, as Rupert pointed out to Dorinda, a grave doubt whether he would speak at all, when informed that his presence in Barship on the night of the murder was known. Hendle intended to question the barrister on this point and hear what defense he could offer, but before doing so, desired to see his cousin and enlist his aid. It was even more to Mallien's interest than to Rupert's to bring Carrington to book, and only by the cousins joining forces could they accomplish their end. And that was, to learn for certain who had murdered the vicar. It assuredly seemed as though the barrister was the guilty person, and should the crime be brought home to him, his evil scheme to acquire money by blackmail would be frustrated. Instead of accusing Mallien to the police, it was probable that Carrington would be forced to fly lest Lawson should lay hands on him. Dorinda returned home in a much more comfortable frame of mind, since Rupert thus placed matters in a better light. She was also more content because affairs were in her lover's hands. He, if anyone, would be able to make the crooked straight.

One of Hendle's last injunctions to the girl was that she should say nothing to her father about her visit to The Big House. He warned her not to repeat what she had heard, and not to question her father in any way regarding his dealings with Carrington. Rupert arranged matters thus because he intended to call on his cousin next day and have a complete understanding with him. Mallien therefore was much annoyed, and very illogically so, when his daughter no longer implored him to be plain with her. On Sunday evening and Monday morning she saw him looking gloomy and disturbed, yet made no effort to cheer him, or, as he put it, to bear his burden. Dorinda laughed outright when her father made this last remark.

"Really, father, you are unreasonable," she observed, when putting on her hat to go shopping in the village. "How can I bear your burden when you won't tell me what it is?"

"I have told you," growled the little man crossly, "that blackguard Carrington dares to accuse me of murdering Leigh."

"Well," said Dorinda lightly, "as you didn't murder him what does it matter?"

"You talk rubbish. Carrington can tell serious lies which may endanger my liberty."

"What are those lies, father?"

"I shan't tell you," snapped Mallien.

Dorinda shrugged her shoulders and took up her sunshade. "Then how can you expect me to bear your burden, as you put it? You tell me enough to make me anxious, yet not enough to enable me to help you."

"You can't help me."

"In that case there is no more to be said."

This speech was so unanswerable that Mallien could find no reply and retreated to his own particular room, feeling—rather inconsequently—that he was not receiving the attention and sympathy which was his due. It never seemed to strike him that his daughter could scarcely administer to his comfort while she was ignorant of necessary information. But nothing irritates an unreasonable man more than being treated reasonably, and Mallien scowled blackly when he saw from the window Dorinda tripping lightly in the direction of the village. He was quite sorry for himself.

"I did think that my own daughter had some decent feeling in her," he meditated sadly; "but she's like everyone else—selfish in the extreme. Oh, it's no wonder that I hate everyone. People think only of themselves. Now what the dickens do you want? Hang you!"

This last question he asked aloud, being still at the window, he saw Rupert open the little garden gate and walk briskly up to the door. As Dorinda had gone one way and Rupert had come another, Mallien never dreamed that there was any understanding between them, or that his daughter had departed so as to afford her lover a chance of speaking to her very egotistic parent. This had been arranged between the two on the previous day, and to carry out the scheme Hendle knocked at the door of his cousin with the will in his pocket. Before he left the cottage he was determined to force Mallien into plain speaking. Things were much too dangerous to permit any further beating about the bush.

"Well, and what do you want?" said Mallien, repeating his former question as he opened the door to the visitor.

"I want to see you," said Hendle very pointedly. "It is time we had an explanation."

"About what?"

"About this," and Rupert pulled the soiled and crumpled parchment out of his pocket—"the will of John Hendle."

"Oh! So you have it. And how did you get it, may I ask?"

"You can ask in your own room," said Rupert politely. "I can scarcely give you an explanation on the door-step."

"Afraid of consequences to yourself," grumbled Mallien, nevertheless yielding so far as to lead the way into his sanctum.

"Oh, dear me, no," replied the visitor, seating himself. "Afraid of consequences to you."

"To me!" Mallien dropped into a chair before his desk. "What do you mean?"

"I think you know very well."

"I don't," said the man doggedly and determined to leave all necessary explanation to his cousin. "You speak in riddles."

"We must solve them together." Rupert spoke dryly, then thrust the will under Mallien's nose, "Read that, and tell me what you think."

Out of sheer contrariety the host would have refused, but his curiosity and greed got the better of him, and he eagerly read the document to learn if indeed the Hendle property would come to him. The Squire leaned back in his chair, filling his pipe and watching the various emotions expressing themselves on Mallien's face. Doubt, amazement, satisfaction and exultation all appeared in turn, and when he had mastered the will, he looked at Rupert with an expression of triumph. Mallien felt that he was top-dog at last, and took a malicious delight in emphasizing the agreeable position.

"The property comes to me," he said, beaming with self-satisfaction. "There isn't the least doubt about it."

"So I gather after reading that will," answered Rupert calmly. "John Hendle certainly left everything to Eunice and her descendants. Frederick was illegally in possession of the property."

"And it follows that *you* are illegally in possession."

"I admit that. But of course as the younger branch, represented by me, has been in possession of the estates for nearly one hundred years, it is quite within my rights to take advantage of the Statute of Limitations."

"Oh, no, you shan't," said Mallien, rolling up the will and thrusting it into his desk, "I am not going to be done out of my rights."

"Am I the man to try and do you out of them?"

"Yes, you are," retorted the other unjustly, "since you talk about this Statute of Limitations."

"Why should I not take advantage of the Statute, when I run a chance of being made a pauper, and not through my own fault?"

"Because it isn't honest," said Mallien virtuously. "You and yours have been wrongfully in possession of what belongs to me. I'm going to have my own, if I spend the last sixpence in the law-courts. I thought you were honourable, Rupert, yet here you talk of putting me to a lot of expense to get my own estates."

Hendle stared at the greedy heir, for such selfishness in taking advantage of an innocent person's misfortune was inconceivable to him. But he knew only too well that argument was useless. Mallien could only see things in his own way, and did not care who suffered so long as he benefited. However, he made one effort "Put yourself in my place, Mallien," he remarked mildly. "Would you surrender everything without a struggle?"

"That is not the question," retorted Mallien, evading a reply after his usual fashion. "The property is mine, and I intend to have it. I shall keep the will, as it is not safe in your hands."

"Indeed. Why not?"

"You would benefit too much by its destruction."

Rupert laughed. "I could have destroyed it while it was in my possession and without your knowing anything about it. Instead of doing so, I have brought it to you. Does that look like dishonesty on my part?"

"You bring it to me because you are aware that I know all about it," said Mallien doggedly. "Mrs. Beatson told me about the will, as you know. If she hadn't, you would have thrown it into the fire."

"Oh, would I? Well,"—Rupert shrugged his big shoulders,—"you are such a misanthrope that you can believe no good of your fellow-creatures, so have it your own way."

"How can I believe any good when everyone is so selfish?" said this amazing man. "Even Dorinda leaves me to bear my troubles alone. I wanted her to comfort me this morning, and she went out shopping."

"How could she comfort you when you refuse to explain things to her?"

"What things?" demanded Mallien alertly and frowning. "How do you know that I have anything to explain?"

"I know more than you think," replied Hendle dryly. "I know that you told her how Carrington was threatening you and—hold on—yet refused to supply details. How then can you expect her to sympathize with you and help you when there is not perfect confidence between you?"

Mallien did not answer directly, as he was too surprised by his cousin's mention of the barrister. "Who told you that Carrington threatened me?"

"Dorinda told me yesterday, and for that reason I arranged that she should go out this morning and allow me to have an uninterrupted conversation with you. Now don't lose your temper, Mallien. I am here to have an explanation, and I don't leave this place until I get it."

"I shall make no explanation," shouted the other savagely; "and Dorinda had no right to tell you about my private affairs."

"She told very little, as she knows very little."

"I don't care how much she knows, or how much she doesn't know," raged the angry little man, shaking with wrath. "I shan't have you meddle in my affairs."

"Will you prefer Lawson to meddle instead of me?"

"Lawson won't dare," answered Mallien, but in a more subdued tone.

"Oh, yes, he will, when Carrington tells him what he knows."

"Carrington knows nothing."

"He does. If he didn't he would scarcely have had that interview with you at *The Hendle Arms* after I kicked him out."

"You kicked him out, did you?"

"Yes, I did, because he wanted me to bribe him into holding his tongue about the will. Failing getting the money from me, he attempted to get it from you at that interview. Dorinda told me that you had one, since you informed her about Carrington's threats. Come now, Mallien, the time has come for plain speaking if you wish to keep your liberty. Did Carrington ask you for five thousand pounds? That was the sum he asked from me."

Mallien was forced to give in, and did so sullenly. "He did ask for that sum."

Rupert nodded. "I thought so. And what did you say?"

"I didn't say anything. I have taken a week to think matters over."

"I see," Rupert pondered; "and at the end of the week, if you don't agree to give Carrington five thousand pounds when you get the property, he will tell Lawson that you murdered Leigh."

"He says he will, but how can he prove it?" sneered the other uneasily.

"Well, you see, you lost that opal in the matrix which I found on the verge of the hole where the will had been buried."

"What does that prove?"

"That you were in the grounds of the vicarage on that night."

"I might have lost it on another occasion," argued Mallien desperately.

Rupert smiled dryly. "I don't think Lawson will be of that opinion. Come now, don't you think it is best for us to join forces and crush Carrington? For Dorinda's sake I don't want you to get into trouble."

"If we join forces, what will you ask for your services?" demanded Mallien, suspiciously. "That I should surrender my claim to the property, I suppose?"

"I ask nothing. What do you take me for?" Rupert looked highly indignant. "Do you think that everyone is so sordid as you are, Mallien? We can fight out the question of the will on its own merits. But, for Dorinda's sake, I wish to save you from Carrington's machinations. It is little use your getting the property if you are in danger of arrest."

"I am not."

"You are. Carrington is aware that Mrs. Beatson told you about the will; he was with me when we found the opal. He says that you are guilty, and when in London sent that anonymous letter—but I forgot you don't know about the letter."

"Yes, I do," snarled Mallien, wiping the perspiration from his forehead. "Carrington was very explicit at the interview." He paused for a moment, then continued: "I may as well tell you everything, since you know so much. But I warn you, Rupert, that nothing you can say or do to crush Carrington and help me will prevent my claiming the property."

Hendle waved his hand lightly. "That's all right. I am aware that you are a thoroughly ungrateful man. Let that pass."

"I am not ungrateful," cried Mallien hotly. "What have I to be grateful for?"

"In the first place for many sums of money I have given you; in the second for my offer to save your liberty and perhaps your life. Were it only for your own sake, Mallien," added Rupert with scorn, "I should leave you to Carrington's tender mercies. As it is, I must consider Dorinda. Now, no more talk, if you please. Let me know exactly what took place between you and that blackmailing thief."

Mallien did not argue further. Not that he felt any shame, but he saw that Rupert was too strong for him, and felt that his cousin had right on his side. Mallien would never have admitted the right, as his nature was too ungracious to ascribe honor to anyone but himself. In a sulky manner, and as if Rupert was trying to do him harm instead of good, he related what had passed between himself and the barrister at *The Hendle Arms*. The Squire thus learned for the first time that Mallien had been in the Vicarage grounds on the night of the murder, and had lost the opal ornament during the struggle with the unknown man in the avenue. "And I believed that the fellow was you," protested Mallien earnestly. "You had every right to murder Leigh."

"Every right," echoed Rupert angrily.

"I mean every reason," said Mallien, correcting himself hurriedly, "and, after the man ran away, I went to look in through the Vicarage windows. There was a light in the study, and, as you know, the window had neither curtains nor blinds. I saw Leigh lying dead on the floor, and went home without saying a word, lest I should be accused."

"You acted the part of a brave man, I must say," said Rupert contemptuously, "but it appears that you didn't murder Leigh."

"No, I certainly did not. Why, I only left this cottage as the church clock chimed eleven, and, as Leigh was murdered at that hour, he must have been dead before I reached the Vicarage. I expect the man was hunting for the will, and only managed to escape with it when I ran up against him in the avenue."

"But who was he? I don't suppose Mrs. Beatson dressed herself as a man to—"

"No! No! That is ridiculous. Mrs. Beatson was made a catspaw by the same man to get the will without throwing suspicions on him."

"I didn't write that anonymous letter, if that is what you mean," said Mallien tartly and uneasily.

"I am aware of that. It was Carrington who—"

"Carrington!" Mallien started to his feet. "Impossible! He was in town on the night of the murder."

"He was in Barship, and he was the man you ran across in the avenue," said Rupert grimly. "No wonder he pointed out your opal on the verge of the hole wherein the will had been buried. He dropped it there while my back was turned and allowed me to find it, so as to incriminate you."

Mallien was thunderstruck. "Carrington!" he muttered, sitting down again. "Oh, it is impossible."

"Not at all. Dr. Tollart came down with Carrington in the train which arrives at Barship shortly after nine. He wasn't with him, you understand; but he saw him both at Liverpool Street and at Barship."

"Then why didn't Tollart say so at the inquest?"

"Why should he? Tollart never connected Carrington with the crime. He believed that he came down to see me, and, as Carrington was with me the next day, of course that gave color to Tollart's belief. However, he mentioned the matter to Sophy, and she told me and Dorinda. For that reason Dorinda came to see me yesterday, and we arranged that I should see you. Now you can understand, Mallien, that we must join forces to have Carrington arrested. I have not the least doubt but what he murdered Leigh to get the will and extort money for it, either from you or from me."

"The scoundrel!" cried Mallien, highly indignant; "and to think that he should have dared to accuse me—me—me!"

"I was in equal danger of being accused," observed Rupert coolly.

"Oh, I don't care about you," retorted the other selfishly. "I must look to myself. I shall see Lawson and have Carrington arrested."

"If you do you are sure to make a mess of things," warned Hendle, accepting his cousin's egotism with a shrug. "We must lay a trap for Carrington and get him down here. Otherwise he may escape and then matters concerning the murder will never be cleared up."

"What sort of a trap?"

"You must write to Carrington asking him to come down here—to The Big House—for an interview with yourself and with me. Say that you and I wish to adjust the rights of the property. Carrington knows that you cannot give him his pound of flesh until we are agreed about the will. Also he will never suspect that he was seen in Barship on the night of the murder, or that we have put two and two together regarding the opal. He will come down."

"Will he enter The Big House seeing that you have kicked him out?" asked the host doubtfully.

"Oh, Carrington has no shame where his own interests are concerned, Mallien," replied the Squire quietly. "He wants money, and is prepared to go to any lengths to get money. Let us get him to ourselves and force him to confess. Meanwhile, we will send Kit to Tarhaven for Lawson, and when the Inspector arrives we can have Carrington arrested. Do you understand?"

"Yes," said Mallien, in a rather subdued tone, for Rupert dominated him at the moment. "I shall write as you suggest, and you may be sure that I shall so word my letter as to trap the beast. What a scoundrel," cried Mallien in a state of virtuous anger, "to try and accuse me of a crime which he has committed himself."

"He looks after Number One, as other people do, Mallien."

"Self! Self! Everyone is eaten up with self, Rupert. No wonder I hate the human race. When I get the money, I shan't give anyone a single penny."

"Oh, I am aware of that," rejoined Hendle, contemptuously; "and I shouldn't throw stones at other people if I were you, seeing in what a glass house you live yourself, Mallien. Now don't argue, but do what I tell you. If you don't, I shall wash my hands of the whole affair, and leave you to extricate yourself as best you can."

Mallien grunted an assent and scowled as Rupert left the cottage. He was not in the least grateful for the help thus afforded, as he hated the idea of his cousin doing anything for him. Besides, being extraordinarily vain, Mallien never liked anyone to be sharper than himself. And Rupert had proved to be sharper, as he had so cleverly solved the mystery of the vicar's murder.

"You think you are a fine fellow, don't you?" growled Mallien, shaking his fist at the retreating form of his cousin; "but you won't get a penny out of me, and you shan't marry Dorinda if I can help it. I'm not going to have you crowing over me"; and thus grumbling ungratefully he retired to his room to write the letter which was to trap Carrington.

Meanwhile, Rupert returned toward The Big House through the village in the hope of meeting Dorinda. He came across her just near his own gates, and in a few words reported all that had taken place. The girl listened attentively, and when her lover mentioned some of Mallien's selfish speeches she looked pained.

"I wonder you do anything for my father," she said sadly.

"I don't do anything for him, dear. I do it for you. Besides," added Rupert with a shrug, "how can one be angry with a child—and a greedy child at that."

"Will you give up the property, Rupert?"

"I fear I shall have to, dear. However, we can discuss that matter when this question of Carrington's guilt is settled."

"Father shall do you justice, Rupert," said Dorinda determinedly. "I shall not allow him, if I possibly can prevent it, to leave you without a penny. And, then"—she broke off with a shrug—"well, it doesn't matter. As you say, we can talk of these matters later. Just now I have something to tell you Rupert. I met old Titus Ark."

"Yes!"

"You know that he was Mr. Leigh's shadow. Well, he tells me now that he was lurking about the Vicarage on the night of the murder and that he saw Mr. Carrington there."

"The deuce! Why didn't he say so before?"

Dorinda shook her head. "He refuses to say."

"I shall question him myself, then," said Hendle briskly; "anyhow, he will be a new and important witness. I am afraid Carrington's goose is cooked."

"Poor creature!" sighed Dorinda, always tender-hearted. "Oh, poor creature!"

CHAPTER XIX

RESURGAM

Next evening Rupert received a curt note from Mallien stating that Carrington had replied to the effect that he would come down to Barship on the ensuing day, and would reach The Big House at twelve o'clock. Pleased with the information, since the interview was likely to settle the question of the vicar's murder once and for all, Hendle took it upon himself to arrange matters. To compel plain speaking on the part of the slippery barrister, it was necessary that witnesses should be present for the purpose of proving beyond question his presence in Barship on the night of the crime. Without doubt Carrington would twist and turn like an eel in his efforts to escape from the corner in which the procurable evidence would place him. Rupert, weary of mystery and worry, made up his mind that the man should be finally brought to book, and therefore went in search of Dr. Tollart. Now that Inspector Lawson was to be dragged into the matter, for the purpose of arresting the culprit, there was no need for further secrecy. And, besides visiting the doctor, Hendle intended to call on Ark for his testimony. Faced by these two witnesses, it would not be easy for Carrington to win free.

Mrs. Beatson duly went away for her so-called holiday, which was simply a preface to her dismissal. Her presence was not required at the coming interview, as what she knew and what she had done did not touch immediately on Carrington's guilt. Also, neither Dorinda nor Sophy was to be present, as they could give no first-hand evidence. Rupert himself, Mallien, Ark and the doctor were the necessary people to prove that Carrington had struck the blow, and the Squire employed Kit to bring Lawson from Tarhaven for his share in the proceedings. And so that everything should be prepared beforehand for Lawson's action Rupert arranged that the officer should not arrive at The Big House until one o'clock. This would give Rupert and his friends sixty minutes to bring Carrington to bay.

Tollart was both startled and surprised when the Squire called to explain why his presence was required at The Big House. He had thought little of Carrington's presence in the train on that fatal evening, and had not in any way connected his presence in Barship with the tragic death of Leigh. This he explained to his visitor, and suggested that, after all, some mistake had been made in crediting the barrister with the commission of the crime. But Hendle determined to put an end to all mystery, explained to Tollart all about the discovery of the will, and pointed out what a leading part the document had played in ensuing events. Tollart, who for once was sober, expressed his amazement and regret, less for the vicar's death than for Rupert's probable loss of his property.

"And surely," said Tollart, in his husky voice, and with his big red face expressing sympathy, "surely Mallien will not take everything from you even if this will proves to be legal."

"Oh, the will appears to be legal enough, doctor. And, knowing my cousin as you do, you may expect him to grab everything."

"He'll make a bad Squire."

"That's his lookout," replied Hendle with a shrug.

"A bad lookout for the parish, Hendle. I don't set myself up for a saint, as I have my failings; but Mallien,"—the doctor made a face—"why, he'll ruin the place. Don't give in to him, if only for the sake of Barship. Fight him to the bitter end."

"Oh, I'll protect my interests as best I can, you may be sure," answered Rupert, pleased that Tollart was on his side. "But that matter can be attended to later. What we have to do now, is to force Carrington into confession. I take it that you are sure it was Carrington who came down in the same train with you, doctor?"

"Certainly. I know him well by sight, as he called on me, when he first visited you, to get some remedy for toothache. I never forget a face, and I saw your friend both on the Liverpool Street platform and at the Barship station."

"Did Carrington try to escape observation?"

"Well, I hardly know. He did not see me, so far as I know, and he had a heavy overcoat on, which was strange considering how sultry was the evening. The collar was turned up, I remember," mused the doctor thoughtfully. "Well, yes, I think he was anxious not to be recognized. I never thought anything about the matter, you know, Hendle, as I believed he was coming down to stay with you. As he was with you the next day, my belief was natural enough."

"Quite so," assented the Squire; "but he must have returned on the same night to Town, perhaps by the midnight express from Tarhaven. His visit to me only dated from twelve o'clock the next day, when he arrived by the midday train."

"Hum! And he knew about the will?"

"Mrs. Beatson told him. I expect he wished to get it, to sell it to me."

"Ah! he doesn't know what an honest man you are, Hendle."

"He knows now," responded Rupert dryly; "however, I understand that you will come to The Big House at twelve o'clock to-morrow to give evidence."

"Certainly; certainly."

"And—" Rupert hesitated with an awkward look.

"Oh, I'll be sober," said Tollart with a defiant laugh. "I'm not quite so bad as people make out. You can depend upon my doing everything I can to help you, Hendle, as I have a great regard for you," and the burly doctor shook hands warmly with the Squire.

Rupert went away feeling sorry that a man with such a good heart should be a slave to a despicable vice, and wondering if there was no way in which he could be reformed. Tollart when sober was a clever physician, but when in his cups made endless mistakes. And for a medical man to make mistakes is dangerous seeing that he is dealing with matters of life and death. However, much as Hendle wished to assist Tollart to lead a better life and give his undoubted abilities a chance, this was not the moment to attend to the matter, as there were more immediately important matters to be looked into. So having secured Tollart as a witness, the Squire walked to Ark's abode.

This was a tumble-down cottage on the verge of the churchyard, which stood in a well-kept garden surrounded by a wall of loose stones. Here lived the old sexton and his grandson in tolerable comfort. The neat looks of the garden were due to Tobias Ark, for his grandfather took no interest in such things.

Tobias himself was a lean dark-faced man, taciturn and rather melancholy, perhaps by reason of his funereal employment. He was digging in the flower-beds when the Squire approached the gate and hastened to come forward with a surly touch of his forelock. In answer to Rupert's inquiry he admitted that his grandfather was in the cottage and said that he would send him out to hear what the Squire had to say. Hendle did not mind waiting at the gate, as he had no wish to enter Ark's stuffy abode.

"Whoy, it be the Squoire," piped Titus when his grandson went in and he came out, like the little old man and woman in the weather-gauge. "And what be you here fur, Squoire? There bain't be no funereals, surely."

"No, Titus, no. I have come to ask you about what you said to Miss Mallien."

"Aye." Ark looked tremendously cunning, and his face wrinkled up like that of a monkey gloating over a nut. "And what might that be, Squoire?"

"You told her that you saw Mr. Carrington near the Vicarage on the night Mr. Leigh died."

"Muster Leigh bain't dead I tell 'ee, Squoire."

"Yes, yes, Titus; we know all about that," replied Rupert soothingly, for he was well aware of the fixed idea which dominated the old man. "But you saw Mr. Carrington about the house?"

"Yus, I did, when walking round the Vicarage, not being able to sleep, me being old beyond telling, young sir, and the night being warm like. Yus," continued Ark garrulously, "I see him sure enough. He come down the road in the moonlight dressed as if t'were winter and went into the Vicarage gardens. But, Lord bless 'ee, Squoire, I did think as he'd gone to see the vicar, and nivir thought aught of him being there."

"But the next morning, Titus, when you heard the vicar was dead—?"

"He bain't dead, I tell 'ee, Squoire," persisted the ancient crossly.

Evidently it was useless to try and beat sense into the old creature's head, so Rupert argued no further. Ark could evidently swear to Carrington's presence in the vicinity of the Vicarage on the night in question and that was the main point. "Well, Titus, we won't talk about the vicar being alive or dead. I want you to come to-morrow to The Big House to tell Mr. Carrington that you saw him on—"

"Be Muster Carrington there to-morrow?" inquired the ancient, his eyes glittering and evidently eager.

"Yes. At twelve o'clock. Can you swear that you saw him on that night?"

"Before the King and the Lord Chancellor," grunted the sexton. "Aye, fur sure I can say so, Squoire. Oh, I'll be there, sir; I'll be there." He rubbed his old wrinkled, gnarled hands gleefully. "I'll tell what I know, Squoire."

"We think that Mr. Carrington killed the vicar."

"Muster Leigh he bain't dead, I tell 'ee," said Titus for the third time and very irritably, after which he shuffled back to the cottage annoyed that his constant statement was not accepted. And it was queer that the old man should persist in declaring the vicar to be alive seeing that he had assisted to lay him in the family vault, which was visible from his abode.

However, Rupert, having impressed upon Ark that he was to be at The Big House at twelve o'clock next day did not trouble himself with the ancient's fancies. So long as Ark could swear—as he evidently could—that Carrington had been haunting the Vicarage on the night of the murder, what he believed about the vicar not being dead mattered little. The man was senile and was crazy on the one point, although he appeared to be clear enough on that other concerned with Carrington's presence at the Vicarage. Rupert did not trouble his head further about the matter, but returned home satisfied that the two witnesses would confound Carrington in the moment of his fancied triumph.

Nothing of any moment happened during the rest of the day, or next morning, when the meeting was to take place. Kit appeared with a spick and span machine before midday, and was sent over by Hendle to Tarhaven to bring back the Inspector by one o'clock. And Rupert informed the boy that while on the way back he could tell Lawson all that had been discovered so as to obviate the necessity of explanations. In fact, as Hendle said, it would be best for Kit to relate everything immediately he arrived at the police-office in Tarhaven, so that the Inspector could get a warrant for the barrister's arrest.

So Kit went off in high glee delighted at being able to do something for his hero and Rupert returned thoughtfully to his library where Mallien was already waiting.

"Suppose Carrington doesn't come?" suggested the Squire, who was very nervous.

"Oh, he'll come right enough," explained Mallien grimly. "I said in my letter that to-day you intended to arrange here about the transfer of the property to me under John Hendle's will, and that we both wanted him to be present."

"You don't suppose that he has any suspicions of the truth?"

"To be sure he hasn't. After all but for Tollart's evidence and that of old Ark, we should never have been able to nail him. I tell you, Rupert, that Carrington has not the least idea of what is about to happen."

"Poor devil! And yet he deserves his fate. The murder of Leigh was cowardly in the extreme."

"It was," assented the other. "Don't be a tender-hearted fool, man."

"I would rather be a fool according to my light than a wise man according to yours, Mallien."

"And I am quite content," chuckled the little man, "for no one but a fool would give up the property as you are doing."

"I haven't given it up yet," said Rupert, disgusted with this brutal speech, "and I may not be the fool you take me to be."

For all his insolence Mallien was plainly disconcerted by this frank statement, and began to think that he had gone too far. A muttered apology was on his lips, but was cut short by the entrance of Dr. Tollart. Immediately behind him shuffled old Ark, who seated himself near the door, chuckling and rubbing his hands with the air of a man who was highly pleased with himself. Mallien and the doctor, who were by no means friends, exchanged a curt greeting, and Tollart, turning his back on the prospective Squire of Barship, talked ostentatiously to Rupert.

"Mr. Carrington will be here almost at once," he declared, drawing off his gloves slowly; "he walked up behind Ark and myself as we reached the gates."

Even as he spoke the footman appeared to announce the barrister. Carrington, evidently considering himself master of the situation, walked in with a victorious air. He looked smart and alert, being quite in his best form. In a well-cut suit of blue serge, with a straw hat and brown shoes, he had apparently arrayed himself in his best to receive the money he expected. Of course, he did not anticipate that the five thousand would be handed to him at once; but when things were arranged between Hendle and Mallien as to the possession of the property, then Carrington intended to get a promise in writing of his share of the plunder. Not for one moment did he think that anything was wrong, and he even offered his hand to Rupert with an insolent air of pity.

"Every dog has his day, Hendle," he said maliciously. "This is mine."

"Don't be too sure," replied Rupert, rejecting the proffered hand. "There's many a slip between cup and lip, remember."

"You are full of wisdom," sneered Carrington. "Well, you will need it all to earn money when you are a pauper."

Hendle stepped forward until he towered over the smaller man and spoke slowly. "Don't tempt me to give you the thrashing which I let you off with the other day, Carrington," he murmured. "Let us get to business, and rid me of your presence as soon as possible."

"Oh, I am ready to go into business as soon as you like," retorted the barrister, still triumphant. "But why is Dr. Tollart here?"

"I am here," said Tollart gruffly, "to state to your face that you were in Barship on the night when Leigh was murdered."

Carrington started, and, in spite of his self-command, winced at the plain speech. His swarthy face grew slightly pale, but he still maintained his air of bravado. "Well, then, I am not here to talk about Leigh's murder," he said viciously, "but to see about this transfer of the Hendle estates to my friend Mr. Mallien."

"Don't call me your friend," growled Mallien, ferociously. "You are no friend of mine. All you want is to get money out of me."

"Take care," said Carrington, glancing at the others, "remember what I know."

"And what do you know?" demanded Mallien coolly.

"Something you would not like anyone else to hear."

"You can say what you like, and before anyone you like."

"Ah!" Carrington now began to see that things were not so safe as he had imagined. "You mean to go back on your bargain?"

"I never made any bargain, you beast. And what is more, I don't intend to make any. Yonder is Dr. Tollart, who can swear that you came down to Barship on the night Leigh was murdered; and yonder is Titus Ark, who saw you enter the Vicarage grounds."

"They are both liars," cried Carrington, taken off his guard.

"I bain't a liar," said Ark, rising, and tottered toward the barrister, "and wor I a younger man I'd make 'ee pay for saying so." He shook a gnarled fist in Carrington's face. "I did see 'ee round about the Vicarage. I swear to it, if needs be, before judge and jury. I bain't afeared."

"And you *will* be required to swear before a judge and jury," said Hendle, in a cold, measured tone, "when Carrington is in the dock."

"In the dock!" Carrington stepped back, trying to command his nerves, for he now began to understand the full extent of his peril. "And on what charge?"

"You killed Leigh," growled Mallien savagely. "Yes, you did, so don't deny it, you criminal. And you dare to accuse me."

"I do accuse you," said Carrington, driven to bay, and becoming fierce out of sheer desperation. "It was you who killed Leigh to get that will. I accuse you in the presence of these witnesses."

"Pshaw!" said Rupert, contemptuously. "What is the use of your talking, Carrington? The game's up. We have got you down here to have you arrested."

"You can't arrest me," said the barrister, with an air of bravado. "I shall go at once to Tarhaven and give information against Mallien."

Rupert got between the barrister and the door toward which he was retreating swiftly. "Stop where you are," he commanded. "There will be no need for you to go to Tarhaven. In an hour Inspector Lawson will be here, and then, if you dare, you can lay an information against Mallien."

"Oh!" Carrington winced and grew very white. "This is a trap."

"It is," said Mallien, with malignant satisfaction, "and I have lured you into it. You accuse me, do you? Ha! We'll see what you'll say when the handcuffs are on your wrists."

"Hendle,"—Carrington turned to his former friend with a cry, half of rage and half of fear—"will you stand by and hear this said of me?"

"Why should I interfere?" said Hendle stolidly. "You are only reaping as you have sown. To get money you were prepared to accuse me as you have accused Mallien. And all the time you are the criminal, as we now know."

"I am not!" shouted the miserable man, trembling. "You can't prove that I did the deed."

"I can prove that you came down to Barship on that night," said Tollart.

"And who will take the word of a drunkard?"

Tollart rushed at the barrister and would have struck him, but that Rupert pushed his big body between the two. "Don't lose your temper, Tollart. What does it matter? Carrington will have plenty to do to clear himself without calling anyone silly names. You understand," he added, turning toward the lawyer, "that both Ark and the doctor can swear to your presence in Barship on the night when Leigh was killed. You knew from me about the will and came down to murder the vicar."

"I did not. Even if I had wanted the will, I should not have murdered him."

"Pshaw!" said Rupert again, and pushing his advantage relentlessly, "all this denial will not serve you. Perhaps you may not have intended to murder the vicar when you struck the blow. I will do you that justice. But, as Leigh had a weak heart, you went too far and he died. Then you took the will and buried it under the sundial—"

"I didn't know where the sundial was," interpolated Carrington, shivering.

"That's a lie!" snarled Mallien swiftly, "for on the first day I met you I took you round the garden and, among other things, pointed out the sundial. You buried the will there, and then sent an anonymous letter to Mrs. Beatson so that she might find it and avert suspicion from yourself. You believed that Rupert would buy your silence to keep the property, and, failing his doing so, you came to threaten me."

"And I do. You were at the Vicarage on that night?"

"How do you know that?"

Carrington saw that he had said too much and glanced toward the door in the hope of getting away. But Rupert was between him and safety, and Rupert looked as stern and determined as a destroying angel. "You needn't think you will escape, Carrington," he said. "As you have sown, so you must reap."

"And your reaping will place a rope round your neck," said Mallien grimly. "You came to have me hanged, but you will go away under Lawson's escort to be hanged yourself. I was at the Vicarage on that night. I wanted to see Leigh about getting the will. But I did not leave my cottage until eleven, and by that time you had murdered Leigh."

"I did not! I did not!" and Carrington winced and cringed and shivered with all the courage oozing out of him.

"You did. It was you I struggled with in the avenue when you came out after burying the will under the sundial. You snatched at my watch-chain and got the opal in the matrix—"

"Yes," said Rupert, taking up the story, "and when we went to examine the hole where the will was buried, you dropped the opal when my back was turned and allowed me to find it, so that the blame might be thrown on Mallien."

"It's a lie," said Carrington, folding his arms and looking dogged, "and I wonder at you defending a man who is going to rob you of your property."

"I dare say you do wonder," retorted the Squire acidly. "Honest behavior is always a mystery to you. No wonder you followed Mrs. Beatson and induced me to do so, Carrington. You had written that anonymous letter to her and knew that she was going to find the will. Your plot was a very clever one, but it has failed completely."

"And I dare swear it has failed," said Tollart in his booming voice, "because the Squire is such an honest man."

By this time the perspiration was streaming down Carrington's face. He was now in danger of his life and knew it only too well. Yet the man was brave enough, and doggedly refused to admit what was said, in spite of the overwhelming evidence. Rupert had no cause to love his treacherous friend, and regretted that he was obliged to have him arrested; yet he could not help admiring the persistent way in which the man fought for his liberty and life.

"Who accuses me of being in Barship on that night," he demanded, raising his head, "a drunken doctor and a senile sexton. Those are nice witnesses. They have been bribed by Mallien to save his own skin."

"I don't waste money in unnecessary bribes," snapped Mallien.

"And I don't take money for performing my duty," said the doctor frowning. "I have one great fault which everyone knows of. I may be a drunkard, but I am not a murderer," he finished scathingly.

"I am not a murderer," persisted Carrington, fighting desperately, and gaining courage, now that he found himself with his back to the wall. "I never came down to Barship on that night. I can prove that I was in London."

"You will have every opportunity of clearing yourself at the trial," said Rupert, glancing at his watch. "Lawson will be here soon with a warrant for your arrest."

"No! No! No!" The cry was forced from the barrister against his will. "It is impossible for Lawson to arrest me. I never saw Leigh on that night."

Titus Ark rose in a creaky manner from his chair, and shambled toward the miserable man. "I do say as you did see 'um," he croaked.

"And so does Tollart," snapped Mallien; "that is, he can say you were in Barship on that night. Hark, Hendle. I believe Lawson has arrived."

Rupert hurried to the window and saw a vehicle pass round the corner toward the front door. "It's a trap and not a motor," he said puzzled. "Who can it be, I wonder?"

"I know; I know," said Titus, shuffling toward the door. "I know one as can say you saw Muster Leigh on that night"; and he disappeared.

"More lies," said Carrington, wiping his face. "Oh, I'll make you all pay dearly for this day's work"; and he wiped his face, while he set his teeth to battle to the end.

There was a shuffling noise in the hall, and Rupert stepped toward the door.

He opened it and then fell back with a cry of amazement. Supported by Titus and his grandson, Simon Leigh staggered into the room.

"I said as he worn't dead," chuckled the ancient. "Now didn't I, Squoire?"

CHAPTER XX

A WEIRD STORY

The unexpected appearance of a man who was supposed, and with every reason, to be dead and buried was so startling that for a few moments no one could speak. Had it been night time, those present might well have been excused had they taken the newcomer for a ghost. But a ghost would scarcely reveal itself in broad daylight, supported by two flesh and blood mortals. Amazing as it seemed, the wan person, who was placed in a convenient armchair by his guides, was actually the Rev. Simon Leigh. His head was bandaged; his face was bloodless, and he appeared to be listless and exhausted. Never was there such a dramatic entrance, or such an uncanny situation.

"Leigh!" gasped Rupert, hardly able to pronounce the name.

"Yes," replied the parson, faintly smiling. "I am alive, you see."

"I said as he worn't dead," chuckled Ark again, and rubbed his horny hands with comfortable glee, while his grandson Tobias stood mute and grim behind the man who had returned from the other world.

Carrington, equally startled, was the first to recover himself entirely. He saw in the reappearance of the clergyman a chance of escape from his dangerous position. "You accuse me of murdering Leigh, and Leigh is alive," he said, regaining swiftly his native impudence. "What do you say now, Hendle?"

Rupert turned his eyes from the vicar to Tollart, whose big face was purple with astonishment. "What do you say, doctor?" he asked, feebly.

"It's a dream," muttered Tollart, rubbing his eyes. "He must be dead. I examined the body; I saw him buried; I gave the certificate of death."

"I'm sorry to disappoint you, Tollart," murmured Leigh with a weak attempt at a smile; "but you see I am still alive. Tobias!"

The grim man knew what was asked for and producing a flask of generous proportions administered a stiff dose of brandy to his patient. The ardent spirit made Leigh cough, but brought the blood to his cheek and a more lively light into his dim eyes. Also when he opened his mouth he spoke with a stronger voice. "Yes, I am alive. I was buried by mistake."

"It's impossible, I tell you," cried the doctor, still struggling with his astonishment. "You were as dead as a door-nail."

"So you thought, Tollart, but you are not the first medical man who has mistaken catalepsy for death."

"Catalepsy?"

"I have been subject to it all my life, but I never told anyone about it—not even you, Tollart. Only Titus knew, and that was why he was what was called my shadow down in the village. I always dreaded being buried alive."

"Yet you were," said Rupert, staring with all his might at the resuscitated man, and wondering if he was asleep or awake. "Titus wasn't much good, after all, in spite of his watchfulness."

"And what could I do, Squoire?" demanded the ancient shrilly. "I said as Muster Leigh warn't dead agin and agin, but none heeded me."

"If you had used the one word catalepsy," protested Tollart, who was annoyed that Leigh should reappear to give the lie to his skill, "I should have known what to do."

"I bain't no scholard," croaked Titus sulkily. "I said as Muster Leigh warn't dead and he warn't. On the night of the day when he was buried, me and Tobias got him out of his coffin and he hev bin in my house getting well."

"You should have told me, Titus," expostulated Rupert reprovingly.

"Now the Lard help me, Squoire. Didn't I tell 'ee times wi'out number. I said as Muster Leigh warn't dead and you laughed; you know you did. But he warn't dead; he warn't dead"; and the ancient repeated his favorite phrase again and again with angry gestures.

"No, he warn't dead," mimicked Carrington, strolling easily toward the door, "and now that we know he warn't, I suppose there is no objection to my leaving this pleasant little party."

"Stay where you are," commanded Leigh in a much stronger voice. "It is no thanks to you that I am alive. Stop him, Hendle."

Rupert took Carrington by the shoulders and pushed him across the room and into the chair he had vacated. "You stay here," he said sternly.

"Oh, I'll stay if you wish me to," replied Carrington, making a virtue of necessity, and shrugging his shoulders contemptuously. "You can't get me into trouble now."

"We'll see about that," replied Leigh, who was breathing heavily. "I haven't much time to live, as the shock of being buried alive has given me my deathblow. But I shall live long enough to see that justice is done. Now let me explain what I owe to Mr. Carrington."

"One moment, before you change the subject," remarked Tollart sharply. "You told me that you had heart disease."

"I did," admitted the vicar dryly; "but I never allowed you to examine me, or you would have found that my heart was perfectly sound. I made that excuse to account for anyone finding me in a cataleptic trance."

"You should have told me the truth," rejoined the doctor sternly. "But that I thought the blow on the head had killed you, along with heart disease, I would have opened your body to be certain of the cause of death. As it was, Mr. Leigh—"

"As it wor," interrupted the old sexton aggressively, "you warn't sober, Muster Tollart. That you warn't."

"How dare you say that!" cried the doctor, flushing angrily.

"Aye, but I do say it," retorted Titus valiantly. "You saw double, you did, and not being sure of your larning said as Muster Leigh wor dead when he warn't. And if 'ee'd tried to cut Muster Leigh up, I'd hev knocked 'ee down. Yus, I would, and no mistake."

"It seems to me that we are not getting on very fast," said Carrington lightly, yet anxiously, for he desired to get away before Inspector Lawson arrived from Tarhaven. "Suppose Mr. Leigh speaks, and relates his experiences in the other world."

"I shall deal with you later," said Leigh meaningly and with an unpleasant look. "You are not going to escape punishment because you failed to carry out your evil design. First, I shall explain about my catalepsy. I have always been afflicted thus, Hendle," he added, turning to the young Squire, "and for that reason I rarely went away from my house. Titus knew that I was subject to these trances, and I always liked to have him at my elbow in case I fell into one. Also Titus had the key of my family vault, so as to rescue me should I be buried alive by any chance. The blow on the head did not kill me outright, although it was severe enough very nearly to do so. I was stunned for the time being and then passed into a trance. Owing to the warm weather, unfortunately for me, I was buried hastily, else I might have recovered."

"You were as dead as any man could be," persisted Tollart sullenly, for the revival annoyed him beyond measure.

"I was not, yet, although you, in your confused state, thought so. And you were confused with drink, Tollart, as Titus assures me. Let this be a warning to you, my friend, to abandon this vice, as you may not so easily escape again from dooming a man to a terrible death."

Tollart tried to speak, but could not, as he knew very well that he was entirely in the wrong, and that the consequences of his too hurried examination of the body might be serious for him. He stammered, stuttered, and turned very white, then walked silently out of the room. He had received a lesson which he would not easily forget. Rupert started forward to stop him, but Mallien, who had been too startled to speak hitherto, laid a detaining hand on his arm. The man was nervous and less aggressive than usual, which was not to be wondered at considering what had taken place.

"Let him go, Rupert," he muttered. "We can deal with this matter among ourselves. I want to hear how Mr. Leigh was rescued from his terrible position."

"Titus rescued me," said Leigh thankfully. "On the night of the day when I was buried he came with Tobias to the vault. He had the key, as I said before, in case of such an accident. These two"—he jerked his head right and left toward his supporters—"unscrewed the coffin and carried me into their house, which is, as you know, near the churchyard. Gradually I revived from my trance, but suffered greatly from the blow in the head which confused me. Feeling that I was not myself, and knowing that serious matters had to be dealt with, I ordered Titus and his grandson not to say anything about my being alive. Since the day of my burial I have been hidden in that little cottage, and Titus has nursed me back to health. But I fear," ended the vicar plaintively, "that I shall not live long. The shock has killed me."

"Well, at all events," said Carrington coolly, "I didn't kill you."

"Indirectly you have," said Leigh indignantly, "and I shall have you punished before I die."

"That is a nice Christian feeling, I must say," retorted Carrington uneasily.

"Men such as you are, who go about attempting murder, should be locked up," was the stern reply. "You intended to kill me."

"I did not. I intended to stun you, and thought I had done so," protested

Carrington sullenly. "No one was more astonished than I was, when I heard next day from Hendle there that you were dead. I thought the heart disease had killed you."

"I had no heart disease, and—"

"We know all about that," interrupted Mallien restlessly. "But tell us how that scoundrel managed to knock you down."

"Give me another dose of brandy, Tobias," said the vicar, and when he felt stronger after taking the spirit proceeded slowly to explain. "I was in my study on that night, and as it was after ten o'clock, Mr. and Mrs. Jabber had retired to rest. I had found the will, which I had mislaid, and was reading it, when I heard a tap at the window."

"I don't know about your reading it," said Carrington insolently, "as I watched you for some time through the window before I tapped. You were holding a parchment over a candle. I believe that you intended to burn the will."

"Perhaps I did," said the vicar with a queer smile. "There is more to be known about that will than you guess. At all events when I heard your tapping on the glass I blew out the candle and put down the will. I opened the window—you know it is a French window, Hendle—and looked out to see who had come at such an untimely hour. When I recognized you and you intimated that you wished to speak to me, I admitted you. I believed that you had come down to stay with Hendle and had arrived late."

"Did you lock the window again after admitting Carrington?" asked Rupert.

"I snicked it, certainly," replied Leigh quietly. "Not that doing so mattered, for, as there was nothing to steal at the vicarage, I paid little attention to bolts and bars."

Carrington laughed cynically. "And for that reason I was able to slip out of the front door and leave it unlocked without exciting suspicion," he remarked. "It was easy to get away."

"Very easy," assented Mr. Leigh. "The front door was never locked either by day or by night, as I did not fear burglars. And I did not fear you, Mr. Carrington, as you said that Rupert had told you about the will, and you wished to speak to me concerning it."

"Oh, you were brave enough," retorted the barrister carelessly. "Well?"

"I think you had better be less flippant, my man," cried Mallien, highly indignant. "You are not out of the woods yet."

"There's gratitude for what I have done for you," sneered Carrington. "But for my appearance at the window the vicar might have burned the will so as to allow Hendle to keep the property."

"Yes, I might have burnt the will, as you say," remarked Leigh with another queer smile; "and perhaps it would have been as well, seeing what an excellent Squire our young friend here makes."

"And what about me?" asked Mallien indignantly.

"You are not fit to govern the parish," said Leigh coolly. "You think of self and of self only."

"Well, the will is safe in my desk now," said Mallien complacently, "and, self or no self, I will be Squire of Barship as soon as the lawyers can arrange for the transfer of the property."

"You count your chickens before they are hatched, Mr. Mallien. There is much to be said before you step into your cousin's place."

"I don't see that," said Mallien doggedly. "Rupert knows that I inherit by that will you found in the muniment chest, as I am the legal descendant of Eunice Hendle. He makes no objection to giving me the property."

"Is this so, Hendle?" inquired the vicar.

"Yes," answered Rupert quietly. "I can scarcely keep what does not legally belong to me."

"You will be a pauper."

"I can't help that. I must act honestly."

Leigh was silent for a moment and cast a look of admiration on the young man. "You shame us all by your honorable nature," he said after a pause. "I am glad that I am spared to do you justice."

"What do you mean by that?" asked Carrington curiously.

"Never mind what I mean. I shall explain in due time. Just now I have to tell these gentlemen of the cowardly assault you made on an old man." Leigh turned toward Rupert to whom he chiefly addressed himself. "He held me in talk, Hendle, and all the time he was keeping his eyes on the will. I refused to let him take it away, as he wanted to do."

"I only wished to look after Hendle's interests," muttered Carrington.

"To look after your own, you mean," retorted Leigh tartly. "Had you meant well you would have gone away after I refused to give you the will. But you waited until my back was turned, and then struck me with the loaded stick you carried. The blow fell on my right temple and I dropped stunned to the floor, while you—"

"While I," cried Carrington, rising and speaking insolently, "snatched up the will and walked out of the front door cautiously, so as not to waken those servants of yours."

"After which," put in Mallien viciously, "you went through the jungle and buried the will under the sundial."

"I did," admitted Carrington recklessly. "You know so much that you may as well know all, for Leigh being alive you cannot touch me in any way. I buried the will, as you say, and afterward wrote that letter to Mrs. Beatson, so that she might find the will and avert suspicion from myself."

"Why Mrs. Beatson?" asked Rupert, disgusted with his former friend's brazen assurance.

"Because, according to you, she had overheard the conversation between you and the vicar. I guessed that, if she produced the will, suspicion would fall on her. Our meeting her on that night, Hendle, was pure chance, but it helped on my plans. I wished her to procure the will to you, and thus bring suspicion on herself as having killed the vicar."

"You infernal villain!"

"Oh, I don't see that," said Carrington carelessly. "Mrs. Beatson would be none the worse for having her neck stretched. But I would not have allowed things to go so far as that. All I wished, was for her to give you the will, and then when you consulted me, as I knew you would, I intended to persuade you to burn it in order to keep the property and pay me five thousand pounds for holding my tongue. You understand."

"Yes," said Rupert quietly, "you explain your villainy so carefully that I can scarcely help understanding. It was you, then, who dropped a clue near the sundial to incriminate Mallien?"

"It was me," replied Carrington, with cynical hardihood. "I snatched the opal by chance from Mallien's watch-chain when we struggled in the avenue. Only when I got away and found what was in my hand did I see how I could get the upper hand of him. I recognized the ornament at once as the one he had shown me on the first day we met."

"You scoundrel!" shrieked Mallien furiously, and would have struck the barrister, but that he swerved. Then Rupert interfered.

"He will have a much worse punishment than a blow," said the Squire, holding his cousin back with a strong arm.

"I won't have any punishment at all," sneered Carrington insistently.

"It is for me to say that," remarked Leigh, who was growing very weak in spite of the dose of brandy which Tobias administered. "So you met Mr. Mallien in the avenue of my place after you had buried the will?"

"I did. There is no reason why I should deny it, seeing that I am safe. And when I got away from him I walked to the next station and caught the night express from Tarhaven which does not stop at Barship. Next day—"

"You came down to play the part of a friend," said Rupert scornfully; "but you soon showed the cloven hoof, Carrington. Your plot was very clever, and had I been a less honest man it would have succeeded."

"It never would have succeeded," interposed the vicar, speaking with labored breath, "for I was alive all the time and intended to speak when necessary, as I have done. Titus kept me informed of all that went on."

"Aye, that I did," said the old man, patting Leigh's hand; "and they'll find in the village as the old 'un don't tell lies and bain't no fool either. I told 'em as you wor alive, didn't I, Muster Leigh?"

"Yes, Titus, yes. But I think you will very soon have to tell them that I am dead," said Leigh with a weak sigh. "After all, it is for the best. I shall never regain my health after that awful experience. And as my successor has been appointed, it would be wrong of me to deprive him of the living."

"Don't trouble about that, Leigh," remarked Rupert, bending over him. "You shall stay here and be nursed back into health again. I'll see that you are all right for the future."

"You are a good man, Hendle; but if you knew—" He stopped abruptly and drew away his hand which the Squire had taken. "But that I can speak of another time. Meanwhile we must finish dealing with this gentleman."

"Do you mean me?" asked Mallien, who felt uneasy because he had an idea that the resuscitated man had, as the saying goes, something up his sleeve.

"I don't mean you at present," replied the vicar, eyeing him with an expression of intense dislike. "I shall attend to your matter later."

"What matter?"

"That," said Leigh slowly, "I shall tell you in my own good time."

"You are very mysterious."

"Oh, I think all mysteries are at an end now," interposed Rupert hastily, for Mallien showed a tendency to make himself disagreeable in spite of the vicar's weak state of health. "We now know that Carrington did come to Barship and did strike down Mr. Leigh."

"Who cares if you do know?" retorted Carrington insolently. "Not me. I have played a bold game and have lost, thanks to your confounded honesty. If you had been wise, you would have destroyed that will and would have kept your money to yourself."

"At the cost of losing my honor," said Rupert flushing.

"Pouf! Who cares for honor in these days?"

"Apparently you don't, you beast," cried Mallien, who was desperately angry at the way in which Carrington had proposed to cheat him. "How dare you speak in this way! I'll have you charged with fraud."

"Fraud!" Carrington laughed aloud and snapped his fingers. "And how do you intend to do that, my good man?"

"Don't call me your good man, confound you!"

"Well, I won't," sneered the barrister; "it is rather a mistake to credit you with any goodness, I admit. You're no more a saint than I am, and would have played the same game had you got the chance. My only regret is that I have not rooked you to the tune of five thousand pounds. And but for the vicar's unexpected appearance I should have done so."

"Not you."

"Oh, yes. You were at the Vicarage on the night of the presumed murder, and I had your opal, which I dropped near the sundial. If I had held my tongue, as I would have done, you would have been hard put to explain your presence there, seeing what John Hendle's will meant to you."

"And you—and you!" shouted Mallien furiously, "how would you have escaped suspicion seeing you came down on that night?"

"Very easily," retorted the barrister in a light and airy tone. "I would have declared that I came down in Hendle's interest to get the will, and arrived at the Vicarage to find you leaving the house after murdering the man."

"Oh!" Mallien rushed forward. "Let me get at him, Rupert. Dog that he is. I want to strangle him."

"And be hanged for the murder of a worthless creature," said Rupert, holding Mallien tightly to prevent his executing his intention. "Leave him to Mr. Leigh. I rather think he knows how to deal with him."

"Oh, do you?" snapped Carrington, wheeling with a contemptuous smile on his dark face, "and what do you propose to do, may I ask?"

"I propose," said the vicar, whom he addressed, "to have you arrested for a murderous assault on me. As a lawyer, Mr. Carrington, you probably know how many years you will get for a contemplated crime."

Carrington grew pale and looked nervous. "I never intended to kill you," he muttered sullenly; "and, as you are alive and well—"

"I am alive certainly, but scarcely well," said the vicar faintly. "All the same, it is no thanks to you that I am not dead. You assaulted me, and you robbed me, so you shall suffer."

"I shan't!" and Carrington made a dash for the door, only to be caught by the Squire, who held on to him grimly.

"You shall," said Rupert stolidly. "As soon as Lawson arrives, and he may be here at any minute, Leigh will give you in charge for assault and robbery."

"Hendle, you wouldn't see me disgraced in that way," pleaded Carrington, who suddenly saw an abyss open at his feet. "If I am arrested, I will be ruined."

Hendle released the miserable man and stood back, rather incautiously as it afterward proved. "You would have ruined me," he said sternly, "so why should you not be done by as you intended to be done by others?"

"There's Scripture authority fur that," grunted old Ark, grinning toothlessly.

Carrington, now at bay, looked round and saw that everyone was against him, so that there was no hope of mercy. He covered his face with his hands and staggered against the wall near the door. For a moment there was silence, for, although neither Mallien nor Leigh pitied the scoundrel, Rupert, having an unusually tender heart, did so. Perhaps the feeling that the man was his old schoolfellow induced him to give Carrington a chance of escape. But be this as it may, when the barrister sobbing near the door suddenly opened it and dashed out, Rupert made no immediate effort to stop him. Mallien did. "Stop, thief! Stop, liar! Stop, murderer!" he vociferated and followed. Rupert was thus compelled to pursue the culprit, although he did so reluctantly.

The two came to the door to see Carrington running down the avenue, and dashed after him. The barrister flew like the wind and speedily outdistanced his pursuers. But he was not to escape after all, for, as he reached the open gates of the avenue, Kit's motor car, containing Lawson, swept round the corner. Running blindly, Carrington tripped and fell under the machine. The wheels passed over him, breaking his back. He was picked up stone dead.

CHAPTER XXI

A FINAL SURPRISE

At the inquest, held on the body of the unfortunate Carrington, the whole story of the events connected with the will of John Hendle was related in detail. This was done by the advice of Inspector Lawson, so as to avert further trouble. As the officer wisely pointed out, it was necessary that the characters of all those implicated in the affair should be cleared once and for all. This could only be done by the truth being made public. And this course of procedure greatly recommended itself to Rupert, who was tired of underhand doings. He was of a frank nature, and the idea of hiding this and concealing that, annoyed him exceedingly. He therefore made a clean breast of the matter when called upon to give evidence regarding Carrington's death, and insisted that everyone else should do the same. Consequently, the whole amazing story appeared in print, and read like a romance.

Mallien was inclined to hold back from giving evidence, as, of course, he should have communicated with the police the moment he became cognizant that a murder had been committed. But both his cousin and Lawson insisted that he should come forward to state what he knew, and, notwithstanding his reluctance, he was compelled to do so. He escaped better than he deserved, as it was seen how difficult his position had been, and the majority of people argued that the man could scarcely have been expected to incriminate himself by drawing attention to the crime at the time when he discovered it. Mrs. Beatson also contrived to elude reproof, as she cleverly stated that, when in possession of the will, she had intended to hand it over to the Squire. Of course, Rupert knew that she had never meant to do this, but for the sake of Kit he did not contradict her statement. And, because of Dorinda's feelings, he was glad to think that Mallien had got off so lightly. The two plotters themselves were much relieved that their characters had not suffered to an appreciable extent, and retired into the grateful shade of obscurity as speedily as possible. Things had turned out better than they had expected.

Carrington's conduct, of course, was condemned, since he had behaved so basely, but not so severely as it would have been had he been alive. Having met with a violent death, it was felt that he had paid for his trickery, and as little as possible was said about him. Kit, of course, was exonerated with regard to the accident, as Lawson proved that the young man had sounded his horn when turning into the park. But Carrington, anxious only to escape before the Inspector could take him in charge, had either not heard the warning of the horn, or had not attended to it. But be this as it may, there was no doubt that he had ran on blindly and thus had fallen under the cruel wheels of the car. Remembering Carrington's two premonitions about walking over his grave in the avenue, Rupert thought it quite uncanny that he should have met his fate on the very spot. But he only remarked on the matter to Dorinda, who was wise enough to hold her tongue. Enough had been said about Carrington and his disreputable doings in the newspapers, so there was no need to say more.

Mr. Leigh did not appear at the inquest, as he lay dying in a comfortable bed under the hospitable roof of The Big House. But he signed a written statement detailing the events of the night when he had been struck down, and this satisfied both Coroner and jury. After all procurable evidence had been sifted a verdict of "Death by Misadventure" was brought in, and the matter ended in the only way it could end. Carrington's sole relative, a clerk in the War Office, came down to take charge of the body, but expressed little surprise at the smirched reputation of the dead man. Carrington had always been a black sheep, and his relative grimly said to Rupert that he was glad things had turned out as they had. Carrington, he observed, would sooner or later have come to prison or the gallows had he lived, being one of those unfortunate creatures who could not run straight. So that was the end of the Squire's old school-friend, who had chosen evil instead of good; and bad as he had been Hendle was kind-hearted enough to regret the man's miserable end. Afterward, he always tried to remember Carrington as he had been at Rugby, rather than as the despicable plotter of his more mature years.

With the departure of the barrister's body in charge of his relative from Barship departed all mystery. It is now known who had struck down the vicar, and why the blow had been delivered. That Leigh had escaped death was not Carrington's fault, and the dead man was practically a murderer. But the villagers, in the excitement of finding their vicar alive, began to overlook Carrington's share in the matter. The question most frequently asked was whether Leigh would resume his charge of the parish seeing that his successor had been appointed. But all talk on this point was ended when it became known that the shocks inflicted on the unfortunate man, both by being struck down and by being buried alive had so shaken his system that he was not likely to live. Tollart was attending to him, and did so in an entirely sober state, as his narrow escape from trouble kept him away from the drink. Sophy, indeed, regarded the whole matter as a blessing in disguise, and hoped that her father would reform. He had every reason to do so seeing what a lesson he had received. With regard to his giving a certificate of death, Tollart's fellow-physicians held that he was perfectly justified, since the vicar had been in a cataleptic trance. But the villagers, headed by Titus, held that Dr. Tollart had been drunk at the time when he examined the body, and this opinion was not favorable to Tollart's reputation. However, when it was seen that he had turned over a new leaf, his conduct was considered more kindly and the doctor began to hope that he would weather the storm. But it had very nearly wrecked him, and the escape he had had greatly improved his character. In time by acting judiciously and keeping strictly sober, he managed to reëstablish his position.

A week later, when everything in connection with the catastrophe was quite settled, Mallien made his appearance at The Big House. He was more subdued than usual, as he also had learned a lesson, but there remained something of his old blustering manner when he entered the library and produced John Hendle's will from his pocket. Rupert guessed that his cousin had come to demand a settlement, and braced himself to face a disagreeable future. It was not pleasant to become a pauper, but there seemed to be nothing for it but to accept the inevitable. Yet it was not so much the loss of the money which the young man regretted as the probable loss of Dorinda as his wife. Rupert knew his cousin well enough to be sure that once in the possession of the estates and income he would not be inclined to permit the marriage to take place. And seeing that he was likely to be poor, it was useless for the girl to insist upon the fulfilment of the engagement. It was with a sad face and a weary heart that Hendle asked Mallien to take a seat.

"I suppose you have called to discuss matters regarding the will," he said, leaning his head on his hand and speaking quietly.

"In a way, though I don't see that there is anything to discuss," retorted Mallien, who was rapidly regaining his former bullying ways. "All you have to do is to clear out and allow me to come here."

"Walk out bag and baggage, you mean?"

"Something of that sort. I don't mind giving you one hundred pounds with which to make a new start in life. If I were you, I would go to Australia with Kit when he marries Sophy Tollart."

"And what about Dorinda?"

"She is not for you," said Mallien resolutely. "As the daughter of the Squire of Barship, she must marry a man with a position."

"Does Dorinda say so?" inquired Rupert quietly.

"Dorinda," said the affectionate parent, "is as obstinate as a pig. She is coming here in a few minutes to argue the matter. I told her that I intended to settle the matter of the will to-day. But she shan't marry you with my consent, and, as I have the money, you can see that it would be wrong of you to drag her down to poverty."

"You put the case very plainly, Mallien."

"How else do you expect me to put it?" said the other, who was not in the least ashamed of the cowardly way in which he was behaving.

"You might have a little more consideration for my position," remarked Rupert, with a shrug.

"What consideration did you ever show to me?" snarled Mallien.

Rupert looked at the little man in amazement. "I have always been your good friend," he said after a pause. "I have given you money and—"

"My own money," interrupted the visitor. "Much thanks for that. It won't do, Rupert. I won't allow you to work on my feelings."

"I never knew that you had any to work on."

"No more I have. I want justice, and justice I intend to have."

"Don't make such a row over the matter," said Hendle contemptuously. "You shall have what you want. But you can scarcely expect me to walk out of this house this very minute. We must take the will to the lawyers and have it gone into. Since you are behaving so brutally, I am inclined to defend my position. There is the Statute of Limitations to be considered."

"And there is me to be considered," said a quiet voice at the door, and the two turned to see Dorinda at the door.

"You have been listening?" snapped her father.

"Yes, I have," she replied boldly, "and what I have heard shows me what a cruel nature you have, father."

"Don't speak to me in that way," stormed Mallien, furiously.

"Oh, yes, I shall"; and Dorinda entered to place her hand on Rupert's shoulder as if to give him confidence. "You have not got Rupert's money yet."

"But I shall get it. The will is plain enough."

Before Dorinda could reply, Rupert rose to his feet and made a gesture that she should be silent. "Leigh has something to say about the will, Mallien," he remarked, "and had you not come over I should have sent for you. Leigh wishes to see you and me and Dorinda."

"If Leigh intends to try on any hanky-panky," said Mallien, uneasily, for the summons seemed strange and ominous to him, "he'll find himself in the wrong box, I can tell you. You've been scheming with him, I expect, since he has been lying there."

"I have scarcely seen him," retorted Rupert, passing his arm round Dorinda's waist. "Tollart says he should be kept quiet."

"Then we shan't disturb him now."

"Yes, we shall. Leigh has something on his mind, and wants to see the three of us. Tollart has given permission, so we can go up to him now. Only I beg of you, Mallien, not to excite him, as he is very weak, and is not far from death. You understand."

"I understand that you want to trick me in some way."

By this time Rupert's long-enduring patience was at an end, and he turned on the selfish little man in a cold fury. "Look here, Mallien, I have had enough of this," he said, firmly. "Don't goad me too far, or you will regret it."

"Oh, will I!" taunted the other; "and in what way?"

"Possession is nine points of the law," retorted Hendle, "and you appear to forget that I am the Squire of Barship. I shall see the lawyers and take all chances I can to prevent you getting possession of the money. I am innocent of any roguery in the matter, and my position is a very unfair one, as I am not to blame. It is close upon a century since that will was made, and if I make use of the Statute of Limitations I may be able to squash the whole affair. Equity, if not Common Law, will be on my side."

"You—you—you!" cried Mallien violently, "you swindler!"

"Don't call names," said Rupert imperiously, "or in spite of the fact that Dorinda has the misfortune to call you father, I shall kick you out of the house. So now you know."

"My own house," foamed Mallien, stamping.

"It's not your house yet, and it never may be."

"Well,"—Mallien drew a long breath—"I never—I never—" He turned on his daughter suddenly and with violence. "What do you think of this behavior?"

"I entirely approve of it," said Dorinda, calmly, "and I am glad to see Rupert stand up for his rights. He has treated you far too well as it is."

"What—what—what?"

"It's no use, father. You don't care for me and you don't care for your honor. All you do care for is yourself."

"I—I—shall cut you off with a shilling—with a shilling."

"So long as I have Rupert, I don't care."

Hendle caught Mallien by the shoulders and pushed him toward the door. "I can't allow any more of this, Mallien. Behave like a human being or I shall turn you out. Now come up and hear what Leigh has to say."

"Oh, I'll come," cried Mallien viciously, but, unable to resist his cousin's superior strength; "but remember that if there is any plot to take away my money I shall make things hot for you."

"Get on! get on!" said Hendle, impatiently, "and don't make a fool of yourself."

Mallien did go on and climbed the stairs to Leigh's room unwillingly. He was beginning to see that there was nothing to be gained by storming, and that his best plan would be to adjust the matters in dispute quietly. Although he believed the will to be legal, he yet had a lurking suspicion that it might be set aside by the Statute of Limitations. Under these circumstances it was unwise to quarrel with his cousin, so he became more subdued. All the same his dog-like temper could not be entirely suppressed, and he entered the sick-chamber growling and muttering savagely. Dorinda and Rupert followed, the girl crying with shame. Her father's conduct was disgraceful.

The vicar was propped up in bed with pillows, looking white and weak. It was evident that he had not long to live, and there was an anxious expression on his face which showed that he had something on his mind. With a faint smile he welcomed the newcomers, and signed to the nurse that she should leave the room. This the woman did, whispering in passing Rupert that Tollart had left instructions that the patient was to be as little excited as possible, since his strength was rapidly failing. She also gave the young Squire a strong stimulant with which to revive Leigh, should he grow faint during the interview; and saying that she would return in half an hour departed softly. When the door was closed, the vicar looked at the weeping Dorinda and her scowling father; also at Rupert, who was cool and composed. Inwardly the Squire was greatly disturbed, but it was necessary that he should keep his emotions under control and he did so.

"Why do you cry, Dorinda?" asked the vicar, softly.

"She's a fool," growled Mallien frowning blackly.

"I am an honest girl," said Dorinda, flushing and drying her eyes; "and I am ashamed of the cowardly way in which you are behaving."

"How is your father behaving?" questioned Leigh with an ironical smile.

"He wants to take everything from Rupert and make him a pauper," said

Dorinda sadly. "He refuses to allow me to marry him."

"And will you obey him?"

"No!" She drew herself up proudly. "I love Rupert more than myself, and if he will marry me I am ready to be his wife at any moment."

"Fool! Fool!" growled her father savagely.

"What do you say, Hendle?" inquired the vicar calmly.

"I wish to marry Dorinda, as I love her dearly," answered the Squire, who was pale but composed; "but if this will is proved to be legal I may lose all, and I can't ask Dorinda to share a life of poverty with me."

"I don't care for your poverty," cried the girl, impetuously throwing her arms round her lover's neck. "I would rather have a crust with you than stay with my father in luxury."

"But I don't think it will be necessary for you to be reduced to a crust, Dorinda," smiled the vicar. "After all, considering the circumstances of the case and that Hendle is not to blame, surely your father will give you half the income."

"Two thousand pounds," said Mallien derisively. "I'm not such a fool. I shan't give Rupert a single penny, and if Dorinda marries him without my consent, which she will never get, she must be prepared to starve."

"Dorinda will never starve while I can work," said Rupert calmly.

"What at? You have never done a hand's turn in your life."

Leigh interposed before Rupert could reply. "Mallien, surely you will not behave so wickedly and selfishly as to keep all the money to yourself."

"Yes, I shall. The money is mine, and I shall not give a penny."

"You are a bad man," said Leigh slowly.

"Pooh! What do I care for your names?"

"Nothing. I can see that. However, I may be able to make you care. Dorinda, give me some of that tonic."

The vicar's voice was growing weak and his eye closed. Dorinda slipped her arm round his neck and gave him a dose of the medicine which shortly took effect. He opened his eyes again and spoke in a stronger voice. "Are you determined to behave in this unjust way, Mallien?"

"It is not unjust, and I do."

"You will keep all the money to yourself?"

"Every penny."

"And—if you can—prevent Dorinda marrying Hendle?"

"Yes. She does so at the risk of starvation."

"But you may ruin two lives, Mallien."

"Pooh! Don't talk rubbish, vicar. I shall do as I like."

"You shall not do as you like," said Leigh steadily. "You are an evil and wicked man, although I am too sinful myself to say so. But I thank God that He has permitted me to live and make reparation for my wrongdoing." The vicar fumbled under his pillow and produced an envelope. "Take this, Hendle, and put it into your pocket. No, don't open it now. When I am dead you can learn how deeply I have sinned. And, above all, don't let Mallien get hold of it."

Rupert slipped the envelope into the pocket of his coat and smiled grimly although he also looked astonished. "I'll take care of that," he said, with a nod; "but what is the paper about?"

"It contains a signed and witnessed confession of my sin."

"Your sin." Mallien began to shake in his shoes as there was something very ominous about these proceedings.

"Yes. I intended evil, and evil has come of my intention. But thank God I am able to nip my wrongdoing in the bud. Mallien"—the vicar shook a reproving forefinger at the man—"I have given you every chance to behave as a Christian should, but you will not seize the opportunity. Now it is too late, and you must abide by your selfish conduct."

"What the devil are you talking about?"

"Hush, father, hush! Don't speak like that," cried Dorinda with a shiver.

"I shall speak as I like. What does Leigh mean by his nonsense?"

"You will not find that paper I have given Hendle nonsense," said Leigh in a faint voice. "It contains an account of my sin and will be your punishment."

"Come to the point; come to the point," stuttered Mallien, nervously angry.

Leigh turned to look at Hendle, who stood beside Dorinda silently amazed at all this strange talk. "My friend," he said, wincing at having to lower himself in the young man's eyes, "I was tempted by Satan and I fell. In the muniment chest I found a bundle of letters written by John Hendle, which showed that he wished to disinherit his son Frederick, whom he hated, in favor of Eunice, the infant daughter of his eldest son, Walter, whom he loved. He declared in the last letter of the bundle—which you will find in the chest where I left it—that he would make a will, leaving the estates to Eunice, who married Filbert when she grew up. But John Hendle died of heart disease, as other family documents show, before he could execute his intention. He made no will in favor of Eunice, and Frederick lawfully inherited the property."

Mallien turned a greenish color and pulled out the will from the pocket—the will which had caused so many disasters. "John Hendle made this—"

"He did not," interrupted the vicar in a strong and triumphant voice. "I made that will. It is forged."

"Forged!" Rupert, Dorinda and Mallien all echoed the word.

"Yes," Leigh went on, speaking swiftly as if fearful that his strength would not hold out to the end. "I wanted money to go to Yucatan, and hoped to get it from Hendle. He was not inclined to fit out an expedition, so I hoped to force him. Satan entered into me, and, taking advantage of what was in those letters of John Hendle, I prepared the will in favor of Eunice. I bought the parchment and wrote out what was wanted to give me a hold over Hendle. When Carrington saw me holding the will over the candle, I was doing so to change the color of the ink and make the parchment appear black and a little contracted. I did not give the forged will to Hendle when I spoke about it, as it was not quite ready. Next day I proposed to give it to him and to offer to allow him to burn it on condition that he gave me enough money to go to Yucatan with an expedition. Failing Rupert, I should have gone to you, Mr. Mallien."

"And you would have gone!" gasped Rupert, amazed by this recital. "I would never have agreed to suppress that will had I believed it—as I did—to be genuine."

"I see that now," said Leigh, whose voice was becoming fainter. "You were too honorable for Mallien and Carrington, and you would have been too honorable for me. My forgery was vain. But God intervened and prevented me from carrying out my wicked plot. Carrington came and—and—you—you—know the—rest. I acted wickedly—and—I—I—" He stopped and fell back on his pillows with a ghastly look on his face.

"He is dying," cried Dorinda, running to the bedside. "Call the nurse."

Rupert opened the door, but Mallien looking like a fiend rushed to the dying man and shook him roughly. "You are a liar! you are a liar!" he screamed, white with thwarted ambition. "This will is not forged; this will is—"

Hendle, furious with the man's inhumanity, caught him by the shoulders and thrust him out of the room. The nurse hurried in and along with Dorinda tried to revive the fainting vicar, but in vain. Dr. Tollart was immediately sent for and came at once to pronounce that there was no hope. Leigh lingered for twenty-four hours and then passed away quietly without ever regaining consciousness. This time, as Tollart took care to prove, the vicar was really dead, and within a week his body was again placed in the family vault. To be certain about the catalepsy, the corpse was kept above ground for the seven days until there was no doubt that the man actually was dead. In vain Titus Ark, overcome with grief, repeated his parrot cry that his friend "worn't dead." Leigh was on this occasion a truly dead man. The blow on the head, the shock to his nervous system caused by being buried alive, and perhaps the shame of having to confess his forgery of the will, had all combined to kill him. He died and Barship knew him no more.

And Mallien? He was almost crazy with rage at his loss. Again and again he tried to prove that the forged will was a genuine document, and saw many lawyers and experts. But the confession of Leigh, signed by himself and witnessed by Titus Ark and his grandson, held good, as it gave all details of how the false testament had been prepared. Leigh confessed therein that he had copied the signature of John Hendle from the letters which first gave him an idea of committing the forgery. So in the end Mallien had to accept the fact that Rupert was the true Squire of Barship, and that there was not the slightest chance of his getting a single penny of the four thousand a year he so greedily coveted.

While Mallien, frenzied with baffled avarice, was moving heaven and earth to prove that he was the rightful heir, the other people who had been connected with the strange affair of the will were settling themselves in life. Mrs. Beatson obtained a situation as housekeeper to an invalid gentleman in Derbyshire, much to the relief of Kit and Miss Tollart. Hendle was so pleased with the way in which these two had assisted him at an awkward moment, that he gave Kit a handsome sum of money; and, along with Dorinda, was present at his marriage to the doctor's daughter. Tollart himself found that, in spite of all efforts, he could not quite do away with the prejudice against him, although more or less he managed, as has been said, to reëstablish his position. But perhaps conscience had something to do with his determination to go to Australia with the young couple, for he felt very uncomfortable among his patients. Sophy, who was unwilling to part from her father since he might take to drink again, suggested that he should emigrate. The doctor did so and shortly departed with Mr. and Mrs. Beatson for Melbourne, where he hoped to redeem himself entirely. And, thanks to Rupert's generosity, a start at the Antipodes was made easy both for him and for the young people.

As to Hendle and Dorinda, they took advantage of Mallien's preoccupation with regard to the will to get married quietly in London. Dorinda was of age and did not require her father's consent. Moreover, after his shabby behavior, she felt that even though he was her father, she could never live with him again. So she became Mrs. Hendle shortly after Leigh was buried for the second time, and, after a short honeymoon, returned to be welcomed by one and all as the mistress of The Big House. Everyone was delighted that Rupert still kept his position, and everyone knew that the will, which had caused so much trouble, had been forged. Hendle would have preferred to keep Leigh's confession to himself out of regard to the unfortunate vicar's memory, but Mallien's action left him no option but to make it public. The amazing story added yet another chapter to the romance of the whole queer business, and the story got into the newspapers. Mr. and Mrs. Hendle were not a little troubled by reporters and interviewers and snap-shot people, but in the end curiosity died away and they were left to live their own simple life, doing good and making everyone around them happy.

In the end, Mallien found that his efforts to prove the will to be genuine were futile, so one day presented himself at The Big House in a very dismal frame of mind. Not being able to get the property, he was secretly pleased that his daughter should have become Mrs. Hendle, even without his consent, as he hoped to use her for his own ends. With the greatest impudence he suggested that his son-in-law should fulfill his old promise and allow him five hundred a year.

"Oh, no," said Rupert, calmly, when Mallien came for a last interview. "I don't think it is good for you to be treated with such leniency."

"Nor do I," chimed in Dorinda, who found it difficult to behave amiably to her father, seeing how badly he had behaved.

"What do you mean?" demanded Mallien, taken aback, for he had quite expected to get his own way. "What do you both mean?"

"I don't think it is so very difficult to gather what we mean," replied Rupert coolly. "You never intended to give me a penny had you got the money, so why should I give an income to you?"

"That's different."

"Maybe. Anyhow, you will have to live on what you have."

"I am Dorinda's father."

"I don't look on you as my father," said the undutiful daughter. "You never have behaved like a father to me, and now that I have Rupert to look after me, I wish to see as little of you as possible."

"And this is my child," moaned Mallien, much cast down.

Dorinda laughed. "It won't do, father," she said calmly. "As Mr. Leigh declared on his deathbed, you had every opportunity of acting honorably. How you have acted I leave to your conscience to say."

"*I* won't," said Rupert sharply. "See here, Mallien. I am a kind-hearted man and wish to help everyone, but for me to give you money for your wickedness would be wrong."

"What wickedness?"

"If you will have it; you threatened to turn me out of this house as a pauper, and you have done your best to prove true a document which you knew to be forged. If you had triumphed, Dorinda and I would have been thrown into the street without a penny. Because you have failed, you come whimpering to me for money. You shan't have any. As you are my wife's father, I should have allowed you enough to live on had you been without an income. But as you enjoy five hundred a year of your own you can exist on that. And, as people here are not very well disposed toward you, I advise you to go away."

Furious at this plain speaking Mallien turned on his daughter. "Do you hear how I am spoken to?" he demanded looking black.

"I hear," responded Mrs. Hendle quietly, "and I am glad that you hear the truth for once in your life. I hope it will make you a better man. I think you had better take Rupert's advice and leave Barship."

"Oh, I shall go. I don't want to stay in such a hole," shouted Mallien, putting on his hat violently; then he became pathetic. "And I go to live a lonely life."

"I think you will find plenty of amusement in playing with your jewels," said Dorinda quietly. "You never cared for me."

Mallien muttering something about an ungrateful child and a serpent's tooth, walked away with a drooping head. It dawned on him dimly when he shook the dust of Barship from his feet that perhaps after all, as he had not given affection, he could not expect affection. But his egotism was much too strong to permit him to understand fully that he was only reaping what he had sown. He took up his abode in London and managed to get along very comfortably on his five hundred a year. But he always persisted in regarding himself as a much injured man and stubbornly maintained that the will forged by Leigh was genuine. Needless to say, he never missed his daughter, as he was far too much wrapped up in himself to desire any company but his own.

"Do you think we have acted rightly, Rupert?" asked Dorinda in a troubled tone, when her father departed after that last interview.

"Yes, dear. He is your father certainly, but he has no right to take advantage of the relationship to behave so selfishly as he has done. It would be wrong to pander to his egotism by giving him money."

"Yes, I suppose so," said Dorinda with a sigh. "People are very hard to understand, Rupert. Besides my father, who puzzled me with his selfishness, there is Mr. Leigh. Whatever made such a good and kind man forge that will?"

Rupert shrugged his shoulders. "A sudden temptation perhaps," he said, after a pause; "but I don't pretend to explain; his act was entirely opposed to his character. If he was in a story people would say that he was inconsistent."

Dorinda agreed. "Very inconsistent. Human beings are strange."

"They are, dear. But you see, as we only see the outside of people we don't know how to account for every action. The majority of people are children and often act wrongly without thinking of the consequences. After all evil is only ignorance, for if wrongdoers knew what they would have to pay for behaving wickedly they would not sin. Now, darling, don't think anything more about the matter. Let us enjoy the peace which has come to us after the storm. There is no more to be said about the past and no more to be done. We are happy and try to make others happy. What more do you want?"

"This," said Dorinda, and kissed him fondly.

THE END

Lightning Source UK Ltd.
Milton Keynes UK
UKHW010701070820
367857UK00003B/740